About

V. L. Heathcote lives on the west coast of Scotland and has a glorious, if somewhat distracting, view from where she sits to write. Having been married and brought up a family, the author has returned to a long-held passion for storytelling. As a lover of theatre, the past has seen a play, written for a young farmers' group and directed by the author, come second in the country finals and four one act plays, again written and directed by herself, performed at the Edinburgh Fringe with some degree of success. Two other novels, one for children, were put on the back-burner when the idea for Colouring In came up. Also an artist, V. L. Heathcote has produced a short, illustrated book for children with an environmental message.

COLOURING IN

V. L. Heathcote

Published by V. L. Heathcote

Copyright © 2015 by V. L. Heathcote

All rights reserved. No part of this publication may be reproduced, distributed or transmitted in any form or by any means, without prior written permission.

V. L. Heathcote
cloudcuckooland9@gmail.com

This is a work of fiction. Names, characters, places, and incidents are a product of the author's imagination. Locales and public names are sometimes used for atmospheric purposes. Any resemblance to actual people, living or dead, or to businesses, companies, events, institutions, or locales is completely coincidental.

COLOURING IN

Chapter 1

CRIMSON LAKE

Arlo diMarco de Pelio squinted up at the early morning sun which was creeping slowly over the grey skyline of the little area of London where he lived. Only it wasn't just grey. To his eyes, the roofs went from the palest pink to a deep bruising purple with the odd splash of brilliant yellow where the light glanced off some shiny or wet surface. So many people, he suspected, missed the subtle hues around them; didn't look closely enough to pick up the ever-changing shades or just didn't give time to truly observe what the world was offering in that moment.

His eyes wandered, taking in everything around him and, as always, brought a smile to his thin, angular face. His grandfather, the first to paint his part of the fire-escape and back door in brilliant colours, must have had the same thoughts and, in his wisdom, decided to make people sit up and notice. Colour! It was everywhere! Sitting quietly on one of the benches in the garden area, Arlo couldn't help but feel he was the luckiest man alive. Everything about the Harlequin triangle, as it had become known, pleased his artistic tendencies because visually, the courtyard was quite stunning.

According to a couple of the older locals, it had come about because, during the war, a bomb had wiped out nearly a whole street. When the authorities came to rebuild, someone in the planning department had gone all creative; left the four remaining houses and built a block of six apartments at an angle from one corner and some shops with flats above at an angle from the other, thus leaving a triangular area of land behind all three builds. To get to it, you had to go through a scruffy alley between the apartment block and a run-down hairdressers.

Inside the triangle, a path ran along the three sides backing onto the yards and gardens of the surrounding buildings and here displayed a myriad of the brightest colours imaginable. Window frames and back doors in rich oranges, clashing fuchsia pinks and searing turquoise blues; fences and railings in piercing acid yellows and vibrant pea greens; drainpipes, guttering and fire escapes in glowering purples and vivid reds. There was nothing in the courtyard that hadn't been touched by colour. Even some of the brick walls had been enlivened by graffiti; a pattern of rainbow soap bubbles here; a silhouette of trees in deep indigo there; a flock of birds flying south; a giant, green beanstalk for Jack to climb.

Arlo's neighbours, so different from himself, had embraced the concept of transforming, what would otherwise have been a colourless prison of dullness, into a fantasy land of Ozwellian proportions.

And then there was the centre, a triangle of ground turned into a garden full of plants of all kinds, from rose bushes to bamboo, sweet peas to runner beans, honeysuckle to rhubarb. There were three benches, painted brightly of course, a swing hanging from an apple tree and a small area of lawn, the latter being used for summer barbecues, firework displays and a winter Christmas tree.

For those who lived around the area, it was a place of great solace and delight. They had helped to develop it, invested in it; a separate world with its own little community; a microcosm of all life with its people entwined, in their own special ways, with the space and other inhabitants. Arlo thought of it as a great big colouring book, with the people filling in the black outlines of their lives with hopes, fears, loves, hates and dreams to create the patchwork shades of their experience.

The pink-framed window of one of the ground floor apartments opened. Arlo caught a glimpse of lacy frill encircling a pale, plump wrist which was then followed by the sleek, satin-furred body of one of Miss Malloy's cats. Another window, this time framed in a deep, cerulean blue, opened to let in some fresh air - air that was already threatening to become heavy and sultry. That would be Trevor, thought Arlo. And indeed, Trevor's pleasant, moon-shaped face appeared at the window and then, a be-ringed hand waved a dainty greeting. Arlo waved back knowing, before long, Trevor would be arguing over the breakfast table with his indolent, over-dramatic, Australian boyfriend, Bryce. They lived directly beneath Arlo on the first floor so he often caught the sound of raised voices. Arlo didn't like Bryce much as he'd detected a spiteful streak. But Bryce had been with soft-hearted Trevor for some time so maybe, Arlo supposed, he was missing something.

Arlo drained the cup of hot, strong tea he favoured in the mornings and went for a last look around the garden. Everything was coming on nicely. Runner beans beginning to twist snakily up their cane wigwams; beetroots flaunting their red-veined leaves and carrots waving feathery antennae in the breeze. Nasturtiums blasted their splashes of copper and gold throughout like some paintballing debacle and the scent of lavender, rosemary and thyme wafted up seductively in the gathering heat of the day. Arlo breathed in deeply and reluctantly headed for the fire-escape which led to his top floor apartment.

A piercing scream stopped him in his tracks.

"Oh my God! Can someone help? Anyone around?"

Arlo was already running towards the alleyway from where the scream had come. Florence Ntombe, still in her nurse's uniform, was crouched over someone lying face down on the ground. As he dropped down next to her, he could see a small pool of crimson forming near the body. For a second, his artist's nature was transfixed by the richness of the colour – and then, he felt his heart pounding furiously as reality hit him.

"Phone the ambulance, Arlo," Florence urged, her dark eyes full of concern. "I don't have my mobile and I tink this man been stabbed."

The next seconds seemed to elongate into minutes as Arlo watched her pull some material from her bag and form it into a pad to push beneath the body and hold against the wound. Then, he was running again and climbing the fire escape two at a time. He noticed his hands were trembling as he dialled and, when asked which service, he stated shakily, "Ambulance and Police." After giving details, he took a deep breath to calm himself and hurried back to where Florence still sat with her hand tucked underneath the man's body. She refused to let him take over so he sat down and put his arm around her, trying to be of some comfort. It seemed like a ridiculously long time before they heard the insistent wailing of the ambulance but it was barely ten minutes. Finally, Florence was able to let go and allow Arlo to take her away from the scene to get cleaned up. She fell against him, shaking and felt that he, too, was trembling. Such an event was too momentous to contemplate but they could think of nothing else – like a nightmare from which you were desperately trying to awaken. The shock waves of violence were all around, palpable, twanging in the bright morning air.

And then, peace no longer reigned. Arlo and Florence sat on one of the benches, their faces stricken, watching the 'to-ing' and 'fro-ing' of members of the local constabulary. They'd been rigorously questioned by Detective Inspector Bulloch and were still shell-shocked as the man, whoever he was and despite Florence's best efforts, had died before they could get him into hospital.

"Such a beautiful day, too," remarked Florence, as though that had any bearing on anything at all.

"I suppose you were-"

"Just comin' home from night duty, yes. We lost a patient there too. This all I needed," said Florence, her West Indian accent becoming more pronounced in her anxiety.

"And you're going to miss it I suppose. You'll need to catch up on some sleep."

She gave him a puzzled look and he shook his head apologetically before pointing up at the sun.

"Oh, that. Yeah, it a nuisance. Still, I don't tink this weather goin' away so maybe I come out later."

Arlo nodded his approval.

"And Arlo, me tomato seeds I plant really coming on. Can they come outside, d'you tink?"

"Probably. I'll keep an eye on them for you. Oh, for fuck's sake!"

"I know," she said and her eyes filled with tears.

Arlo put his arm around her and pulled her close. "Is this what having a stiff upper lip means, d'you think? Carrying on regardless and all that. It feels very odd to me."

"Me, too," sniffed Florence, miserably. "I'm used to seein' death but that – a life been taken – someone's brother or dad or uncle. Awful! And so near our lovely garden. It feel violated."

There was a moment's silence and then, Florence spoke again.

"Not that it important – compare to losing your life, I mean."

"I know what you mean, Flo. It's important to us and just because you're acknowledging your feelings about our precious bit of land, doesn't diminish what happened to that guy."

Another silence and then Arlo again, "Anyway, he could have been a villain for all we know, wreaking havoc on innocent people."

"But we shouldn't judge till we know." Florence had a strong religious gene running through her veins.

Arlo was spared having to comment as Trevor came tripping up the path, his gentle face full of concern. Bryce followed but was having a conversation with his smart phone. Not so smart if you got yourself bought by the likes of Bryce, thought Arlo, uncharitably.

"What *is* the world coming to?" declared Trevor dramatically. "I *mean,* someone getting knocked off, right by our little piece of heaven. It's not on. You can feel the vibes of death everywhere."

He sat down heavily next to Arlo causing him to budge along and squash Florence.

"We were sort of saying the same thing," Arlo explained, trying hard to narrow himself so they all fitted a little better on the bench.

"We being very self-centred, you know," Florence pointed out primly.

"Well, nobody else is going to look out for you." Bryce, the king of self-centredness, came and stood, or rather posed, next to the bench so they could all look upon his magnificent personage and sigh with envy.

"The Marshmallow took it better than I expected," Trevor commented. "I thought she'd freak but no – as long as neither of her darling moggies were harmed, she didn't seem all that... you know."

They all looked over to Miss Malloy's windows and pondered.

"I never could fathom her out anyway," said Arlo. "Strange lady but kind-hearted, I feel."

"Hmm, something about her," said Bryce, lighting up a long cheroot-looking thing. "She's probably the one who done it."

Arlo hurriedly turned a snort of derision into a cough. The man didn't even know his grammar and yet he pretended to be so high and mighty.

They all stared at Marsha Malloy's baby-pink window frames and back door. She was a big fan of pastel shades. Even the flowers in her window boxes and pots were all chosen for their varying degrees of paleness. Pale pink aubrietia and white hyacinth interspersed with wispy London Pride. The occasional lilac hue or very pale blue was allowed but absolutely no garish yellows, oranges, reds or purples. Her home was much the same. Lots of white and cream with the odd touch of pink. Trevor had once been heard to remark that it was like falling into a bag of marshmallows. Their sickly sweetness soon palled and left you with the urge to throw up. It was partly this remark and partly when someone discovered Miss Malloy's first name was Marsha, that was responsible for her becoming known as the Marshmallow. Plus, of course, although quite tall, the woman was soft and plump and pale so it suited her very well. It was noted that she was always very sweet too; her manner always polite and unassuming; her language moderate and genteel. If you called on her, she was welcoming and warm with offers of tea made from loose leaves in a teapot and served in white, bone china cups. But Marsha Malloy didn't get visitors that often. Perhaps because it was all just a little bit too much.

"I never seen Marshmallow lose her cool over anyting. Not even when one of her cats die," Florence remarked, turning to watch a skinny but rather handsome, young police officer run across and disappear down the alleyway. "She just say, it his time and that's that."

"Perhaps she felt the same about the victim in the alleyway," said Trevor, with a shudder. "Have you spoken to anyone else?"

"One or two," said Arlo. "We went back to mine after we'd spoken to the police and we haven't been back out long. It must have happened in the early hours I guess but nobody seems to have heard anything."

"Mr Footlik say he sleep with earplug so he don't hear anyting," remarked Florence.

"Ah yes, no." This, a favourite expression of Trevor's most likely to come out when he was excited. "He told me he wakes about five every morning without fail. It drives him mad apparently because he thought when he retired, he'd be able to sleep in. So he could have been up and awake when IT happened."

"Well, he say he not hear anyting anyway," said Florence, stifling a yawn.

"You should go and get your head down, Flo," Arlo advised. "You must be worn out."

"Why's that then?" sneered Bryce. "You don't think these nurses actually stay awake on their night shifts, do you?"

Arlo was heard to cough again with the word 'tosser' not very successfully disguised in its midst.

"I won't dignify that with no answer," said Florence, prising herself from the bench and moving off to her apartment without a backward glance.

Trevor, deciding it was time to get on with the day's requirements, bustled Bryce away. Arlo was left wondering if he noticed Bryce's spitefulness. He'd never heard Trevor remonstrate with his lover or even blush when he was at his most vicious, which usually occurred after a few too many drinks at a party. Trevor would just change the subject or move Bryce gently aside. Arlo pondered on the day he would land a punch on the young man's mahogany-tanned face before Trevor could step in. He was secretly looking forward to it.

The day wore on and people came and went. Arlo couldn't settle and every time he went back to his flat, he found himself peering out of the window to see what was happening. The community around the courtyard tended to look out for each other and, with the enormity of what had happened, Arlo felt obliged to be vigilant so he could report back to everyone. In the end, he took a sketch pad and pencil out to the garden and made himself available to anyone who wanted to off-load their anxiety regarding the shocking events the morning had revealed.

* * *

Harry Footlik spotted the vicar too late to use his usual avoidance tactics. He tutted loudly, not caring one jot if the man hurrying towards him heard and was offended. Harry was too long in the tooth to worry about what other people thought although, if he were honest, it had never been much of a concern at any point in his life.

"Ah, Mr Footlik," spluttered the vicar, mopping erratically at his perspiring face. "What a shock – terrible shock. How are you feeling?"

Harry viewed the Reverend Ernest Tiplady with an air of extreme contempt. "How do *I* feel? You ask how *I* feel? Just as I always am – absolutely fine. Why on earth wouldn't I be?"

The Reverend Tiplady put up his hand to shield his eyes from the sun, as he tried to look into the other man's face. Footlik was large and, although elderly and walking with the aid of a stick, still formidable.

"I just thought... you know, the horror of – of the – of the body – in the alleyway - that you might be... you know... upset."

Harry Footlik was silent in his contemplation of the shorter, younger man before him. And while Ernest felt himself starting to tremble beneath the steady gaze, Harry was statue-like in his stillness. Finally, the torture ended and Footlik spoke, his deep, sonorous tones filling the space around them.

"Horror," he boomed. "Is that what it is? People are obsessed by horror. Things which have been happening since time began are now deemed horrific... by the press, the politicians, the public. Every bloody film out at the moment is about horror and zombie horror in particular. D'you want to know what I think?"

Ernest Tiplady shook his head violently and then, realising his mistake, nodded so hard his spectacles fell off and were left hanging precariously from one ear.

"I think it's symbolic, the zombie thing. The human race destroying itself, eating itself up. The greed of humanity feeding off itself. The subconscious always knows the truth and it's showing itself in the films we're producing. THAT is what I think, Tiplady."

Mr Footlik swept triumphantly past the vicar, a galleon of a man in a long duster coat and a frayed straw hat. Ernest watched him go whilst retrieving his glasses and wondered, not for the first time, where the Lord was when you needed him.

Fortunately, the next person the vicar bumped into in the gardens, quite literally, was not so formidable; not, at least, in the same way as Mr Footlik. But Giselle Greene always, without fail, affected the vicar's ability to string a sentence together in a way that made any sense at all.

"M-Miss Greene, how are you alright?" he began and noticed a puzzled look travel over her pretty features. "Sorry... I mean, so sorry... what happened... aren't you? I mean..."

"Not your fault, Reverend Tiplady. In fact, I think it was *I*, bumped into you."

"No, no – I mean, the b-body! Sorry to mention the... er..."

"Oh no! Was it someone you knew?" She pressed her full, soft lips together anxiously.

"No! No, oh no, no, no," spluttered Tiplady, quite unable to take his eyes from her mouth. "Sorry did I give... no, no! Just awful though for you... for the females, I mean... and for us men. But for women who... you know... when you're out and about like you are... and..."

The Reverend literally ran out of steam and stood helplessly, looking at the young woman in front of him, wishing he had never heard the rumours. Giselle Greene worked in a massage parlour. It was situated not too far from his church and was rumoured to be a 'knocking shop'. Nothing had ever been proven, of course, but, once aired, the idea was bandied around by those with little else to do. And, it had to be said, Giselle had a certain look about her that made you believe that she could quite easily have been 'a lady of the night.' She did not, Ernest noted, dress modestly; not even when it was cold enough to freeze the snot off the end of your nose. Her cleavage was forever on display, just asking to be admired and appreciated. Her eyes were always ringed by sultry-coloured shadows, her lids just slightly lowered, hinting that it was surely time for bed. The vicar swallowed and attempted to rein in his thoughts. He might just as well have said that having a murderer around must be particularly worrying for a prostitute such as herself. He glanced at her face, anxiously looking for any signs that meant she had taken his remarks in such a way. But Giselle was looking more worried than offended.

"To be honest, I've only just heard about it. I was up late and slept in this morning as I could feel a migraine coming on. I'm afraid I ignored the knock on the door which I suppose must have been the police making enquires. Do we know anything about the victim, Reverend?"

"Not really," replied Ernest, his errant mind still stuck on, 'I was up late'. "Florence found him – stabbed I believe and she and Arlo... I'm sorry you're not feeling well. I hope nothing untoward kept you up. You can always come to me if you can't sleep - I mean, that is, if you have worries... you know... I mean..."

Ernest felt like vomiting with humiliation. It must have been obvious that his treacherous mind kept wandering below waist level. He felt naked and exposed and expected retribution to rain upon him at any minute.

"Oh, there's Arlo on the bench. I might just have a quick chat."

And she was gone. And Ernest was left to contemplate that even his clumsy words had no power to move her to any emotion other than indifference.

* * *

Arlo watched Giselle's approach with the eyes of an artist. Her face was symmetrically almost perfect but it was the luxuriant, tawny mane of hair rippling over her slim shoulders that really caught your eye. He'd heard the rumour, of course, but had never given it much credence. What she did or didn't do had nothing to do with him anyway. He just appreciated she was easy on the eye and it felt right that she was part of the community around the Harlequin triangle. She cared about it as much as anyone and always mucked in when there was work to be done. He smiled a welcome as she sat down next to him.

"Do we know who it was, Arlo?" she asked, her tone neutral.

He shook his head. "Not yet. I expect we'll find out soon enough."

"Mmm." She stared straight ahead giving him a chance to study the lines of her perfect profile.

"Poor soul," she said eventually. "Everyone's nightmare to be found dead in an alley, isn't it?"

Arlo raised his eyebrows. "Can't say the thought ever crossed my mind. Would you let me paint you?"

It seemed to take a few minutes for his words to sink in; possibly, Arlo felt, because she was deep in thought - certainly not because she was slow-witted.

"Did you see what he looked like?"

"Not really. Darkish hair, fortyish. Medium buildish. Sorry, a lot of 'ishes' but he was lying face down. Why? D'you think you might know him?"

"What?" She looked shocked. "No, no. Of course not. I just – well, you know - felt sorry for him. There may be people he's left behind and if he was old, there'd be less likelihood of a lot of people missing him... maybe." She smiled apologetically at the lameness of her explanation but Arlo just shrugged.

"Well, he died from a stab wound so he possibly pissed someone off," he stated a little coldly. Her avoidance of his earlier request ruffled him more than he'd realised.

Neither spoke. Birdsong serenaded them, whilst traffic forced its insistent rumble into the background; an annoying accompaniment proving that whatever ghastliness humans sank to, the world rolled on.

"I take it that's a 'no' then," said Arlo, after a while.

"What?"

"A 'no' to painting you – erm, your portrait that is."

"Well, I didn't think you meant actually putting paint on my body," she said, suddenly grinning. "Although, I've heard worse requests."

"I thought we could do it out here; sit you in the garden somewhere, with the sunlight on you coming through the tree. But it's up to you."

Silence again. Giselle stood up.

"Safer, isn't it? No gossip or rumours if we're out here in full view of everyone."

"No, that's not why I-"

"Yes, I'll sit for you. My pleasure, Arlo. I'll even do it for nothing."

And she was gone; marching down the path in a defiant sort of way, heels clicking rhythmically on the paving slabs. Arlo stared at her disappearing back, a frown of annoyance creasing his face. People and their insecurities! They wore you out. He got up, suddenly desperate for the peace and quiet of his home but before he could even take a step, Reverend Tiplady descended upon him. As always, the vicar held his hands in a strange, begging dog-like way - in front of his chest, hanging down from his wrists – almost as though he expected you to take them and kiss the ring on his fingers; stranger still that the gesture came from a man who appeared to have little confidence and was constantly apologetic.

"Good morning, Vicar," said Arlo, determined to get the meeting over as quickly as possible. "Dreadful business."

"You took the words right out of my mouth, Mr Arco di... di Pellio." He could never get it right. "Do you know what -"

"No no; nothing as yet," Arlo interjected hurriedly. "But if and when I do, you'll be the first to know." A blatant lie, of course, but Arlo was beyond caring. "Oh, look! There's the Kshatryias. They've just been interviewed. Perhaps they can tell you more."

He applied gentle pressure to the vicar's back and was rewarded with the response he desired. Ernest Tiplady moved towards the couple, eagerly and Arlo was able to make his escape. He turned only when he got to the bottom of the fire-escape that led up to his flat. He could see the Indian couple edging away as the vicar tried to prise information from them. Nice people in Arlo's opinion, working hard in their little general store, from early till late, for which convenience many people were extremely grateful. The Kshatryias were far too polite to tell the vicar to bugger off so they would be there for a while. Shaking his head sympathetically, Arlo hurried up the colourful metal stairs to his home.

* * *

The Beekeeper's Arms, more commonly known as The Bee's Knees, was buzzing. This very remark was made by Finn Hunt, sat on bar stools with Benson Clark and Linus Swankey, with whom he shared one of the four terraced houses that backed onto the Harlequin triangle.

"D'you see what I did there?" Finn snorted. "Buzzin' – the Bee's Knees – buzzin'."

"Yes, Finn, we get it. Really, if you have to explain it, it's not funny," sighed Benson.

"It wasn't funny anyway," said Linus, loftily. "I mean, it's not as though it was a first."

"All right!" Finn held up his hands. "Just trying to bring a smile to your miserable faces."

"Erm, dead body; our alleyway; reason not to be cheerful," Linus stated.

The others refrained from pointing out that Linus rarely needed anything that drastic to make him sombre.

"Don't get your knickers in such a twist, Wanks," said Finn. "Just be grateful it wasn't you."

The other two shook their heads.

"Really, you can't let someone else's misfortune ruin your day," he continued, defensively. "It's just not on."

"I think the word 'shallow' must have been invented with you in mind," said Benson. "I mean, a little respect –sympathy – something? Anything!"

"Absolutely!" said Linus, thumping the bar. "Calling someone Wanks just because their name is Swankey is an appalling... Why are you laughing?"

"Because," chuckled Benson. "I was referring to the dead man – not what Finn called you."

"Oh!" Linus was crestfallen. "I thought, for once, you were sticking up for me."

"Dear God, how did I end up sharing a house with two, such self-obsessed people?"

"You know you love us really," grinned Finn.

Benson couldn't argue. He surveyed his two friends, suddenly seeing them with new eyes. What if it *had* been one of them in the alley? How would he have felt? His gut twisted and he got a hint of the misery of loss. He'd known Finn the longest. Arrogant, insensitive but extremely handsome, Finn was always in the middle of some romantic disaster, from which, Benson often had to extricate him. Linus, on the other hand, was too thin with pale hair and troublesome skin. He worked in the city but was vague about what he actually did. Benson suspected that Linus could have afforded a place of his own but knew, if he had, he would be lonely. He was a decent enough bloke if you ignored his occasional sense of humour bypass.

Any arguments usually sprang up between Finn and Linus with Benson inevitably playing the role of peacemaker. Finn was jealous of Linus's financial security. Finn worked part-time on the nearby market plus as many shifts at the pub as he could get. His 'real' job was acting, as he was always quick to point out; a precarious profession, even for a person such as himself. He insisted it was only a matter of time before someone spotted his undeniable talent but, until then, he did what he could to bring in the money; not to mention the girls. It was in this area that Linus experienced *his* feelings of envy. He had no luck with the opposite sex whatsoever and his resentment of the way Finn treated his female 'fans' and got away with it, often bubbled to the surface.

Despite all this, the three men rubbed along very well but the calming influence of Benson Clark had a lot to do with that. Benson was an electrician and ran a boxing and martial arts group for disadvantaged kids in his spare time. That's the sort of guy he was. And he laughed a lot, tending to see the funny side of things. No one could stay grumpy for long when Benson was around.

"First time I've ever been interviewed by the police," Linus admitted. "Can't say I particularly want to repeat the experience."

"Well, at least we're all alibis for each other," said Finn.

"Well, sort of; I mean, we were all in yesterday evening and saw each other go to bed at what? About twelve wasn't it? But one of us could have got up and snuck out of the house." Benson spread his hands in a dramatic gesture.

"But which one of us would have the stomach, let alone the desire, for stabbing someone to death." Linus pulled a face and downed some of his pint.

"I don't even know anyone I hate that much," agreed Finn, doing the same.

"Well, maybe it was me and I've just been putting on a front to fool you that I'm a nice guy. But deep down, I have a need for blood and… Oh, just look at your faces!"

Finn and Linus were staring at him, their eyes widening in horror.

"I give up with you two," sighed Benson. "You're like a couple of three-year-olds."

"Giving you a bit of bother, are they Benson?" Dennis Harris leaned over the bar to wipe up some spilled beer.

"Oh, you know how it is, Dennis," grinned Benson. "Busy tonight, eh?"

"Yeah well, not surprising really. Everyone wants to know if anyone else knows more than them. I suppose you got interviewed, did you?"

"Yes and it's not something I want to experience again." Linus had a habit of repeating himself.

"Do you want me to jump on? It's gone mad," said Finn, noticing another group of people squeezing in through the front door. He enjoyed his shifts at the pub and was always ready to do extras where he could. He likened it to being on stage, everyone looking at you. He'd perfected a few tricks with the cocktail shaker and fancied himself a bit of a Tom Cruise. Linus once rather spitefully pointed out, as he wasn't that much taller, he could certainly fit the bill. But that backfired because Finn had become the focus of the majority of the females present, including the one Linus had been trying to chat up.

"If you wouldn't mind, Finn, that would be great," said the landlord gratefully. "Glenys has gone to get her tablets. She's got one of her heads starting so if you come on, I can tell her to go and have a lie down."

Finn wormed his way through the crowd and appeared on the other side of the bar. He pushed his sleeves right up, undid a couple of buttons to show off his muscles and threw himself into the job at hand. Linus rolled his eyes but Benson just laughed. He knew Finn was a decent sort of bloke deep down and suspected when he did finally settle down, he would be a very loyal and devoted husband.

The evening wore on and the little pub heaved and groaned with the excess of customers. Finn, Dennis and Barbara, the landlord's daughter, flew about like disturbed bats and Glenys appeared again, making a sudden and remarkable recovery once she heard Finn had joined them behind the bar.

Nearly all conversations were centred around the body in the alley. Even an observation on the advantages of such an occurrence for local business was bantered around. Dennis and Glenys secretly agreed but were quick to display their decency by denying such a thought had entered their heads. In truth, their little pub did very well with its proximity to the local market, shops and offices and, of course, the residential areas. Also, the couple were totally suited to their profession. They were blank canvases on which their customers could splash their perceptions and opinions of life. They listened, absorbed, smiled and nodded, validating everyone's point of view and making them feel worthwhile once again. It was easy for Glenys. She was excruciatingly nosy and actively encouraged anyone who came through the door to spill every bean they'd ever stored.

Dennis, on the other hand, couldn't give a 'flea's fart' about anything anyone said to him. But as long as people kept on handing over their money, he was happy to stare glassily into their eyes and make sympathetic noises. After all, he had a wife and daughter to keep in the manner to which they were accustomed and that included at least one luxury holiday every year – usually somewhere hot and exotic. Dennis was ever hopeful that someday, one of these holidays would produce a rich husband for his daughter and he would be relieved of the burden of having her around.

Poor Barbara! It wasn't that he didn't love her – although Dennis wasn't really capable of actually loving anything – but he was acutely aware his daughter had inherited every negative thing about him and his wife and that was hard to live with. She had his large nose and his wife's thin lips; her body was thick like his and yet she had Glenys's skinny limbs on which to support it. Sadly, Barbara did not possess a disposition that meant you could overlook her ungainliness. She was mean, spiteful and moody and, for that reason, kept out of the bar as often as possible. Instead, she was given accounting, ordering and paperwork to do and this, Dennis was quick to admit, she did extremely well.

Needless, to say, Barbara was not oblivious to Finn's attractions and, whenever fate threw them together to work behind the bar, she made the most of it.

"Phew, this is madness," she said, having squeezed past Finn a lot closer than was necessary for the umpteenth time. "I can't remember the last time we were as busy as this."

"Me neither," Finn replied, leaning across the bar to give someone their change. "Need to find a less horrific reason to get people in though."

"Whatever," said Barbara heartlessly. "My parents should get you in more often. Takings always go up when you're on."

Finn flashed his gleaming, white-toothed smile. "Maybe they should invest in a sexy, little barmaid for the lads as well. That would guarantee-" He stopped, realising from the look on her face, the huge clanger he'd just dropped.

"Sorry. I didn't mean... I mean, you... erm, your job is more..."

"Fuck you, Finn!" She said it through gritted teeth. "You just fucked yourself!"

Barbara's plain face was suffused with colour and her mother, who'd just come up behind her and had never heard her use that sort of language in the bar, grasped her arm.

"Barbara, whatever is the matter with you? I won't have that sort of language. Barbara!"

Her daughter wrenched her arm away and threw down the cloth she was holding. She pushed past Finn and made her way to the back entrance where she turned and glared at him.

"Ask *him*, Mother. Just ask him!" she hissed and disappeared through the doorway.

Glenys turned and looked enquiringly at Finn but people were screaming for drinks all along the bar. It was too noisy for anyone to have noticed the exchange between the barman and her daughter and Glenys knew it wasn't the time to pursue it.

"I'll talk to you later," she said and turned to serve the baying crowds.

Finn caught Benson's eye and noted the raised eyebrow, making a black James Bond seem totally feasible. He shrugged and mouthed, "Tell you later", before he too plunged back to see to the demands of his adoring public.

* * *

Most of the residents from the Harlequin triangle called into the pub that evening. Arlo, Trevor and Bryce and Harry Footlik all popped in for a 'swift half'. Tom and Catriona Penworthy, who lived in one of the terraced houses with their two children, joined them halfway through the evening. They gravitated, as the others had, towards Linus and Benson in their little corner by the end of the bar and the now familiar round of questions regarding who knew what, took place. Catriona was looking very concerned but Tom, having patted her shoulder, moved away to chat to someone else.

"Don't look so worried," boomed Harry Footlik, with his usual lack of empathy. "Not likely to happen again. Don't think I've ever heard of a murder happening in the same place twice."

"But it's the children," whimpered Catriona. "It does things to their little minds, this sort of... of occurrence."

Catriona was a teacher so everyone presumed she meant her pupils but she could have been referring to her own off-spring. However, no one imagined that two such monstrous children could possibly be affected by anything as mundane as a dead body in the alley. Sulky Sonia and Nightmare Nigel, as they were fondly known by the locals, rarely endeared themselves to their peers, let alone any of the adults with whom they came into contact.

"How are the children?" The quavery tones of Anya Petrovka, tinged with a Russian accent, wafted in from behind them. A resident of one of the flats, she was rarely seen out any further than Harlequin's triangular garden but had persuaded Hilary Scantleberry, who ran and lived above the charity shop, to accompany her.

"It's pure curiosity, before you ask," she continued, cutting off Tom's reply that his children were in rude health. "They gave absolutely nothing away on the news and I just couldn't bear it. I knew you'd all be here so I thought I'd call in and see vat I could find out. A voman by the door, as I came in, said a man had been stabbed at least fourteen times."

She turned, looking anxiously around, as though the killer was sure to be somewhere amongst the pub's customers. Next to her, Hilary shrugged and looked slightly uncomfortable.

"That's absolute nonsense," said Arlo contemptuously. "He'd been stabbed once – in the chest, I believe. Florence tried to save him but sadly failed. She's very upset about it."

"Oh, vell, that's not so... but still...," said Anya anxiously. "Isn't anyone going to offer to buy me a drink? I've come out vithout my purse."

No one even raised an eyebrow. This eccentric behaviour was quite typical of Anya. She was, Arlo said, an enigma about whom it was difficult to surmise the exact truth. It was guessed she was in her sixties. Always well groomed and elegant, if slightly 'off the wall' in her choice of outfits, she acted as though she was a member of the aristocracy and never had any money on her. She hinted she was of Russian decent and there was the suggestion of ballet dancer in the way she stood, her feet forever in first position. Occasional exotic-sounding names like Diaghilev and Anastasia Abramova appeared in her conversation but no definite statements ever made about a career as a dancer. At other times, she alluded to work in Oxford and someone called Ptolemy - who may, or may not, have been her husband. The stories would change from one day to the next but no one minded. She was a colourful, harmless sort of character and, as such, a perfect addition to the community around the Harlequin triangle.

Others visited that evening and joined the Harlequin bunch in the corner; Reg Prodger, a shy and nervous man in his fifties who lived in one of the flats and Baz and Linda Pugh who had one of the terraces and fostered children. Just before closing time, even Patrick Baxter squeezed his way through the crowd to join them and asked to be filled in on the day's events. Patrick, a flat owner, was rather suave and worked away a lot, causing plenty of speculation as to why. Now, it was his turn to feel frustrated as, of course, no one could tell him much at all.

* * *

In other homes around the Harlequin triangle, the same subject was being discussed. The Kshatryias, in the flat above their shop, spoke of it in nervous whispers and, in number two, Grenville Row, one of the terraces, Frances Arbuthnot tentatively asked her sister, Valerie, if she'd heard anything when she'd been shopping.

"No dear, I didn't," replied Valerie, in her usual sneering tone. "I'm not one to gossip, as you know."

"Well, I hardly think concern over the situation could be classed as gossip," said Frances boldly. "We all want to know we can sleep safely in our beds and, if there is someone out there who gets his kicks from killing, well, I for one, would like-"

"What? What would you like, Frances? Police protection? A gun on your bedside table? For goodness sake, have a little common sense. Why would anyone want the bother of ending your life anyway?"

Valerie, as usual, had made it sound as though Frances was worth absolutely nothing; not even the time or energy of some murderer to come and knock her off. Not for the first time, Frances wondered what madness had induced her to allow her sister to move in. Yes, she'd felt sorry for Valerie when her husband, Hugh Figgis, had died but how come she hadn't remembered what a poisonous, controlling witch her sister could be? But, Valerie had put on a good show of intimating that she was a changed woman, all sweetness and light, and Frances, in her naivety, had fallen for it. An errant thought flashed through her mind. Maybe the murderer *would* come back and maybe this time, Valerie would be in the wrong place at the right time. Frances felt herself blush at the wickedness of her imaginings but had to acknowledge that, at the moment, she felt no love for her sister whatsoever.

* * *

Two weeks on and the murder had not been solved. The victim, however, had been identified as Peter Lowdon, a local councillor. He was a married man with no children and lived in one of the big houses on Peachtree Lane - an area popular with those receiving salaries of generous proportions. It said, in the local paper, that Councillor Lowdon was a well respected figure, not thought to have any enemies and, as he was no longer in possession of his wallet when found, it was difficult to discern any sort of motive other than robbery. This was not strictly true, however, as the first thing the councillor had done on taking up his new post, was to spend thousands of pounds refurbishing and decorating the council offices. With hospital, schools and social services in general crying out for more funds, it had been anything but a popular move. Now, people were tight-lipped and slow to express any sympathy for the man's plight but, for those with a conscience, a shadow of shame that they should feel so little for someone's untimely death, would cross their eyes from time to time.

Things had settled a little though. Finn noticed the subject didn't come up quite so often in the pub but that may have been because he was too pre-occupied with his own troubles. Glenys had finally managed to get him on his own and demanded to know how and why he'd been foolish enough to upset her daughter.

"She just suddenly took umbrage," he offered lamely. "Don't even know what I said."

"What were you talking about at the time?" persisted Glenys, her steely eyes darting over his body as always.

"Umm, I think we were talking about getting more staff. It was extremely busy, if you remember."

"Why was that a concern of yours and why would Barbara take offence at that?"

Finn rubbed his face, knowing she wasn't going to give up. His brain was working overtime in an attempt to come up with a feasible explanation. Finally, he decided to tell her something near the truth in the hope he could claim a misunderstanding if it came back on him.

"It was just a passing remark, Glenys," he said, with a shrug. "As I remember it, one of us – I don't remember who – said if things carried on being so busy, we'd need more staff. Barbara said there were always more customers when I was on, so I suggested getting some more good-looking bar staff... As a joke, you know. I wasn't really boasting – but, maybe, she thought I was being arrogant – disrespectful. From my point of view, it was just banter and I'm really sorry if I've upset her in any way."

And Glenys had to be satisfied with that but she couldn't understand why Barbara was so offended. Speaking to her later, she gleaned no more from her daughter other than the man was a sick bastard and she didn't want to discuss it further. She did hint, however, that her parents might like to look for a new barman but unfortunately, they misunderstood and thought she meant for them to hire an extra person – not to get rid of Finn. And when they hired Daisy May, a pretty, chirpy, twenty something, Barbara's fury knew no bounds.

"You little snake," she hissed to Finn. "I'll teach you to go behind my back and manipulate my parents. Just you wait!"

"But I didn't," cried Finn, reaching out and touching her shoulder. "I swear to you, Barbara..."

But this time, the touch of his warm hand and the puppy-dog look of pleading didn't work as it had in the past. Barbara jerked her shoulder away and stared viciously into his face.

"You are going to be sorry, Finn *Hunt!*" Her emphasis on his surname left him in no doubt as to what she was thinking. "Unless you can find a way to make it up to me. Very sorry!"

And from that day on, Finn found his shifts reduced, changed at the last minute or lumped together so he didn't get a break. Often, auditions had to be cancelled as cover for him could never be found - which he knew, of course, was a lie.

Something had to be done. Work was scarce and money burnt a hole in Finn's pocket at the best of times. Even the level-headed Benson couldn't come up with any answers. In the end, it was Linus who sparked an idea which, had Finn thought it through, he would have known could only lead to disaster.

"Why don't you just sleep with her?" Linus said sarcastically. "Isn't that what you usually do to get yourself out of a hole? Or in one, as the case may be!"

Linus was very pleased with his little joke. Finn heard him chuckling to himself all the way down the hall and into the kitchen where he relayed his amazing witticism to Benson who was cooking Sunday lunch. He heard Benson's roar of laughter and felt somewhat betrayed but his main focus was on the truth of the statement Linus had made. If he was sleeping with Barbara, she would no longer have cause to hate him and life could go back to normal again.

* * *

Perhaps, out of everyone, the Kshatryias were most affected. They had extra CCTVs put in the shop and their eyes constantly darted to one of these whenever anyone came in or even moved around to search for something they needed. It annoyed some of their customers more than others.

"Do you think you could focus on what I'm saying," said Valerie Figgis, through gritted teeth. "Your eyes are shooting about all over the place."

"Sorry - so sorry," said poor Mrs Kshatryia, her eyes suspiciously bright. "I have to make sure no wicked criminals are coming in."

"And what are you going to do if they are?" Valerie countered spitefully. "Challenge them to a duel?"

"No, no. I don't know but Mr Kshatryia-"

"Will come flying in to the rescue no doubt."

"Everyting all right, Mrs Kshatryia?" Florence, her big boobs spilling over a bright, floral sundress, bounded up to the counter, having caught the conversation as she entered.

"Yes, oh yes." Mrs Kshatryia's actions belied her words. Her smooth, plump hand fussed shakily around the scarf draped on her head and neck. The purple and jade in the material brought out the richness of her skin colour and made her eyes look like huge pansies. Florence was touched by her beauty and told her so.

"Honestly, Mrs Kshatryia, that really suit you. I tink you should wear those colour all the time but then I seen so many other colour look good on you too."

"Do you think we could dispense with the fashion babble and get back to serving customers," snipped Valerie.

"Oh, so sorry. One pound fifty-six please, Mrs Figgis. So sorry." Mrs Kshatryia took the five pound note held out to her and scrabbled about in the till for change.

"It me who should apologise, not you," Florence interjected swiftly. "But I tink it good to chat with your neighbour, don't you? I didn't know you in such a rush, Mrs Figgis. You shoulda said."

Valerie opened and shut her mouth several times. Then, snatching her change from the shopkeeper's hand, she flounced out of the shop. The two women remaining, looked at each other and burst out laughing.

23

"We shouldn't laugh but she such a sourpuss," giggled Florence. "And I won't have it - her bully you like that, Mrs Kshatryia."

"Oh, I get worse than that," she replied and, scanning her neighbour's kind face, was encouraged to confide her constant state of fear. Despite her own misgivings, Florence managed to persuade her if she felt like that, the murderer was, in effect, controlling her life.

"You in Britain," she said. "You gotta stiffen upper lip and stick two finger up at everyone who try to mug you off. You take your power back, my darlin'."

Prithyma Kshatryia contorted her mouth and held up the wrong two fingers and Harry Footlik, who had just come in, backed up Florence's words with a sterling rendition of 'Land of Hope and Glory'.

* * *

Arlo moved Giselle's hand a few centimetres to the left. She was staring off into the distance and, he felt, determined not to look him in the eye.

"Giselle, if you don't really want to do this, it's fine," he said gently. "It was just a whim - not the end of the world if it's not indulged."

She turned and their eyes met.

"I don't mind, Arlo," she sighed. "It's just... Oh, you know - other people. The things they say."

"Yes, I know. But, do we really care? I thought you were above all that."

"I try to be but it gets to you in the end - wears you down, you know. They'll be saying I'm flaunting myself; that I'm vain; that I'll do anything for money; that I've seduced you; that we're-"

"Sleeping together? Yes, I've thought of all that, Giselle. But *we* know the truth so isn't that all that matters? The fact is, the reason I wanted to paint you is you're extremely beautiful which, no doubt, has its 'fors' and 'againsts' like anything else."

Giselle nodded vigorously.

"But you know what gets me," continued Arlo. "If you have a good brain, you are applauded and encouraged to use it and if you have strength, the same and so on with any other asset people have. However, if you have beauty, not so much. Not without criticism anyway. It's almost frowned upon that someone uses their looks and sexual magnetism to their advantage; and yet, surely, that's a gift like any other."

She was staring at him now, her green eyes fixed on his. And, to his horror, a tear appeared and dropped onto her perfect cheek. His hand flew to his mouth, his eyes full of remorse.

"I'm so sorry, Giselle. I didn't mean to-"

"No, Arlo, don't apologise. That was such an amazing and profound thing to say, I can't tell you... I'll never forget what you just said. Never."

He looked confused, chewed the end of his pencil and shuffled his feet.

"Glad to help," he said eventually. "Portraits painted and philosophy offered. No extra charge."

There was a slightly awkward silence and then Arlo said very quickly, "You're not wearing exactly the sort of thing to show you up in the best light though..." as if he were unsure how the remark would be perceived.

"No, I know. I wasn't in a good place when I dressed," she agreed, with a smile. "If you'll give me five minutes, I have an off-the-shoulder, white, cheesecloth number. It's a bit see-through but maybe that will add to your picture..."

Her voice trailed off and she gave a giggle as she skipped back down the path. Arlo shook his head and chuckled to himself. His words had somehow brought comfort to the girl which could only be a good thing. He felt suddenly, gut-wrenchingly protective towards her and it was only then, thoughts of a murderer on the loose worked their way back into his mind.

* * *

Marsha Malloy was in the charity shop. It wasn't something in which she often indulged but she had her reasons, not least of which was to chat to Hilary Scantleberry. Better known at Hippy Hilary, the woman was a good-hearted soul but extremely loose-lipped. She admitted to being capable of picking up several conversations at once and remembering all the details later. Hilary often hinted it could have been her clairvoyance at work as she claimed to be highly psychic. Sadly, her eccentricity gave little credence to her claims. Marsha, while open-minded about the possibility of Hilary's capabilities, was more interested in her ability to pick up random bits of information and her willingness to pass them on.

"Hello, dear," chirped Hilary, in her high, reedy voice. "Not seen you for a while."

"No, I've had one of those rotten summer colds," replied Marsha, holding a floral handkerchief to her nose.

"Were you looking for anything in perculiar?" Despite frequent difficulty in finding the correct word to express her meaning, Hilary found it impossible not to talk to anyone in her shop.

"Just something to read really," said Marsha, scanning the shelves. "Although I might have a general look round while I'm here."

"Well, just help yourself, dear. Let me know if you need any help."

There were but a few seconds silence before Hilary spoke again.

"Dreadful business - that chap in the alley. And no signs of 'em catching anyone for it. I still feel the vibrections of that death. Stops me sleeping at night."

"I'm sorry to hear that, Hilary, but I don't think you need be afraid. As someone said, it's not likely to happen in the same place twice."

"You say that," said Hilary darkly, "But it really all rests on the reason *why* the man was killed. You know, if someone had reasons to want the homes round the Harly to drop in value, then local violences would be a good place to start."

Marsha let go of the pink curtaining she'd spotted and turned with amazement to stare at the little woman. Hilary was busy putting some ladies' clothing into a bag. Her long, greying hair was piled on top of her head and held together with a large purple clip. Her cheeks were a little over-rouged and little splodges of mascara could be seen around her pale blue eyes. Her clothes, always purchased from the charity shop itself, were slightly crumpled. She wore long a skirt and little top in an array of mismatching colours but somehow, on Hilary, it worked. The woman was bordering on super-skinny and smelt of tobacco beneath a mist of lavender and patchouli. But, more to the point, despite her demeanour and appearance, Hilary was not as green as she was cabbage looking.

"I hadn't thought of that," said Marsha. "However, there has to be easier ways to discredit an area."

"Oh, I agree but - a murder! No one will want to buy property round here for months - if not years. And getting rid of someone as horrible as that Lowdon character – well, you're killing two chickens with one rock, if you ask me."

Marsha bit back a smile. For someone who was such a hippy and constantly preached peace and love, Hilary Scantleberry could be quite venomous in her condemnation of anyone who contravened her particular code of ethics.

"That's one thing we do agree on," said Marsha softly. "He was a vile man. I doubt if even his mother would miss him. His wife certainly won't."

Hilary's head came up sharply. "Oh, d'you know 'em then? His mother and his wife?"

"No, no," said Marsha hurriedly. "I just meant... I was being, erm - sarcastic. You know."

Hilary held her gaze just a little too long and Marsha hurriedly changed the subject.

"Is that a pink skirt you're putting in that bag, Hilary? That could be just the shade I'm looking for."

"This is for Podge. I mean, Reg - Prodger," said Hilary, with an apologetic smile. "He came and chose some stuff the other day – for his mother, of course – but he didn't take it at the time cos he was off to town for some do or other."

"I see. Of course. No problem."

The subject was dropped but the truth hung in the air between them like a party balloon, each wondering if the other had seen it. Reg Prodger's mother had been dead for many years.

* * *

Trish had been on holiday and it hadn't been a great success. She hadn't found love; she hadn't even found much fun. What she did find was that the crude antics of some young Britons abroad were both disgusting and shameful. It occurred to her that perhaps she was getting old. Her thirtieth birthday was looming and, to Trish, it was all downhill from there. To make matters worse, her finances were in a shocking state, a fact which always seemed to slip her memory when she saw something she wanted. To escape the gloomy thoughts that descended on her return home, she took herself to the Bee's Knees to spend the last remaining pounds in her purse.

Sadly, Finn wasn't behind the bar. Trish liked his pretty face and amusing chat as much as the next person. Instead, Glenys served her and, after enquiring how she'd enjoyed her holiday, regaled her with news of the body in the alley. Trish, still irritated by how little attention Glenys had paid to her holiday woes – she'd hardly finished the bit about the Spanish waiter who'd promised paradise but delivered disappointment – didn't really take on board the enormity of Glenys' disclosure. Dissatisfied with her customer's response, Glenys repeated herself, speaking slowly and with a slightly raised voice. She was then rewarded with a squeal of horror from Trish who nearly fell off her bar stool.

"What do you mean? A dead body?" she wailed. "Did somebody just keel over or… or what?"

"Stabbed!" said Glenys dramatically. "Councillor Lowdown – cut down in his prime."

'Lowdown' was a popular nick name for the councillor. 'Bin Lowdon' was another.

Trish's hands were shaking as she took her glass and gulped down some wine.

"How am I going to sleep at night?" she said. "I'm on my own in that flat. I'm going to be terrified."

Glenys shrugged. "Well, I don't think you need feel that bothered. You've locks on your windows and doors, surely? Aah, Daisy, at last. You need to be a bit more punctual, dear. Lateness for work is not something we tolerate at the Bee's."

Trish turned her gaze to the girl who'd just appeared. She was far too pretty for Trish's liking, despite her face appearing to be virtually devoid of make-up. She had white blonde hair, cut short and spiky in an elfin sort of way and she wore a cream, broderie-anglais blouse and cut-off denim shorts that showed her neat figure to its best advantage. She flashed Trish a dazzling smile before assuming an expression of contrition for the benefit of her employer.

"I'm so sorry, Mrs Harris. The traffic was truly awful. I really need to find somewhere nearby to live. I'll look in the paper for something at the end of my shift, I promise."

"Yes, well make sure you do," said Glenys sniffily and disappeared into the back.

Daisy went to the other end of the bar to serve someone. Trish watched her every move, an idea beginning to form in her mind. Daisy had an easy, friendly manner but didn't seem too full of herself despite her obvious beauty. In fact, she seemed quite unaware of all the admiring glances. Trish went through a little scenario in her mind and imagined the two of them in her flat; maybe exchanging magazines, watching TV together, having girly nights in with their jim-jams on, drinking wine and painting their toenails. She imagined Daisy handing over a wad of money for her rent and standing in front of her if anyone tried to break in, ready to sacrifice herself for her flatmate. Daisy's face suddenly appeared before her, making her jump.

"Oh, sorry! I didn't mean to startle you." Daisy looked genuinely concerned. "I just wondered if you were ready for a refill?"

Trish made up her mind.

"Did I hear you say you were needing somewhere to live, nearby?"

"Yeah. Do you know somewhere?"

"Well, I've been thinking about taking on a flat mate - a lodger. We could give it a go – a month's trial perhaps?"

"Erm, where do you live exactly?"

Trish hadn't expected anything less than having her hand bitten off by the girl and felt slightly peeved.

"In one of the flats down the road, on the Harlequin triangle."

Daisy let out a high-pitched shriek causing many heads to spin round in her direction and Flannel, the pub's Border terrier, to flee yelping from his special cushion in the corner. She leant over the bar to grab Trish, pull her forward and kiss her soundly on the forehead.

"Oh, my God! My prayers have been answered. I soo wanted to live round there. It's just beautiful - with that little garden and everything. I just love it. Yes, please."

No one could help getting drawn into the girl's enthusiasm and Trish found herself grinning from ear to ear. She jotted down her address and phone number and told Trish to call in after her shift.

"I have to admit, it's not a very big room I'm offering you," she warned.

"Don't need a big room. I travel light," giggled Daisy excitedly. "We're going to have a brilliant time."

And for the first time in ages, Trish experienced a slight feeling of optimism.

* * *

Sulky Sonia Penworthy stormed into number three Grenville Row and flung her school bag across the room.

"Are you alright, darling?" asked her mother tremulously, her heart already sinking.

Sonia stomped over to the fridge, flung open the door and grabbed a carton of smoothie which she proceeded to glug down thirstily.

"That fuckin' Freddie kid," she hissed. "He's an absolute-"

"Sonia!" Her mother was genuinely shocked. "Please don't use that sort of language."

"Mum! I'm fifteen. Everyone says it these days – even little kids. You're living in the dark ages."

"I don't care. I will not have that word used by my family. It's that school. I knew we should have sent you to the private."

"Well, I'm beginning to think you should," retorted Sonia. "Then, I wouldn't have to put up with tossers like Freddie!"

"Again, Sonia, please moderate your language." Catriona spotted her daughter rolling her eyes and decided to ignore it. "So what has Freddie done to ignite such passion in you?" she asked.

"Mum, would you please just talk like a human being instead of some eighteenth-century novelist. It's embarrassing. I mean, I know you're a teacher but really! Do you have to?"

Catriona kept her head down and said nothing. Nobody tells you, she thought, that your children will one day inflict such pain on you.

"Anyway, to answer your question, it's just him. He thinks he's so clever and he's always making some smart-arse remark or other – and usually at my expense. I'm sick of it."

Catriona scanned her daughter's face. She would have been quite pretty if she wasn't always scowling, she thought.

"Can't you talk to him about it? After all, he only lives a couple of doors away."

"Are you mad? I wouldn't give him the satisfaction. Anyway he'd probably kill me. I wouldn't be surprised if it was him bumped off Councillor Bin Lowdon, he's such a psycho. Perhaps he'll get sent back to his real parents soon – with any luck."

Freddie was fostered by Baz and Linda Pugh who lived next door but one to the Penworthys. They'd fostered a few children in their time and all quite successfully until Freddie came along. Freddie was a damaged boy and something of a challenge but they weren't the type to give up. Catriona found them a little coarse for her taste but there was no denying they were good-hearted people. Salt of the earth, her husband Tom called them but Catriona preferred her salt a little more refined.

"That seems a little far-fetched, Sonia, but these days... Well, you never know. Anyway, if you want to use the kitchen table for your homework, you'd better get on with it. Nigel will be home soon."

"Where's the little scrote today then? Doing something amazing as usual, I suppose."

Catriona sighed and gave up the fight. "Whatever! As you would say."

"Don't. That's just sick. I'll go upstairs and do it in my room. I don't want to bump into the creep."

And she flounced off, making every step on the staircase sound like someone was taking a hammer to it. Catriona put her head in her hands and tried to calm her breathing. Soon, Nigel would be home. Nigel with his brilliant brain, capable of passing exams meant for pupils at least two years older than himself and yet with absolutely no concept of social grace whatsoever. Why, she thought, had the good

Lord saddled her with such difficult and unpleasant specimens of humanity. It just wasn't fair. And Tom - who managed to avoid contact with them far more often than was reasonable and then, had the temerity to criticise her parenting skills. She bit her lip to stop herself speaking out loud but didn't manage to stop the thought – bugger the lot of them!

Soon, it would be the summer holidays and they'd be around all the time. And she, Catriona, would be at home unable to escape into the world of work. She'd be faced with the stark reality of what her life had become and the haunting prospect of how much worse it could get. And then, of course, there was the summer barbecue...

Chapter 2

PURPLE

The Harlequin barbecue was traditionally held on midsummer's evening, a decision forced into flexibility by the unpredictable British weather. But the warm, if somewhat oppressive, temperatures held so, despite one or two comments regarding the suitability of a party after a recent, violent crime in the vicinity, it was decided, by the majority, to go ahead.

Offerings of food and drink were expected from all, although size and quantity weren't stipulated as everyone appreciated earnings differed. On the whole, people were generous.

On the morning of the barbecue, preparations were underway and Harry Footlik had taken up his usual role of offering everyone unwanted advice but not actually doing anything. Arlo had the task of starting the barbecue which he'd fashioned out of a big, old oil drum. Florence, Anya and the Marshmallow were busy fixing material over two pasting tables borrowed for the occasion from Hilary's charity shop. Trevor and Bryce were sorting out a music system and Linus and Benson were putting up bunting, a new addition to the decorations made by the fair but arthritic hand of Frances Arbuthnot.

"It's not very well made," her sister said, when she brought it along.

"I'm sure it will be fine," replied Benson, inspecting it. "Tell Miss Arbuthnot we're very grateful."

The look on Valerie's face conveyed that was the very last thing she intended to do as she marched off to 'chivvy Frances along'.

"What's her problem?" said Linus, from up the ladder where he was attaching the first length of bunting to the apple tree.

"Dunno," shrugged Benson. "Some people are just like that. They're unhappy, I suppose."

"You have a very generous heart, young man." This from Hilary who, having just delivered extra cutlery, had overheard the conversation. "You deserve, and will receive, great joy in your life."

And she whisked away, all chiffon scarves and long, floaty skirt.

"I can't vait to see vhat she turns up in later," said Anya. "Ve have similar tastes, Hilary and I, but she is, I think, a little more bohemian."

Anya's accent was suddenly more heavily Russian but, as Florence pointed out, that often happened on big occasions like the barbecue, as though she felt it helped to make her more noticeable.

Everything was ready by six and the Quinners, as they had become known, started to gather. Some, who were having to work and expected a little later, had plates of food put by for them. The smokey smell of the barbecue combined with the aroma of sausages, burgers, chicken and trout cooking away, soon had everyone's mouths watering. People were gravitating to the tables and picking at the nibbles. Bowls of salad glistened invitingly, ready to accompany the cooked foods to come. Hilary had come up with the idea of making a rainbow of salads and was proudly explaining the ingredients of each different coloured bowl.

"For purple, we have red cabbage, red onion and beetroot," she said enthusiastically. "And the orange salad is shredded carrot, orange pepper and, of course, oranges."

"That's genius," said Arlo. "And just the thing for the Harlequin barbie. Did you make all these?"

"Oh no," replied Hilary, delighted with his praise. "Marsha, Florence, Anya - lots of people helped. So here, the green salad is obvious - lettuce mainly, with green peppers and herbs. And the red is tomatoes and pickled red peppers. Yellow is peppers again and sweetcorn and yellow tomatoes and white is the potato salad with onion."

"No blue?" Bryce peered over Arlo's shoulder and shook his head as if deeply disappointed.

Deflated, Hilary moved away but Arlo could have sworn he heard her mutter, "Fuckwit" under her breath.

Soon the food was ready and everyone piled their plates high.

Glasses were clinked and the air was filled with laughter and chat. All seemed to be going well. Even some purple clouds gathering on the horizon didn't elicit comment as they might have done on an ordinary day.

The atmosphere was quite highly charged, Arlo noticed. It was always a well anticipated event but there was something in the air this time, that was different. Voices seemed more strident and drinks were being sunk at quite a rate. This was the first communal event they'd had since the discovery of the body in the alley. Maybe it was that or maybe, because it was horribly close and stormy. That often set people on edge, he mused. Ever the observer, he wandered around the different groups trying to get a feel for the situation.

"Damned if this isn't the best weather we've had for decades," declared Harry Footlik, his voice booming out across the area. Harry was always the first to comment on the weather.

"I wouldn't speak too soon, Harry," said the Marshmallow, resplendent in a pale lavender two piece. "If you ask me, storm's abrewin'."

"It is a bit sticky," agreed Anya. "I must be careful how much I drink. This sort of veather alvays gives me head pain anyvay. Oh look, here comes Hilary. Oh my, she has flowers in her hair."

"Hilary, come and join us," called Arlo. "Can I get you a drink? Pimms?"

"Ooh yes, I'll say," cried Hilary gleefully. "I've decided I'm going to let my hair down tonight."

"We can see that," said Marsha, glancing at the wispy, greying locks hanging round her shoulders. "Doesn't it make you feel hot round your neck?"

"Well, I've got my clips in my bag if it does. I just felt, after what we've all been through, I wanted everything to be free and flowing."

"She be telling us she got no knickers on next." This was Florence whispering in Arlo's ear. He snorted with laughter and nearly spilt the Pimms he was preparing.

"Behave, Flo," he hissed. "You'll get us into trouble."

"Trouble? Oh, not more trouble, surely?"

Arlo froze as Ernest Tiplady's dulcet tones wafted over his left shoulder. The vicar was not a Quinner as the vicarage was a couple of streets away but somehow he always managed to turn up when something was on.

"Just came to see how you were all doing now it's a few weeks on after the er, body, you know... Sorry to er, mention-"

"Bit difficult to ask how we're doing without mentioning it, Reverend." Bryce had already had too much to drink and the spite in him was emerging. "Anyway, we're having a bit of a do so we're fine. But you can see that, as you appear to have gate-crashed as usual!"

Arlo and Trevor spotted the danger simultaneously. Trevor moved as swiftly as his plump body would let him and put an arm round Bryce's waist.

"Come and tell me what you think of Hilary's new look, darling," he said and led his loud-mouthed lover away.

At the same time, Arlo said firmly, "Won't you join us for a drink, Ernest? There's plenty of food if you're at all peckish."

"Too kind. Too kind," said the reverend, eyeing up the laden tables appreciatively. "Just half a shandy, if you can do that for me."

"No trouble," replied Arlo stalwartly. "Flo, would you take Hilary's Pimms over to her."

She smiled and nodded, mouthing, "You're a saint," as she walked away, leaving Arlo the arduous task of chatting to the vicar.

More people began to arrive. Trish turned up looking as pretty as a picture in a new fifties-style sundress that had cost her an arm and a leg. The extra income from Daisy's rent had given her a feeling of security and she was wasting no time in utilising that feeling to make herself poor again. She gravitated to Benson and Linus who were chatting to Patrick Baxter.

"We *are* honoured," she laughed, gazing up into Patrick's steely grey eyes. "No business trips at the moment then?"

"Actually, Trish, I made the last three events if you remember. I deliberately try to keep these weekends free now. I feel it's important for all of us living around the Harly to mix from time to time and have some quality contact."

Trish blushed. She'd forgotten he'd been around for the more recent get-togethers. She could have kicked herself.

"Silly me," she giggled. "I was probably wasted."

It wasn't what she'd wanted to say but stuff always came out of Trish's mouth without any prior warning. She blushed even deeper and Benson, taking pity on her, gave her a hug.

"Quite right too, sweetheart," he chuckled. "That's the whole point of these occasions, is it not? By the way, where's your new flatmate?"

"Working," replied Trish, disappointed he'd mentioned Daisy when all his focus should have been on her. "I suppose that's where Finn is too."

"Oh, yes," said Linus smugly. "Barbara gives him all the rotten shifts these days."

"Really? Why's that then?" asked Patrick, intrigued.

"Silly sod upset her in some way and now she's making him pay for it."

"You shouldn't gloat, Linus," admonished Benson. "It's unattractive."

Linus immediately looked guilty and changed the subject.

"Oh my God, look who's just turned up," he said hastily.

"It's only Tom and Catriona," said Trish, puzzled. "What's wrong with them?"

"Nothing, nothing!" said Linus "But you can be sure their horrible children won't be too far away."

"And there they are!" Benson actually shuddered.

"Are they that bad?" Patrick enquired. "I've not had much to do with them."

"Well, Sonia's going through puberty and Nigel's a child genius," Linus pointed out. "Doesn't make for a good combination really."

"Hmm, well I suppose I really should try to get to know them better," declared Patrick and moved off to welcome the Penworthys.

"Hey, Patrick, it's good you could come along," said Tom Penworthy, shaking his hand vigorously.

"I've just pointed out to someone else that I've actually made the last few get-togethers," said Patrick, laughing. "I must be extremely forgettable!"

"Oh, I wouldn't say that." Sonia came forward, holding out her hand and looking at him from under eyelashes weighed down by a tonne of mascara. The teenager was dark-haired and had a slightly thick-set body but you couldn't say she was unattractive. Her eyes were huge and luminous and her mouth a pretty shape, when she wasn't pushing it into a fashionable pout.

"Umm, don't know if you remember the children," said Tom, rolling his eyes at Sonia. "This is Sonia and this... Oh, where's he gone now? Oh there!" He pointed to a bespectacled boy with a pudding basin haircut. "That's our son, Nigel."

Patrick was obliged to take Sonia's still-extended hand. She held onto his just a little too long until he was forced to pull it away. She grinned at him, wickedly.

"So, what do you want to do when you grow up?" Patrick said pointedly.

"Can't make up my mind," Sonia replied, her expression turning nasty. "Brain surgeon or prostitute? Speaking of which..."

Everyone turned to where she was looking and saw Giselle Greene walking up the path. There was the slightest of pauses in the babble of conversations. Heads turned and then, quickly back. There was no doubt that Giselle looked stunning. Her simple turquoise dress enhanced her golden skin and showed off her perfect figure. The Reverend Ernest Tiplady's legs took it upon themselves to forge towards her, whereupon his mouth offered to get her a drink.

"I'm on it," said Arlo and handed Giselle a glass of Pimms. "This stuff isn't going to last all evening the way everyone's going at it, so I thought you should get one down you at least."

"Oh I say, they look rather nice," said the vicar, staring closely at the fruit-filled glass. "I wouldn't mind trying one of those myself."

Arlo cleared his throat and, as intended, alerted Ernest to the fact that Giselle was holding the drink just in front of her splendid breasts. It didn't look good. The Reverend Tiplady leapt back in a panic, crashed into Catriona Penworthy and, living up to his name, did indeed tip the lady over. Catriona was compensated for her fall by having Patrick lift her swiftly to her feet and concern himself with her ability to cope with such a shock.

The vicar, meanwhile, was turning himself inside out in his attempts to apologise for his clumsiness.

"I'm so very sorry, Miss Greene. Lisa... No, no, it's not Lisa... Sorry, I've forgotten. I'm so stupid. Catriona, can you forgive...? I mean, how can I ever...?"

"Arlo, get the vicar a Pimm's," said Giselle, loud enough to interrupt Ernest's attempts to excuse himself. "He obviously needs something for the shock. Please don't be upset, Reverend. These things happen, admittedly usually after a few bevvies but there... You've started the ball rolling."

Ernest visibly relaxed at the soothing sound of Giselle's voice and he smiled at her gratefully. For him, she then took on the persona of an angel. Not only was she incredibly beautiful but she had a pure and compassionate heart. And, in that moment, the Reverend Ernest Tiplady lost his own heart, just as many others had done before.

* * *

The evening wore on and the Harlequin's triangular courtyard echoed to the sound of laughter, music, conversation and the chinking of glasses and cutlery. Everyone was merry; everyone except perhaps Frances Arbuthnot and her sister Valerie. They arrived with Valerie making a great show of her sister's disabilities. Frances struggled out of their back door on two sticks, determined to leave her wheelchair behind for once. She made no fuss but her progress was naturally slow. Valerie walked just behind her sister, her hands outstretched as though ready to catch her when she inevitably fell.

"You really should have used your chair, Frances."

"You're so stubborn, Frances."

"Why don't you ever listen to me, Frances?"

And so on and so on went Valerie's sharp little voice in her ear. But Frances blotted it out and focused on the laughter and chatter ahead. She knew if she'd had her way, Valerie wouldn't have let her come. Too often these days, Frances gave in to her sister just for a quiet life but, she'd decided, NOT when it came to the Harlequin barbecue. She would go if it was the last thing she ever did.

"Miss Arbuthnot! How gorgeous do you look?" Benson turned to greet her as she reached the party-goers. "And that beautiful bunting you made... Well, it just finishes the whole thing off, don't you think?"

"Yes, I suppose it does." Frances looked around at the colourful, little flags she'd so carefully sewn, despite her painful joints.

"What would you like to drink, Miss A?" Linus asked.

"Oh, I'm not sure. What would you recommend?"

"I think you would enjoy a Pimms," said Benson. "But don't have too many. They can be lethal."

"I really don't think you should be indulging in alcoholic beverages..." began Valerie, seething with jealousy at all the attention her sister was getting.

"Nonsense dear, one won't hurt," returned Frances. "And if it does, it does. You only live once."

"And even if you don't." Florence had joined the welcoming group. "Why worry? There a place on the bench when you want to sit."

"Arlo's put a special cushion on it for you," laughed Linus. "It's got a picture of the Queen on it or something. Seems rather disrespectful to her Maj but I'm sure he meant well."

Frances chuckled and allowed herself to be led to one of the benches where she joined Hilary and Anya who were well on the way to losing their inhibitions. She was soon sharing a toast with them which went from "Bottoms up!" to "Bums up!" to "Arses up!" in a matter of minutes, causing great shrills of laughter. She didn't look back to see what her sister was doing and didn't search for her in the crowd as the evening wore on and grew darker. Frances was content amongst her friends.

*　*　*

Baz and Linda Pugh turned up later than they had hoped. Freddie, their foster child, trailed behind them looking mutinous. He'd had 'discussions' with Baz and Linda regarding his behaviour at school. Of course, they didn't understand – he'd had to put some kid in his place; a kid who was just too smug and up his own backside. Freddie couldn't allow anyone else to be 'cock of the walk'. That was his position. It had to be. In his fifteen years of life, he'd learnt you had to establish your place as top dog pretty quickly or you'd be down there with the rest of the pack, being kicked and abused. He knew all about it and wanted no more experiences of that kind. His new foster parents meant well. A little piece of his heart warmed to their attempts at understanding him but how could they know what it was like to have someone stub their cigarette out on your arm whilst spitting their bile into your face? It was the worst feeling... And yet, something in him craved the adrenalin that filled his body during those moments and made him want to inflict his pain on someone else. Of course, Freddie didn't understand why, when he saw a weaker being than himself, he had this urge. It was just what he was used to – had become part of him and yet, the gentle, wise counselling given to him by the Pughs, messed with his head; confused him and made him angry, frustrated and unsure what to do with those feelings. His eyes lit up as he spotted Sonia but before he could make his way to her, her tiresome brother, Nigel approached him.

"Ah, Freddie," he said, sounding like a little old man. "Tho good to thee thomeone nearer my own age at latht. Although not nearer my IQ of courthe." Nigel gave his hiccupping sort of laugh.

Freddie put his arm around Nigel and, having lulled him into a false sense of security, found a nice, plump bit of back to pinch.

"You're not that clever, Niggle," he hissed. "You can't even thpeak thenthibly coth you can't thay your etheth tho you thound like a thilly thod!"

And with that, he pushed the little boy forward so he tripped and his spectacles ended up sliding down his nose. Nigel turned and looked balefully at his attacker, wishing that he could spin round and turn into one of the superheroes he loved so much. One day, he thought, he would get his own back. He would invent something that would show up the bullying gene in people and, by then, he would be Prime Minister and he would get a law passed that all bullies be exterminated at birth. Nigel watched as Freddie moved away chuckling to himself and knew the gut-churning feeling of pure hate.

* * *

Finn and Daisy finally pitched up just as it was decided it was dark enough to light the lanterns.

"Ah see, just for us," cried Finn, indicating the strings of lights with a flourish of his hand.

"Oh, my Lord, that looks so pretty," breathed Daisy, showing her perfect teeth in a smile of delight.

"Just like you."

"Oh, you!" she laughed and punched him on the arm. "I'll be needing the sick bucket."

Sonia, who was surreptitiously sneaking some wine nearby, caught a glimpse of the pretty newcomer and decided she hated Daisy even more than she hated Trish and Giselle and began plotting her downfall.

Benson and Linus spotted their friend and, more to the point, his gorgeous, little companion and made a bee-line for them. Trish, who always followed the young men of any group, trotted after them.

Patrick was having difficulty taking his eyes off Giselle who, to his amazement, seemed more interested in chatting to the older members of the crowd. Out of everyone there, he was the one person who'd never heard the rumours about her and couldn't believe that someone so stunning appeared to be on their own. He'd done his duty in chatting to Tom and Catriona who he found somewhat dull. Catriona, in particular, was as nervous as a racehorse and he felt he had to constantly reassure her. Maybe, she was still in shock with the vicar careering into her like he did but he suspected it was more than that. She seemed intent on getting, and keeping, his full attention. Her daughter was obviously a hormonal, teenage nightmare and, he was sure, quite a handful. Catriona's eyes constantly darted about as though trying to locate her children but there was something in her expression that said she didn't really want to know what they might be up to. Her husband had no interest in any of them. He barely glanced at his wife but spoke with great affection to every other person who joined them. Out of the four Penworthys, Patrick had the most sympathy for Nigel. Despite his obvious intelligence and geekiness, he was just a lonely little boy who wanted someone to talk to.

Patrick decided the time had come to introduce himself properly to Giselle. A few drinks had given him that little bit of extra courage he needed and he turned to go over to her. Too late!

"Whoa, Patrick! Good to see ya. Hey, Linny, look who's here. Glad you could make it, man."

Baz Pugh had grabbed Patrick's hand and was pumping it remorselessly. He only stopped to put an arm around his wife when she hurried over to join them.

"Patrick! How are you?" squealed Linda. "Look at your handsome face. We don't get to see that often enough."

"Easy tiger!" roared Baz, with a guffaw of laughter.

"Actually, I was here last year," said Patrick wearily. "And Christmas. Although I was, admittedly, rather late for that celebration."

"Well, never mind. You're here now. We were a bit late gettin' here ourselves - some issues with the boy, you know." Linda pulled a few gurning expressions – a habit for which she was well-known – indicating that Freddie was the boy in question.

"Yeah, apparently we missed some tricks; like the vicar falling for Giselle's charms. You know, like literally!" Baz's raucous laugh rang out into the night and one or two people turned to stare crossly at the culprit. Baz, as always, misinterpreted their expressions and waved to everyone in his usual friendly manner. He and Linda continued to engage Patrick in their loud, overbearing way until he could bear it no longer. They were decent enough people; nothing wrong with them at all. They just weren't his type. He muttered his excuses and finally made his escape. But now, Giselle was nowhere in sight.

* * *

Harry Footlik was enjoying himself enormously. Through his beer goggles, he felt he was king, his little entourage of ladies all around, gazing up at him adoringly and hanging on his every word. Reg Prodger who, in Harry's opinion, could often monopolise the conversation, had not appeared so the audience was all his. In truth, Reg was very shy and quietly spoken which had the effect of endearing him to their female friends who much preferred that to Harry's loud blusterings. It was not for the want of trying but Harry had never married; not surprising, Marsha Malloy pointed out, when you possessed such a surname.

"I mean, who in their right mind would want to be called Mrs Footlik," she observed, when Harry was otherwise engaged at the drinks table.

"I'm surprised he never changed it," remarked Anya. "It's not that difficult, you know."

This raised a few eyebrows in Anya's direction and she swiftly diverted the attention elsewhere.

"You have been married, Marsha, have you not? And Hilary, vat about you?"

"Yes, I was married - briefly," admitted Hilary, stretching her arms above her head and leaning back over the bench only just missing punching the vicar in the stomach. She continued her stretch for a few seconds while the others admired her bendiness and vowed to take up yoga as well. Tiplady, alarmed by Hilary's position and the proximity of her hands to his crotch, scuttled away not wanting to be the perpetrator of any further incidents.

"Dear Stewart, he was a real eco-warrior. I've not had him for ten years now," Hilary continued, still at full stretch.

"Oh, I'm so sorry, dear," murmured Marsha. "How did he die?"

"Oh, he's not dead," said Hilary, springing upright again. "But you know, a lot of those types tend to believe in free love and I lost him to... well, several people really, including a farmer who supplied veg to the local health shop where he worked. Stewart said he was a very organic man but I think he meant orgasmic. Still, you know, onwards and upwards. No good looking back."

There was a short lull in the conversation while people digested this forthright revelation.

"And you Marsha? You alvays keep quiet about your private life." Anya, nonplussed with Hilary's story, decided on another avenue.

"That's why it's called private," Marsha retorted, pressing her lips stubbornly together. "So you can keep quiet about it."

Anya and Hilary both began protesting at once until Harry walked back into the fray, holding a tray-load of drinks.

"Ladies, ladies," he boomed. "Come, come! We're supposed to be enjoying ourselves. What's with the raised voices?"

Marsha ignored the temptation to mention kettles, pots and

blackness and stated her position very clearly. "Our friends want to snoop into my private life and I'm afraid I'm not playing."

"Well, Marsha, I have to agree you're a very intriguing character and the longer you keep quiet, the more desperate for information we're going to be." Harry handed round the drinks and turned his rather bleary gaze onto Marsha once again.

"I don't care how desperate any of you are," she said, shrugging. "Anyway, I have to see to Toodleoo and Toodlepip, so I'm off. If I don't make it back, enjoy the rest of your evening."

And with that, the Marshmallow got up from her seat in quite a sprightly manner. She was a tall woman and, in that moment, appeared taller as she discarded her usual stoop and marched off defiantly towards the flats and her precious pets.

"Oh dear. D'you think we offenended her?" said soft-hearted Hilary.

"No, she vill be fine. I've asked her thinks before and she alvays clamp up," said Anya, with a sigh.

"Well, come on then Anya," said Harry eagerly. "Tell us about yourself because you're another cagey customer I seem to remember."

"Me? Ah, nothing to tell," replied Anya, annoyed the focus was back on her. "Or perhaps too much to tell, eh? Many lovers in many place, many times. There, does that satisfy your fantasies, Harry Footlik!"

And with that, they had to be satisfied and turned their attention to a very faint rumble of thunder that could be heard in the distance.

* * *

Patrick finally tracked Giselle down. He spotted her coming down the stairs from her flat above the hairdressers. He stood transfixed for several seconds and just watched her. She even moved beautifully. She made her way to a group of people and he remembered he wanted to talk to her on her own. He moved swiftly but it was too late. Benson was smiling and making a gap for her to join the group. Patrick swore under his breath.

"Whazupwiyou?" said a voice at his side. Sonia!

"Sorry, I didn't understand what you said," he snapped.

"You should be nice to me or I could make things very awkward for you," she said, through gritted teeth.

Alarm bells rang.

"What makes you think I'm not being nice to you, Sonia?" he said pleasantly.

"Hey, you remembered my name." She smiled, altering her sullen face completely.

"Of course I remembered your name. Why wouldn't I? You're a..." He was about to pay her a compliment but something stopped him. He had to be careful here; very careful indeed. Girls like Sonia were a dangerous breed. It occurred to him he'd rather be swimming with sharks.

"I think your mum was looking for you." He knew this wasn't going to go down well but he was stumped for anything safe to say.

"So?" Sonia stared at him belligerently.

"Just saying," he said, trying to sound nonchalant. "Hey, I need the loo. I'll catch you later."

"Okay," she said huskily, moving towards him so he could see how thickly she'd applied make-up to her somewhat spotty, teenage skin. "I'll make sure I don't run too fast."

Patrick gave the briefest of smiles, hot-footed it up to his flat and then, had a horrible thought. Please God, she didn't follow him there.

* * *

Daisy hadn't met Giselle before. She stared at her, unblinking, for some time until Giselle, unable to stand it any longer, turned her own gaze on Daisy. Daisy's hand flew to her mouth in consternation.

"Oh, I'm so sorry. I was staring. It's just you're so beautiful."

"That's okay." Giselle was taken aback by the girl's honesty. "Thank you for such a lovely compliment. I'm Giselle Greene. I live over the hairdressers. There! The cherry red paint job."

"Daisy. Daisy May."

"Really? Daisy *May?* Sorry, that was rude! Now it's my turn to apologise."

"Oh, it's okay. It's a sort of nickname... well, part of it's my own. Anyway, I've moved in with Trish. The fuschia pink-"

"Oh yes, I know where Trish lives. That's nice for you both."

"Well, we hope so." Trish moved in to join them. "It's not been long but so far, we've got along okay, haven't we Daisy?"

"Yes but to be honest, I get along with everyone. You'd have to work really hard to fall out with me. I'm so laid back, I'm horizontal."

"That's interesting," remarked Giselle. "I've never met anyone that easy-going. I'm intrigued now. What makes you so... you know, chilled."

Daisy shrugged. "I just never found anything to get that upset about. Life's... too short."

She turned away, holding up her glass to sip at her drink, making Giselle wonder if she was hiding something.

"Hey, you sound like the perfect partner," joined in Benson. "No nagging, no moaning, no emotional black-mailing. What a girl!"

"I was just going to say the same." Linus squeezed between them, determined to be included. "I'm very easy-going myself."

Benson gave a snort of derision and looked over at Finn to see if he'd heard Linus's declaration. But Finn was gazing at Daisy. He had a fuzzy sort of look about him and there was a stupid grin on his face. Linus, who'd glanced at Benson to tear him off a strip for laughing at him, followed his friend's eyes and also caught the expression on Finn's face. Trish spotted it too and pursed her lips in annoyance. Trust Daisy to bag the best looking bloke in the Harly. She should have known the girl was trouble. Giselle stood back and watched them all, sighing at the complexities of human relationships and wondering where it would all end. It ended, at that time, with Daisy's giggle as she spotted Patrick zigzagging across the area towards them.

"What on earth is he up to?" she cried. "Does he think he's in the SAS or what?"

Patrick arrived at the group, having alarmed several other guests on his way. He realised they'd been watching him by the expressions on their faces and couldn't help grinning.

"That must have looked mad," he admitted.

"What? Why? Who?" laughed Finn, shaking his head.

"The Penworthy girl. She's stalking me, for God's sake."

"Ooh, I'd be careful," said Giselle. "That could be a very dangerous situation."

Patrick turned to her and, finally, found himself looking deeply into her amazing green eyes.

"My thoughts exactly, Miss Greene," he breathed. "And that's not the sort of danger I'm interested in."

His words were swallowed up by another low rumble from the purple skies.

* * *

The Kshatryias turned up very late but at least they turned up. Everyone made huge efforts to engage with them, a mistake really as the Kshatryias didn't drink and were then forced to endure other people's alcohol fuelled boisterousness. Even the Reverend Tiplady had had enough to make him much more confident and verbose than usual.

"We should get together some time," he suggested, his hands hanging limply from his wrists in front of his chest. "Have a good old exchange of our beliefs. I bet you we'd discover we have a lot more in common than you might think."

Prem Kshatryia put a protective arm around his wife's shoulders. "We know all about your religion, Reverend. There is no point in any discussions. It is not the religion that is important but the character of those practising it."

"Yees." The vicar stroked his jaw and tried to look like he knew what was meant.

"Words can be interpreted in many ways," Prem continued. "Those who *feel* the teachings in a way that benefits all, they are the true holy men."

"Ah yes, of course. How very true." Ernest struggled to move on from the subject. "Can I get you anything? A drink perhaps... not a, you know... I know you don't... I mean, a non-alco... a soft drink..."

"We're fine, thank you. We can get our own if we need to. But very kind, thank you."

"Hi, Pretty! How we doin'?" Florence bounded up, full of the joys of spring and quite a lot of cava.

Prem looked at her. "What is this? Pretty?"

"It's nothing, Prem. Florence and I are friends and that's how she's interpreted Prithyma."

"We call that a nickname, Mr Kshatryia," said Ernest, trying to be helpful.

"Yes, I know what it is." Prem said. "I have lived here many years and I am not a stupid man."

"Prem trained as a solicitor when he was a young man back in India." Prithyma looked up at her husband, her face full of pride.

"Oh I'm sure. I didn't mean to say-"

"Why you not doing that now then?" asked Florence, interrupting the vicar's stammering attempts to make amends.

"Well, you see, he-"

"There are many reasons, none of which we want to go over again – especially at a celebratory gathering." Prem's tone was gentle but very firm and his wife nodded and said no more.

"Course," said Florence and, holding his gaze, she smiled at him. "Understand. We just be friends."

It was a simple statement but held within it a wealth of meaning and Prem inclined his head very slightly and smiled back. Ernest, watching them, learnt something; something about acceptance, truth and respect. He felt it deep in his guts, the energy of it shifting around and reaching his heart; a message shooting from his heart to his brain. Prem did not feel the need to explain himself, let alone apologise for anything in his life and his respect for himself somehow radiated out to those around him and gave them a feeling of being respected too. Ernest, on the other hand, was constantly apologetic and needing to explain himself. He knew it irritated people and the more it irritated them, the more flustered he became. And here was a man who held himself with calm dignity; who knew who he was and was comfortable with that. The reverend felt a tremor of envy run through his body.

"I need to go home," he said suddenly. "I have things to think about."

And for once, he didn't apologise. He just held up his hand in a farewell gesture and began to make his way out of the garden. He stopped briefly to clap Arlo on the shoulder and thank him for allowing him to stay and then, he was gone.

His exit was followed by a flash of light and thunder rumbled once again.

* * *

Looking back, it may have been beneficial if everyone had decided to abandon the celebrations at that stage but such is the magic of alcohol that less is never enough. The drinks still flowed and food was still being picked at. Tongues wagged and new information was shared.

Hilary had stumbled over to the younger crowd and was regaling them with stories of how drugs had enhanced her youth and brought out her creativity.

"There's nothing wrong with it," she cried, waving her glass around and spattering them all with wine. "Shamans used mind... en... enchanting drugs to diagalose and previct and make wise judgementals, you know. And as for the sex... WELL! What can I say?"

Everyone flinched and prayed that Hilary Scantleberry never discovered what she could say.

"In fact, I would go as far as to say..."

Everyone held their breath.

"I would go as far as to say that if anyone could get hold of some stuff for me," And here she winked several times in quick succession making her look like she had a nervous tick. "I would go so far as to say, I would be extreeemly grateful!"

She began winking again but this time it seemed to affect her balance and she started to topple. Benson and Linus moved swiftly and managed to catch her before she hit the ground.

"I think we'd better get you home, Hilary," said Benson, scooping her bird-like body up into his arms. Hilary smiled beatifically and snuggled into his neck.

"Oh, yes please," she sighed. "I always liked a black man."

"Come with us, Linus," ordered Benson, his eyes widening in alarm. "I may need you to er - open doors."

Linus tutted but did as he was bid.

"Well, they say the sixties was where it was at," laughed Giselle, watching them go. "I wish I'd been there."

"I'm glad you weren't," said Patrick recklessly and was puzzled to see the shutters come down on her face. He was unable to question her expression however, as raised voices rang out from the other side of the garden.

"I think it's a bit much that you're blaming Freddie when it's quite obvious to everyone that your daughter's nothing but a-"

"How dare you! How dare you disparage our child like that!"

"Look love, just because you swallowed a dictionary doesn't make you better than the rest of us!"

"Now, we really all need to calm down here-"

"Yeah, well you try calming down when someone's accusing your child of something it's just not in his nature to do."

"Oh, don't make me laugh! Not in his nature! Dear God, do you even know him?"

And then screams and shouts and no one could bear it any longer. They all rushed over to where the Pughs and Penworthys stood; only they weren't all standing any more. Linda had wrestled Catriona to the ground and she, in turn, was doing a grand old job of yanking cruelly on her attacker's hair. Baz was trying to find two arms belonging to different females so he could pull them apart and Tom was hopping from one foot to the other, obviously undecided on what action to take.

Arlo, on the other hand, knew exactly. He soon had an arm around Catriona's skinny waist and lifted her from the ground. This left Linda panting and growling on all fours so her husband was able to get to her.

"Oh, *please!*" said Trevor, the back of his hand on his forehead. "I can't bear all this violence. This is *not* what living around the Harly is all about."

"Quite right, Trev," said Arlo. "Ladies, what on earth got into you?"

"They were fighting over their children, that's all," said Baz, in quite a subdued voice for him. "You know what women are like when they're defending their kids."

"She attacked me!" exclaimed Catriona. "I was putting forward a point of view. It didn't warrant that sort of reaction."

It did seem a bit extreme. Catriona's face was covered in tears interspersed with a little blood from a cut on her forehead. Her nose was running and her clothes, streaked with mud and grass stains. Linda had the grace to look a little ashamed although she herself was holding her head which was intensely sore from the handful of hair Catriona had removed.

"She's been pushing it," she said gruffly. "Ever since the murder, she's been trying to say our Freddie had something to do with it or if he didn't, then he'd grow up into the sort of person who would do that sort of thing. I can't have that. She wouldn't shut up so I had to make her."

No one knew what to say. Not until Bryce stepped unsteadily forward, giggling uncontrollably.

"Oh my God, what a hoot! The Harlequin triangle's first bitch fight. Hilarious. When's the next round?"

Trevor's move towards Bryce wasn't quick enough. Baz got in first. He grabbed the younger man's shirt in his hefty fist and pulled him close, snarling, "Hey! You think people getting upset is funny, do you Bryce? Well, how about I upset you and you can find out how funny that is, yeah?"

The tension crackled like lightning in a bruise-coloured sky, echoing the vibrations of the oncoming storm. It was rare to see congenial Baz lose his temper. Everyone held their breath and if Anya Petrovka hadn't chosen that moment to faint, anything could have happened. She keeled over spectacularly, knocking Valerie Figgis forward so she spilled her drink over Giselle's beautiful turquoise number. It was chaos but somehow it broke the tension and everyone moved, rushing to bring solace to the afflicted and calm to everyone in general. Florence went swiftly to see to Anya whilst Harry Footlik took Valerie's arm and led her to sit on one of the benches. She was rather ungracious in her acceptance of his ministrations, annoyed that all the younger men seemed pre-occupied seeing to other women.

Baz Pugh very wisely escorted his wife and young Freddie back home. His arm was protectively around Linda's shoulders and he was heard to speak to her in gentle tones. Catriona glared at their retreating backs, resenting the kindness her enemy was being shown by her husband. Her own had sloped off to the drinks table and was pouring himself a large glass of red wine. Suddenly, she felt a warm hand take hers and turned to see Daisy smiling at her.

"Why don't you come and sit down? Just till you get your breath back. I've some wipes in my bag and I'll get a drink to steady you."

The kindness in Daisy's voice set Catriona off. Tears coursed down her cheeks as she allowed herself to be led to one of the folding chairs donated for extra seating. Daisy gave her some tissues from her bag, plus the packet of wipes and a small mirror and went to pour her a drink. Tom was still lurking by the table and he looked uncomfortable as Daisy approached. But she just smiled at him.

"Pretending a situation doesn't exist, doesn't make it go away," she said eventually. "It's like a boil. It'll just keep growing until you take notice. You need to lance it as soon as you can."

Tom had had far too many drinks to really take this on board and decipher the message but he stared at her bleary-eyed and tried to commit her words to memory. He had a funny feeling they might make a lot of sense one day.

The rumbling continued but so far the rain held off. Everyone was suddenly very merry, fuelled, no doubt, by adrenalin brought on by the dramatic events of the evening. Trevor continued to have problems reigning in Bryce and Valerie had no success at all in getting Frances to go home. She even tried for sympathy, pointing out how shaken she was with that woman crashing into her but Frances countered her argument by saying it was up to Valerie to leave and that she, Frances would see to herself.

Patrick had gone off to get a cloth for wiping down Giselle's wine-soaked dress, despite the fact she'd assured him it was quite unnecessary.

"D'you know, the world would be a much better place if people just worried about themselves instead of fussing over what they think others need," Giselle remarked to Arlo.

He nodded. "No doubt, Gee, but the problem is they want to feel needed so they try and make themselves indispensable."

"I never thought of it that way," she murmured, absently scrubbing at her dress with a serviette.

"Well, I'm not saying everyone does but you know how good it feels when someone sincerely and wholeheartedly thanks you for something. It's really great, yeah?"

Giselle's face softened and her eyes misted over as she smiled at Arlo. "You're a very wise creature, Arlo diMarco de Pelio. A very wise creature indeed."

Patrick, returning from his flat with several towels, saw the look and was stopped in his tracks. He could feel the warmth of her expression from where he stood and wondered if she would ever confer such a look on him. He couldn't believe she had any feelings for the artist. Why would she? Arlo was tall and lean with rather a gaunt look about him. He had to be in his fifties. His hair, which was thinning at the front and too long at the back, was peppered with grey and his face, although nut brown from gardening in the sun, was deeply lined. His best features were his eyes which were a deep, brilliant blue.

Patrick felt a primeval surge in his belly and subconsciously prepared for the fight ahead as he moved forward with his offering of clean, fluffy towels with which to wipe Giselle's outfit.

The night darkened, turning a deeper shade of purple and the rumbling continued.

* * *

Trish refilled her glass with the dregs from two bottles of wine and wandered around the garden pretending to be interested in various plants. In fact, she was hoping to bump into Benson or Finn who seemed to have mysteriously disappeared since Anya Petrovka's fainting fit. She spotted the swing hanging invitingly from the apple tree and made her way over to it. Her plan was to place herself decoratively on it and hope the boys would spot her when they returned. It was well lit as the tree had been adorned with fairy lights and would, she hoped, show her up to her best advantage. Had she looked in a mirror she would have quickly realised that it would take more than a few fairy lights and a magical setting to do that. Her make-up was sliding from her face and her hair was only piled up on one side of her head, the other half having toppled down some time earlier. Even the fifties dress had lost its crispness and looked limp and crumpled.

Trish neared the tree and entered a dark patch hence she couldn't quite see what was at ground level. It was thus she missed the legs she tripped over and found herself falling towards the swing. She managed to catch hold of it however and saved herself from crashing painfully into the ground.

"What the. . .?" Trish turned to peer into the darkness to see what had been responsible for her trip. There was movement, a groan and Sonia hauled herself into sitting position.

"What on earth are you doing lying on the ground?" cried Trish, shock sobering her a little.

"Dunno. Think I must've pissed out... I mean, passed..."

"I think you were right the first time," said Trish, sitting herself in the swing. "How much have you had?"

"Dunno. Think've 'ad quidealod," slurred the girl. "Don' tell mum an' dad, will you?"

"Maybe you should tell them yourself," advised Trish and immediately knew how ridiculous that must have sounded. "No, I won't say anything but they're going to realise as soon as they see you."

"You keep 'em talking! Jus' keep'em talking... and I'll sneak back'ome, yeah?"

"Well, I suppose. Can you even walk though?" Trish suddenly spotted Benson, Linus and Finn strolling down the path, chuckling. An idea came to her and she stood up, waving her arm frantically. Having got their attention, Trish beckoned furiously, obliging them to come over.

"Whatchoodoin'?" growled Sonia, through clenched teeth. "I don' wanna be seen like this."

"It's okay, Sonia. They'll help. Don't worry about a thing."

Trish didn't pick up on Sonia's concern over her appearance and drunkenness in front of the boys despite the fact she would have felt exactly the same had she been in that position herself. As it was, she was unaware of her own sorry state, too excited to have something in which to engage the three bachelors. Fortunately for both girls, the young men had also imbibed a fair amount and didn't notice the less than perfect condition of the females before them.

A plan was quickly made that Trish and Finn – she'd been very specific that Finn be the one to stay with her - start up a conversation with Tom and Catriona Penworthy. Meanwhile, Linus and Ben were to escort yet another female guest – this time, the other end of the age scale – home.

Catriona was still shaken when Trish and Finn found her with Daisy who was talking gently to her. Trish looked round for Tom. She took a firm grip on Finn's shirt sleeve and pulled him along.

"We'll leave Daisy to talk to Catriona," she said brightly. "She seems to be doing a grand job of taking her mind off things."

"Well, I could just-"

"No, Finn. I need you with me. Look, there's Tom. Let's check he's okay. Tom! We were just saying what a rotten thing to happen on a night like this. What caused it do you think? Too much booze? What?"

And so she went on. Tom stood listening in amazement but when Finn got the giggles, decided he'd had enough.

"Look, thanks for your concern," he said tartly. "But I really don't want to talk about it. It's bad enough your wife starts brawling at an event like this. I just want to forget about it."

And he was off before they could stop him. Trish looked around frantically but there was no sign of a drunken Sonia being hauled home by Benson and Linus, who were only minimally more sober. She breathed a sigh of relief and turned to Finn.

"Mission complete," she said, smiling up at him.

"You were amazing Trish," Finn replied, grinning back. "God knows how you thought of so much to say."

"You helped too," replied Trish. "Just by being there." And she took her reward by throwing her arms around his neck and kissing him passionately.

Lightning rent the air, illuminating the little area and all its glorious colours. The brightness lit up Trish and Finn's kiss which was seen by Daisy. It showed the expression on Daisy's face which was spotted by Catriona who started crying again. This was seen by Tom who wondered how he could ever tell such a highly-strung person like his wife that he didn't love her. In another part of the triangle, Arlo caught a look of malevolence in Patrick Baxter's eyes and wondered what he'd done wrong and Florence spotted Giselle touching Arlo's arm yet again. Tucking her hand through her husband's arm, Prithyma Kshatryia wondered what Florence was so interested in and Valerie, noticing Prithyma's action, sighed sadly and wished for a different life. Harry Footlik heard her sigh and wondered what was making her sad. Bryce, terrified of storms, jumped at a crack of lightening. He just missed stepping on Harry's toe and Trevor held out a hand to steady him. Seeing this, Frances finally got to her feet, having decided it was time to go. Benson and Linus caught the kiss between Finn and Trish and nudged each other, mercilessly. And then, thunder crashed mightily and the first drops of rain fell.

The lightning struck again, this time for longer, giving an even brighter view of the arena below. A cry went up as a new character appeared on the scene.

"My God! Is that Reg?"

And sure enough, coming gingerly down the fire escape, was Reg Prodger - only it was difficult to be a hundred percent sure. Reg was wearing full female regalia and he stopped and posed on the stairs, despite the rain, proud and carefree for all the world to see. This is who I am, he seemed to be saying. Take it or leave it.

And then the storm began in earnest.

Chapter 3

DOVE GREY

Harry Footlik carefully twisted a bit of honeysuckle around the trellis. It was very quiet. He had hoped someone would be out in the garden but it seemed everyone had the Monday morning doldrums and had stayed in bed; except those already at work, of course.

It was one of those days when he felt his loneliness deeply; one of those times when he wished he hadn't lived quite so much for the day and thought a little more about his future. He'd always been a bluff sort of fellow, brushing off sentimentality and vulnerability as terms concocted by therapists and tree-huggers. An army man, Harry was a whole-hearted supporter of the stiff upper lip and fire in the belly. Now, he was surrounded by an abundance of women who seemed to talk rather a lot about *feelings*.

Harry's first experience of women came from a mother who was a gung-ho hunting, shooting, fishing type and had never shown the slightest compassion for any living thing other than herself. As he matured, he went on to engage with the sort of females grateful for being bedded and 'given a good seeing to' and certainly not bothered about *commitment*! At least, that's what he'd always presumed.

At the barbecue, Hilary, in her inebriated state, had shocked him by telling him that he was a "prime example of the worst kind of masculity" and that he would "do the world a favour by purchasing a blow-up doll to salidify himself". Having deciphered her words, he tried to remember what had prompted the outburst and was uncomfortably convinced he'd made a lewd comment on how many women he'd serviced in his time and how he may easily have fathered an army. He'd been so busy laughing at his own remarks that he hadn't, at first, noticed the silent glares coming from those around him. But now, in the quiet beauty of morning in the Harlequin garden, it all came crashing back.

Women were strange creatures, he thought, and yet, remembering a past invite to afternoon tea at Anya's, he concluded there was a lot to be said for having them around. He remembered the occasion vividly; the sweet smell coming from a bowl of pot-pourri, quite alien to him when compared to the mustiness of his own flat; the soft colours of the walls, lilacs, mushroom and creams and how comfortable on the eye, the blending of her furnishings with those colours. So different from his own mish-mash of stuff, thrown together over the years. He remembered the gentle chink of china as she brought in the tray; the pleasing ritual of placing cups on saucers and the pouring of milk from a dainty jug. He would never have bothered with all that; why mess up another container when the stuff was already contained? But, as he watched, he became mesmerised and felt himself relax back onto the soft, feather-filled cushion behind him. Even so, he was unimpressed by the size of the cup which he could drain in a single gulp but then, found himself sipping slowly and savouring each mouthful – a new experience which Harry found surprisingly satisfying.

He remembered soothing music playing softy in the background and the swish of her skirts as she moved around the room; a gentle breeze from an open window, wafting through the white gauze of the curtains, filtering the light to a level which was kind on the eyes. All those little things, Harry would have deemed "a load of twaddle", or worse if no ladies were present. But now, he rather longed for the scent of femininity to waft past his nostrils and to feel the gentle touch of a warm hand brushing his arm. There was something deeply nurturing about such things that Harry had missed out on in his life. And now, in his late sixties, he'd begun to regret the choices he'd made as a young man. Stories of his sexual prowess only lingered in his own memory and meant nothing to those he told. Those stories brought him no comfort when he sat alone in his flat. That's what it was too, he thought. It was flat. His place offered no vibrancy for the visitor; no comfort, no feeling of welcome or joy. It was just a place where someone resided; someone who hadn't cared for others nor had been cared for himself.

It was all a bit too depressing so he turned his mind to the spectacle of Reg Prodger in a dress and tried to work out whether the man was under the influence, creating a humorous scene or just horribly troubled.

* * *

Trish couldn't believe her eyes when, a week after the barbecue, there was a knock on the door and it turned out to be Sonia, standing there, all puffy-eyed and red-nosed.

"Nobody likes me," she whimpered, when Trish brought her through to the lounge. "My parents hate me, my brother despises me and I'm never going to get a boyfriend because I have no freedom of choice. I might as well be in prison!"

Trish opened and shut her mouth several times as she wondered how to say, "Why are you telling me?" without sounding callous.

"I'm sorry to hear that," she said eventually, scanning Sonia's face for any adverse reaction. "I expect it'll all get better though."

"Get better! How will it get better?" shrieked the distraught girl. "I have the most vile parents in the world. My mother is just a hysterical attention seeker, my dad's never around and my brother is a freak. So, what the fuck?"

Trish bit her lip and looked around for inspiration.

"I really don't know what to say," she said nervously. "I don't have children and I don't have brothers or sisters so I'm probably not the best person to-"

"But I thought you were my friend!"

"Did you? Well, I mean, of course I am... sort of..."

"Well, you helped me at the barbecue, didn't you? So I thought you wanted us to be friends so here I am. And I need your help and you're not being... you're just standing there, looking thick."

"So what do you want her to do?"

They both jumped. Neither of them had heard Daisy come in. She stood in the doorway, all pretty and petite in her summer dress and sandals but her face looked drawn and pale.

Sonia's eyes flashed with anger at the interruption.

"Advice!" she snapped. "I want some advice as to what to do about my appalling situation at home."

Daisy dropped her bag onto a chair and slowly walked up to the teenager, looking her up and down as she did so.

"You look alright to me," she said finally.

"Well of course, I *look* alright," hissed Sonia, her face contorted with frustration. "But mentally, they've really fucked me up. I'm desperately unhappy. I need to spread my wings and experience... stuff! And I'm restricted. They won't let me do *anything*!"

"Oh dear. What a shame. Poor you," said Daisy, her voice completely devoid of all emotion. "You'll get over it. Just hang in there."

"What?" Sonia was aghast.

"Sonia, you don't have a problem. Believe me. If you think you have problems, just wait and I promise you, you'll find out what problems are. Now, would you leave please. I need some peace and quiet."

She marched over to the door and held it open pointedly. Sonia stared at her in disbelief for a few seconds and then walked over to her. She stopped and pushed her face into Daisy's.

"You are going to regret this, you bitch," she snarled.

And to complete Sonia's humiliation, Daisy burst out laughing. But when she'd gone, Daisy wiped the spittle from her cheek and burst into tears.

* * *

Finn had made a mistake. He knew it was a mistake and he knew it was huge. To get back into Barbara Harris's good books, he'd turned his charm ray on full beam. At first, she'd sneered at his attempts; told him she knew exactly what he was doing and that it "wouldn't wash with her". But, from past experience, Finn knew it was only a matter of time. He was a master in seduction. He let her catch him watching her, making sure he had a soft, gooey look in his eyes. He touched her at every opportunity; a hand on her arm, a squeeze of her shoulder, a brushing of his body on hers as he passed by her in the bar and his piece de resistance, a gentle moving of a strand of hair from her eyes. He could tell it was working. She began to smile more often in his company and their conversations became less stilted. He waited, like a spider, for just the right moment before he caught her in his web and then told her he couldn't bear it any longer; his feelings were too strong; he had to have her. And just as he'd known she would, she succumbed.

Barbara didn't allow herself to analyse the situation. For whatever reason, Finn Hunt was, without doubt, making a play for her and she, having held off for as long as she could so as not to look pathetically desperate, was going to enjoy herself while it lasted. Life owed her that much. She could count her sexual encounters on one hand or, if she was honest, on one finger - unless she allowed for Miranda Hargreaves from her school days with whom she'd had an embarrassing fumble in the girls' lavatories. Then, at college, she'd had six confusing months of Angus Chappell whom she'd met at a party. Neither of them had managed to get into conversations with the other students there, most of whom seemed to be talking about their sexual exploits, brushes with the law or experience with the latest drugs. Neither Barbara nor Angus had anything to offer on these subjects and, feeling more and more out of touch, had gravitated towards each other. What followed had been an uncomfortable and inept event, made possible only by the consumption of a large amount alcohol. The pair had persevered - and, at least, they had each other, enabling them to feel a degree of self-worth amongst their peers. It was a situation destined for failure however, as they drained each other of energy with their neediness. Also, lacking in charm, looks and personality, both put a great deal of store by their academic prowess and ended up vying for supremacy in the intellectual department. The ensuing rows reached levels which neither could handle and they parted swiftly and acrimoniously.

And so Barbara forgave Finn his many faults and took him to her bed but, once she had him there, inevitably she didn't want to let him go. It was then he realised it would be easier to rid himself of a terminal disease than this woman who he'd tried to manipulate. And almost simultaneously, he fell in love for the first time in his life; passionately, deeply in love. But Daisy hadn't got over his kiss with Trish at the barbecue, so was she ever going to understand how he'd got himself entwined with a vengeful harpy like Barbara Harris?

* * *

Catriona stood by the window and looked out over the gardens to where Freddie sat idly throwing stones at a few cans he'd set up. It wasn't right to hate a child with such a passion but she didn't know any other way to describe her feelings about him. The children she taught were a lot younger than Freddie but she knew, without a doubt, there were some she didn't warm to as much as others. There were also some who stole her heart and, given the opportunity, she would devote all her time. She mulled over that thought, debating whether or not it was acceptable to admit how she felt or whether she could condition herself to love all children unconditionally.

Catriona closed her eyes and said a little prayer. Not that she really believed in such things but, like most people, she was prepared to hedge her bets. It came as somewhat of a surprise when, a few minutes later, she answered a knock on the door and found Linda Pugh standing there.

"Could I er... could I come in and talk to you for a minute?" Linda was forced to speak as Catriona had said absolutely zilch.

"I suppose," said Catriona ungraciously. "Is the devil child safe to be left then?"

Linda bit her tongue and walked through to the kitchen. Unlike her own, it was scrupulously clean and neat.

"You have everything so nice," she said, with a smile. "I'm afraid my place is a tip."

Many thoughts passed through Catriona's mind but she refrained from comment.

"I wanted to apologise," Linda continued. "For the other night. It was unforgivable. Really. I er... I'd had a few drinks. Alcohol doesn't agree with me, you see. It has a bad effect and brings out my violent streak, I'm afraid."

"They say it brings out your true colours - who you really are," said Catriona triumphantly.

Linda looked directly into Catriona's eyes, sighed and gave a slight shake of her head.

"Yes, I'm sure it does. But then, I already know exactly who I am, Catriona. I know why I can lose my rag and get physical. It's because of what I suffered as a child. And that's fine because I know what I'm working with; what I can do to improve. That's what I teach the children I foster, to help them. Accept your circumstances and then, you know what you're working with. Freddie's circumstances are extremely difficult for him to accept which makes him behave the way he does but he's trying really hard."

Catriona surveyed the woman before her. Red-haired and pale-skinned, she was short and a little on the plump side. She could have been generous and described her as voluptuous but that wasn't in Catriona's nature. Linda wore a short-sleeved blouse which Catriona would never have done had she had possessed such flabby arms. Neither would she have chosen jeans – not that she ever wore them anyway – if she had an ample behind like the woman in front of her. But, there was something about Linda's eyes; something that invited you to offer yourself up to her embrace and lay your head on her motherly bosom. An involuntary sigh escaped Catriona's lips as she remembered her own mother's bony chest and the perfunctory hug she'd occasionally managed.

"Well," said Linda, fed up with the lack of response. "I've said what I came to say. I'll leave you in peace."

Linda started on her way out, feeling she had wasted her time, when Catriona's voice halted her in her tracks.

"Do you... I mean, did you actually like all the children you fostered?"

Slowly, Linda turned and took the two steps back into the kitchen.

"Like?" she repeated. "No, I can't say I really liked many of them at all. Freddie certainly isn't likeable. But I loved them."

"What do you mean by-"

"What I believe, Catriona, is that the core of us all is one and the same; an energy if you like, that permeates all things. And that's what I love because that core is pure and... unadulterated, I think is the right word. It's our true spirit and that's what I aim to reach and remind each child that whatever's happened to them to make them behave the way they do, that's not who they really are."

It was obvious that Catriona was deep in thought, for again, she said nothing. Once more, Linda made a move to leave.

"Thank you for coming to apologise." Catriona's voice was a little shaky. "I er... I didn't mean to-"

"It's okay, Catriona. It's all good."

And Linda Pugh left feeling more sad than triumphant at what was obviously a breakthrough. There was something quite tragic about Catriona Penworthy and she had a horrible feeling yet more tragedy was on its way.

* * *

Reg Prodger felt himself go hot with mortification as memories of barbecue night re-emerged. But, however often he played it, he couldn't make the scene any different. It had been the silence that had thrown him; the open-mouthed looks of disbelief. Unsurprisingly, it had been Bryce who'd broken the spell by bursting into great cackles of laughter and shouting, "Hey, mate! What cruel bastard told you it was fancy dress?" And ironically, that had given him an out; an out he needed because, after the initial burst of bravado fuelled by a large brandy, he'd dissolved into a ball of sheer panic.

Joining in the laughter, Reg had gratefully lied and told everyone he was convinced someone *had* said it was fancy dress although he couldn't remember who. Of course, they'd accepted his mistake and insisted he join the party in his outfit. So, Reg had experienced what life could be like if he was allowed to dress as he wanted but also, what it was like to lie to his friends and neighbours. Fortunately, the rain had become heavier and everyone got fed up with feeling wet and packed up, so his time at the party had been short.

He hadn't been out much since then. He couldn't think what had made him take such a decision after so many years of keeping his penchant for wearing ladies clothing in the closet, so to speak. Although, that wasn't entirely true. He *had* been thinking of going public for some time but always talked himself out of it. Then, on the morning before the party, he'd called in at Hilary's charity shop to collect his latest purchases 'for his mother'. There'd been a look in her eye as she'd handed over the carrier bag and he'd sensed she was about to say something he would find uncomfortable. He'd tried to hurry out of the shop but his bulk and the chaotic placing of the stands and rails made a quick getaway nigh on impossible.

"It's good your mum doesn't mind second-hand clothes," Hilary had said cheerfully. "It makes such sense to me, you know, cycling and helping charity and a bit of retrail therapy all in one go."

Reg had nodded vigorously and backed into a rail full of nighties and bras. The hangers jingled like a bell ringing time on his lies.

"Plus, of course, one can be so much more inderidual. Put together things from different times and cretate a whole new look. I bet mum's really good at that, isn't she?"

"Well, I'm not sure she even thinks about... you know...," said Reg, struggling to understand

"I s'pose not cos you buy her stuff. But Podge, I've noticed how well you choose for her. You have a real eye for fashion. Perhaps you missed your vacation." The more Hilary talked, the more she muddled her words. "You should have been a designerist."

"Me? A designer?" Reg had said, still grappling with wire hangers and bra straps. "That's a bit far-fetched even for you, Hilary."

"Nonsense! I've a feeling you were brain-wished to go down a certain path when you were young. I think there's more to you than greets the eyes."

Reg had stopped, mid-untangling, and held his breath.

"So this morning's advice from the Scantleberry school of wise words, is that you should follow your passions; be who you really are and to hell with all those who say different!"

The hanger had finally given up its hold on Reg and he'd catapulted out of the shop, with a wave of his hand and a, "Good advice. Can't stop. See you later".

Her words rang in his ears for the rest of the day and throughout the hours before the party and somehow affected him enough to give him the courage to make his appearance on the stairs.

* * *

Hilary, having watched his frantic departure, had wondered if her advice would have any impact at all. Reg Prodger was one of her favourite people and hadn't even objected when she'd come up with the nickname, Podge. She cared about his happiness but knew his choices were none of her or anyone else's business. However, in Hilary's world, there was no room for anything but the truth, the whole truth and nothing but the truth - apart, that is, from one little thing that she'd buried; buried so deeply she was convinced it must have happened in another life.

* * *

Trevor swept past Bryce and into the kitchen. Bryce could hear him clattering about and wondered if he would be offered any breakfast. He knew it was unlikely. Their row after the barbecue had only been matched in ferocity by the storm which raged outside. Bryce knew Trevor didn't like it when he became drunk but they usually got around it in the end. This time, it felt different and it was all down to that stupid tosser, Reg Prodger. He liked the sound of that and sang it under his breath a few times.

"Reg Prodger, stupid tosser, tiny todger! No, that doesn't work. Start again. Stupid tosser, Reg Prodger. Cos he's got a tiny todger. Reg Prodger, stupid tosser, dress crosser! Haha! I'm a poet and I know it..."

Bryce's voice faded, suddenly realising that Trevor was standing in the doorway, hands on hips, listening to him. He giggled. He couldn't stop himself. But Trev remained grim.

"Aah, come on, sweetheart. It was just a joke."

"Oh really? And was it a joke the other night when you went around telling everyone you'd never seen Reg look so comfortable?

Constantly intimating that he was, in fact, a tranny. In fact, you didn't intimate, you actually called him that."

"Oh come on, Trev, we've been through all this. It was patently obvious the guy loved being in those clothes."

"So bloody what!" Trevor was now shaking with rage. "I was hoping you'd come to this on your own but it appears not."

"Come to what, Trev? You're not making any sense."

"Come to *the point*!" yelled Trevor. "And the point being, it's irrelevant! Irrelevant whether he likes wearing women's clothes or not. It's nothing to do with anyone else."

"Yes but-"

"No buts, *darling*! We know Reg. We like Reg. He's never given us any reason not to like him. So why are you now judging him and-"

"Hey, hang on! Who says I'm judging him?"

"Well, you were certainly getting some mileage from taking the piss out of him. You - of all people - who get so irate if gay people suffer any injustice and yet, you're prepared to sneer at Reg."

Bryce shrugged and looked down at his perfectly manicured hands.

"I think you're making mountains out of molehills, Trevor. Get over yourself."

"No, Bryce, it's you I have to get over," replied Trevor, in a dangerously quiet voice. "And I think this time maybe, finally, I have."

"Oh come on, sweetheart. Don't be like that. I didn't realise I'd upset you so much."

Bryce moved forward, his hand outstretched to take Trevor's but Trevor was having none of it and moved away.

"No, Bryce, leave it. Go to the pub or something. I want to be alone. I need to think."

* * *

And, in many of the households around the Harlequin triangle, the same prickliness and tensions permeated the air. There seemed to be a cloud hanging over the area; a small, pale, dove grey cloud maybe, but a cloud nevertheless. The storm didn't seem to have cleared the atmosphere at all. Things, Arlo was heard to say, were afoot. A strange wind sprang up which, although giving some relief from the humid weather, also appeared to be ruffling a few feathers. People were looking anxious and snapped if asked a question. Florence remarked that the hospital seemed full of folk who'd 'lost it'; some who had attempted suicide or been in a fight for the first time in their lives; and some who'd lost concentration, being too focused on their troubles, and had accidents.

Anya Petrovka had been found walking around the Harlequin triangle in her nightdress but had no idea how she'd ended up there. Whilst there was no shortage of people offering to lend a hand and keep an eye on her, the incident was alarming to everyone who knew her. Giselle contracted a debilitating virus which put her out of action - whatever that action was - for nearly two weeks. Speculation was rife when Patrick Baxter came back early from a business trip with a very similar complaint. Valerie Figgis continued her bullying tactics on her sister, Frances, who uncharacteristically wondered how easy it would be to poison someone. Freddie was caught shop-lifting, unusual only in the fact that he'd been caught and Sulky Sonia's tantrums reached epic proportions when she pushed her brother's head into the toilet and flushed. Only the Kshatryias seemed reasonably unscathed by the negative energies that abounded at that time. They heard everyone else's horror stories but had remained friendly and polite, providing a comforting sense of calm to all who entered their shop.

And then, disaster struck again. On waking, the following Saturday, the residents around the Harlequin triangle discovered their precious gardens had been trashed.

Chapter 4

BURNT SIENNA

Once again, it was Florence who, on her way home from night shift, had the dubious privilege of discovery. She walked swiftly through the alleyway, feeling the usual shudder as she remembered what had happened a few weeks ago. She supposed it would fade one day if, and when, the perpetrator of the crime was apprehended. In the meantime, she kept her mind on the anticipation of seeing the garden in all its early morning glory. She liked to have a quick wander round before she went indoors, breathing in the aromas and seeing if she could spot new growth. At first, it didn't register. Then, gradually, the devastation in front of her came into focus as she blinked rapidly to clear her vision.

"Oh my Lord! My dear Lord," she whispered, moving slowly forwards. "Who would do this?"

Plants had been trampled or pulled up from their earthy beds. Pots had been smashed, the swing cut down and branches broken off the apple tree. A can of brown paint had been swirled around covering nearly everything with dark trails and spatters. Even the small area of lawn had been hacked and stomped on until it was more mud than grass.

Florence sank to her knees and sobbed.

Sometime later, she became aware someone was standing behind her. She turned swiftly and gasped with relief when she saw it was only Benson. He was visibly shocked and even as he came forward to help her to her feet, he couldn't take his eyes off the devastation before him.

"How long have you been here?" he asked. "Did you see anyone? I can't believe this."

"No, honey. I just turn up five, ten minute ago. There was no one, just this mess. I don't understand, Benson. Why someone do this?"

"God knows," he replied, shaking his head. "We've just got over one shock and now this."

They stood holding each other, gaining comfort from the fact they were united in the condemnation of such an act. Around five minutes later, Arlo descended the fire escape clutching his mug of tea and found them, silent, staring and hanging on. He'd been so fascinated to see what he thought was a romantic embrace, he hadn't looked over at the gardens. But as he approached, he felt the vibrations of their distress and swung round to see what was upsetting them.

"Fuck!" The mug fell from Arlo's hand and smashed on the path. His mouth open in disbelief, he walked towards the mayhem.

It was all he could say.

* * *

That was the strangest thing; the silence. It was as though all words to describe or express how everyone felt had been sucked out of them. They just stood and looked. Even the birds and insects seemed to have clammed up, for not a chirp or buzz was to be heard. When he eventually turned up, Constable Hargreaves was hard pushed to get a statement out of anyone. People just shook their heads or bit their lips and sighed and sighed and sighed. In the end, it was Marsha Malloy who shocked everyone out of their catatonic states.

"We'll get to the bottom of this. And when we find the culprit, they'll regret their actions. You can be quite sure of that. They will regret their actions until their dying day!"

Arlo later admitted the ferocity behind her words had stunned him. There was an edge to Marsha's voice he'd never heard before and a new steel in her eyes. It was as though she'd dropped the soft, pastel overcoat of her outer persona and an entirely different person had emerged. Even her walk was different as she'd marched around, fists clenched and feet angrily stomping the ground.

Having emerged from their Sunday morning stupor to confront the debacle before them, some of the Quinners started to examine the damage more closely to see what could be salvaged.

Trevor was quite overcome. He pulled out a sparkling white handkerchief and dabbed at his eyes.

"I can't believe it," he gasped. "I just can't believe it."

Bryce took him to one side and spoke to him. Linda Pugh later reported he'd reprimanded Trev on making such a fuss over a few bits of vegetation but Trev had told him to piss off if he felt like that and not come back. Bryce then had little choice but to change his attitude and, when it came to it, offer to muck in and help like everyone else.

"Quite a few of the plants that have been pulled up, may have a chance if ve get them back in the ground quickly," said Anya, tenderly caressing a fallen begonia.

"And give them lots of water," added Harry Footlik.

Linus, who was straightening up a fuschia, observed, "I reckon this little baby will survive with a bit of TLC."

"What do we do about all this yukky brown paint?" asked Trish anxiously.

"We'll have to cut the bits out, I guess." Daisy hooked arms with her flatmate's, thus resolving some of their recent relationship challenges.

"We can mend the swing, I'm sure." This was Benson.

"The lawn can be pressed back down and reseeded," Arlo stated. "It'll take a bit of time but we'll get it back to its former glory."

"Hey, we should get cracking right now!" yelled Baz. "I'll get some tools from the shed and-"

"Here, I've got some! Let's get to work, Quinners."

Everyone turned from the garden to where Reg Prodger, once again, made a grand entrance; only this time, he was in a pair of buff-coloured dungarees and a checked shirt and held an armful of forks, spades and secateurs. For some reason, everyone started to clap, giving Reg a huge round of applause, although whether it was for bringing the garden implements or just for turning up, no one was quite sure.

It was the blackest of hours but, as is so often the case, disaster can bring people together. Even Valerie Figgis appeared in her wellies, gardening fork in hand. Frances followed on with her sticks at a much slower pace and sat on one of the benches to give encouragement and advice.

"These benches could do with a new lick of paint anyway," she observed. "I'll buy some if someone will volunteer to do the work."

"I think we have quite a lot of this orange paint left," said Tom Penworthy, sitting down next to her for a well-earned break. He wiped the sweat from his brow and grinned at her. "Sunburst it was called, wasn't it?"

"Something like that," said Frances, thinking what a nice smile he had and wondering if the rumours of a troubled marriage were true.

"Slacking again?" snipped Catriona, coming up behind them. "People will talk."

Frances felt the tension in his body and heard him suck the air through his teeth.

"Just getting my breath back, Trina," he replied, before getting to his feet and grabbing a spade.

Frances watched him. He hadn't even glanced at his wife. His shoulders were bowed, his head hung down and he dragged his feet a little. There was nothing about his demeanour that suggested that he was, in any way, a happy man but turning to Catriona, she was not surprised. The woman wore a glowering expression as her gaze followed her husband's departure.

"That's the most common view I have of him," Catriona said sourly. "The back of him as he walks away."

Frances desperately wanted to tell Catriona her attitude wasn't helping but felt it would be unacceptable. Anyway, what did she know? She'd never even been married. In the end, she just said, "Well, why don't you run after him, dear? Show him you're not going to let him go."

Catriona threw her a look that plainly said Frances must be off her trolley and walked away in the opposite direction.

In another area of the garden, Linus was on his knees, carefully unearthing some bedding plants before replanting them more firmly.

"Anything I can do?" Trish stuck her fork into the ground, narrowly missing Linus's hand.

"Hey, watch it!" he yelped.

"Oh, sorry. I'm so clumsy," apologised Trish. "I just don't know what to do to help. I'm not much of a gardener, I'm afraid."

She looked miserable and Linus felt sorry for her. She wasn't the sharpest tool in the box but there was no harm in her.

"Okay, well if you get the watering can you can follow me along. As I plant, you water in. Some of these have had it but we may be able to save a few."

Trish, eager to help, skipped off happily to fill the can. Of course, she over-filled it and by the time she got it back, her espadrilles were soaked and muddy and she was less than delighted.

"They cost me such a lot of money," she bemoaned.

"Really?" said Hilary, eyebrows raised disapprovingly. "We had some very similar in last week which would've cost you all of three pounds. Only worn once as well."

"Eeuw, no!" cried Trish. "Someone else's feet!"

"Well, if you want to waste your money..." Hilary gave a shrug and went off to find some secateurs.

Work progressed steadily. The Kshatryias, who'd had to work in their shop and couldn't help, compensated by sending over lots of goodies at midday and everyone stopped for a welcome break. Marsha also came across with a couple of large plates piled high with sandwiches. She looked calmer but her face darkened every time she viewed the garden. It was such a change from her normal sweet, serene disposition that it shocked a few people. Arlo nudged Florence who acknowledged her agreement of his meaning regarding the Marshmallow's behaviour but neither felt they could say anything.

Linda Pugh brought drinks out for everyone when the temperature rose to an uncomfortable level and had raided her freezer to make up a huge bowl of ice cubes. The temptation was too much for Finn and he chased Linus around threatening to put some down the back of his shirt. This caused great hilarity, especially when Daisy joined in and managed to put a dripping cube down Finn's back, having conned him she was on his side. He turned and grabbed her, gasping with the shock of cold and then, they just stopped and stood looking into each other's eyes, leaving no doubt about how they felt. Good job, Barbara wasn't around, thought Benson, who had recently been privy to Finn's woeful outpourings.

It was also a very good job sulky Sonia wasn't around, in most people's opinion. Catriona was at pains to inform everyone that her daughter was at a sleepover at a friend's house and the look in her eye dared anyone to suggest otherwise. Nobody said it out loud but Sonia was high on the list of prime suspects although it was hard to come up with a motive; other than, she was a nasty, vindictive piece of work. Nightmare Nigel was present however, and proved quite useful, if you could stand his constant chatter for more than five minutes.

The only other person conspicuous by his absence was Patrick Baxter. It was presumed he was still incapacitated by his recent virus but, just as they were finishing their communal lunch, Patrick turned up carrying a large box overflowing with plants. He plonked the box down and sank exhausted onto the ground.

"Are you alright, Patrick?" cried Giselle, hurrying to his side. "Where did you get all these from?"

"Local garden centre," he replied, sounding really puffed out. "I'm sorry, I knew I didn't have the energy to put in any work. Wretched virus has knocked me for six. So thought I'd go and buy us a whole load of new plants instead."

Patrick's contribution was met with gratitude in the form of whoops of joy and hearty slaps on his back; the latter of which, he could have really done without. Giselle gave him the best reward by throwing her arms around his neck, kissing him soundly on the cheek and telling him he was an absolute darling.

By the afternoon, there was a big pile of paint-spattered vegetation stacked to one side and quite a few bare patches where plants had been too damaged to salvage. But it was an improvement; a start. And now they had Patrick's contribution, all were convinced, it would soon begin to look as good as new.

"Don't think we're going to get too many veggies this year," said Hilary with a sigh. "But we can start planting for winter crops."

"None o' my tomato plant survive then?" asked Florence tearfully.

"No dear. 'Fraid not." Hilary patted her arm sympathetically.

"It feels like we've lost some friends," said Trish sadly.

"That just shows how everything is connected," said Hilary. "Plants are like animals, they give everything and ask nothing in return – except their basical needs, of course."

"That's all anyone, or anything, has the right to expect. Water, sustenance and shelter," said Daisy thoughtfully. "Everything else is a bonus."

"Except these days, most people seem to expect a great deal more," stated Giselle, a grim look on her face.

"You can say that again," chipped in Linda Pugh. "It's like when we found out we couldn't have kids ourselves, we decided to help the kids who didn't have families to support them. I didn't go demanding someone fixed it for me to have my own babies."

"Well, maybe the urge to have children is a lot stronger in some women," Catriona pointed out. She hadn't found it easy to conceive and was in her thirties before she'd managed to get and stay pregnant.

"Maybe people should learn they can't always have everything they want. It's not a right. Well, not in my book anyway. It's nature's way and we shouldn't be messing with it," said Linda dismissively.

Catriona was starting to frown and a little zip of tension crept into the atmosphere. Baz quickly intervened.

"Hey, let's get this lot bagged up, folks," he suggested. "I'll take it up to the tip. Here, Freddie, grab a sack."

Freddie quietly did as he was told, as he had done all day. This had been noted by quite a few. Many had Freddie down as another suspect but having seen how diligently he'd worked, suspicions had begun to fade.

"Who wants to test the swing?" Benson called and Florence, who was nearest, jumped on.

"Good as new," he laughed, giving her a push.

"I always loved swings," said Anya, coming dangerously near Florence's outstretched legs. "It feels like flying, doesn't it?"

"Here, you have a go, Anya. See if it feels okay again." Florence jumped off and helped the older lady on. Some of her hair had come loose from its bun and her face bore a couple of streaks of mud but she was soon beaming like a child, as Benson gently pushed her.

"I really worried 'bout her," Florence whispered to him. "Her mind keep wandering."

"She's been alright this afternoon, hasn't she? Or, if she hasn't, I didn't notice."

"Yeah, but I tink it help she have work to focus on and people around. It come and go, this sorta vagueness ting. I mean, she always been a bit like that but now, she seem to be goin' back to another time and get confused. It could be the start of someting, you know."

"We should set up a rota. Get people to pop in and make sure she's okay. I'd be happy to do that."

"Good idea, Benson. I'll aks around. There a couple of people who wont, o'course – like Bryce - but most will, I reckon."

The day wore on and melted into evening. It was still warm but a welcome breeze wafted around, cooling the burning faces of those who had worked so hard. Arlo was on his hands and knees firming in a new, healthy-looking hosta. Satisfied it was well bedded, he brushed the rich soil from his hands. As always, the colour fascinated him. Brown, or burnt sienna as it was called in his paint collection, was so easy to dismiss, he thought. And yet, to him it was a mixture of all the colours and if you looked long enough, you could see different hues shimmering in its depths. He picked up a handful of earth and let it run through his fingers, savouring the cool feel and the ripe, primeval smell.

"What are you doing?"

Arlo turned to see Nigel watching him, his eyes large and earnest, magnified by his spectacles.

"Looking and thinking, Nigel," said Arlo kindly. "Just looking and thinking. We take this stuff for granted, you know." He picked up another handful of brown earth and jiggled it about in his hand. "It's the giver of life and so precious and yet, we don't really take care of it on this planet."

Nigel nodded. "Yeth, you're right."

Arlo dropped the soil and grinned at the little boy. Nigel had understood exactly where he was coming from and it felt good to have made a connection with him. Then, Nigel spoke again.

"But you really should wear gloveth coth that'th where all the catth go to shit."

And with that, the little boy solemnly turned and walked off to enquire after someone else's activities, leaving Arlo to digest his advice. Having first been taken aback, Arlo found himself rocking with laughter. Trust a kid to bring you back down to earth when you were offering philosophies on life.

"What's so funny?" Giselle plonked herself down next to him and listened with interest as he relayed what had just taken place.

"Well, the metaphor is interesting," she observed. "Bringing you back down to earth. That's sort of what's happened today, isn't it? You know, it's made us all realise what's important. It's not what people choose to wear or whether they're on the ball or not. It's not even about who gets on with whom. It's about getting on with life and appreciating the simple things we take for granted, as you say. Everything else is just fantasy."

"I couldn't agree more. We create so much drama. I suspect because we're never satisfied with the basics. I don't think all the extras that people crave, make us happy. Well, not for long anyway."

Those working closest to Arlo and Giselle had begun to listen. To some, their words were idealistic and unrealistic but for others, they had a ring of truth and were, at the very least, worth considering.

Catriona silently scoffed and dismissed the pair as idiots. She refused to listen to the little voice in her head which begged her to reconsider. She'd already decided that life constantly gave you lemons and that lemonade would certainly pall if you kept making it, as so often advocated. Money was important. If you had money, when life gave you lemons, you could buy some gin and tonic in which to put a slice. Catriona had imagined herself having that sort of future; big, fancy house, flashy car, exotic holidays, champagne for breakfast. She'd married Tom because she'd been impressed by his apparent lifestyle. He had flashed the cash often and conspicuously. He was going places. He had big dreams and they matched her own.

For a few years, things seemed to go to plan and they were gradually moving up in the world, although not fast enough for Catriona. And sadly, no little Penworthys had arrived on the scene. Nearly eight years after they were married, Catriona had finally managed to conceive with the help of science and a great deal of their hard earned money. For a while, she'd given up her teaching job in order to be a stay-at-home mum. Sonia was not an easy child, even at an early age, and it took all Catriona's energy to deal with her. Catastrophe struck when the advertising agency where Tom worked, collapsed and Catriona was to experience the bitter taste of down-sizing.

Tom didn't get more work; not for some considerable time. They began to fall behind with the mortgage repayments. One day, he dropped the bombshell that they'd have to sell the house and move somewhere cheaper.

Catriona's response was the final straw to Tom who'd long suspected he'd made a mistake in choosing a woman whose ambitions for the future far outweighed his own. But time proved that selling up was the only course of action and they bought one of the four houses that made up Grenville Row on the Harlequin triangle. Catriona resented every brick of it. A three-bedroom terrace was, in her mind, a huge step back. Even her childhood home had been a semi in a leafy, "des res" suburb. And then, shock of shocks, two years after moving there, she became pregnant with Nigel, bringing more expense they could ill afford. No, life sucked as far as Catriona was concerned and her face showed it. In fact, most of the time, her expression looked like she'd been sucking the lemons life had thrown at her. Tom made every excuse to keep his distance.

Trish was another who found it hard to appreciate the simple life that Arlo recommended. She focused very much on what she lacked, mainly based on what others had that she did not, rather than what she actually needed. It made her quite difficult to live with and, consequently, her relationships never lasted very long; another sadness which she would bemoan at every opportunity. Even patient, tolerant, kind Daisy struggled to cope with the relentless whingeing about how unfairly life treated her new flatmate.

"Why our garden?" wailed Trish. "It's so unfair. I don't understand why they chose our beautiful little patch."

"Well, maybe they were jealous. Stupid eh?" said Daisy, hoping Trish would pick up on something here. "You know, instead of envying someone else, why not put your energy into creating something beautiful for yourself."

"Hmm." For a moment, Trish looked thoughtful. "But maybe, they had awful lives where everything was against them and so they never learnt to think like that."

"Then, they're to be pitied," retorted Daisy, battling with her frustration. "Anyone who can't learn to take responsibility for their own thoughts and actions is to be pitied. And personally, I never want to be in a position where people feel sorry for me."

Daisy's voice was shaking and she turned hurriedly back to the honeysuckle she was winding around a metal arch. Trish felt her emotion and, after wondering why Daisy was getting so upset, began to think about what she'd said.

Reg Prodger had nodded sagely at Arlo and Giselle's words. All he'd ever wanted from life was acceptance; acceptance for who he was and what he wanted to do with his time. His love of women's clothing hurt no one and yet, people like Bryce managed to turn it so it hurt Reg, himself.

Bryce hadn't been near enough to hear what had been said. In fact, he'd popped back to the flat to pour a gin and tonic which, he told himself, he richly deserved having worked so hard in the gardens. Bryce resented that work. He resented the brown soil beneath his fingernails and the smell of wet grass and mud emanating from his shoes. He didn't even like the garden that much. He would be quite happy in a concrete jungle surrounded by chrome and glass and modern art. He just wasn't an outdoorsy, nature sort of bloke. He was cold, hard steel and, as ruthless as he was, didn't care who he had to tread on to get what he wanted in life. The only fly in the ointment was Trev. Trevor Byles, who'd rescued him when he was a young and foolish boy. A boy fresh from Australia, who thought he could conquer London society with a bit of attitude and then discovered that very attitude pissed off the sort of people you really did not want to be pissing off; people who'd humiliated him and made him feel worthless and insignificant and that the world was his enemy. And then Trevor had come along and lifted him up and loved him with all his faults and made him feel so much better about himself. Trevor was the one person in the world Bryce could not bring himself to hurt. He would have been shocked to know how often he did.

* * *

The light had begun to dim but the air was still warm, accentuating the earthy aromas. Patrick's plants had been bedded in and there were only a few obvious gaps. People stood around in the fading light as the falling sun dappled the ground with its beams. No one seemed to want to leave.

"I don't mind what get planted, where," sighed Florence. "I just happy to see our lovely garden lookin' better."

"Oh, I agree," said Hilary, linking an arm through Flo's. "But, you know, looking on the positive side, it's brought us all close again."

"I didn't realise we'd fallen apart," said Arlo, before swigging beer from a can.

"Didn't you?" Hilary glanced at him with raised eyebrows. "And I always thought you were such a sensitivial man. Didn't you feel the energize pulling in different directions at the barbecue? Or rushing t'wards each other and clashing? It's never felt like that before."

"When you say energies…?" Giselle had come up to join the group.

"Oh, I can't be bothered to 'splain it all now," said Hilary, with a sigh. "I'm too tired and I'm off to bed. But just think about it, Giselle. You, of all people, should know what I mean."

Puzzled, Giselle watched as the woman walked off to her flat above the charity shop. Hilary was right. Of course, she knew. She read people all the time; felt their sadness and frustration; their anger and their fear. It was all in the vibrations emanating from them. And looking back at the night of the barbecue, she realised there had been some strangeness – a feeling like taut wire twanging in the breeze – but because she'd wanted to switch off from other people's feelings for a while, she'd convinced herself, it had been the stormy weather disrupting the calm.

"Thanks, Reg. For getting us going, I mean." Arlo raised his beer can in a salute to Reg as he bumbled past, clutching a few of the garden tools he'd retrieved.

"Come again?" replied Reg, looking puzzled.

"If you hadn't come out with all your tools and rallied us into action, I suspect we'd have stood here all day just talking about what to do."

"Oh! Oh, right. Really? Well, you know…" Reg stared at the ground and swung his large head from side to side but he was grinning. "One does what one can. Night, night."

"Night, Reg," chorused the remaining few.

"I wonder who did it," said Benson. "And more to the point, why? I mean, has anyone pissed someone off recently?"

"You don't tink it connected to the body in the alley?" Flo's eyes were huge in the twilight.

"None of it makes any sense," said Arlo. "But maybe that's because we don't have enough facts. I, for one, will be keeping a closer eye on things in future."

"Well, we all should," said Linus, throwing down his spade and accepting a can from Finn. "We need to start taking our neighbourhood watch duties more seriously."

"Too right, Linus." For once, Finn did not use the derogatory nickname for his friend. He'd been surprised at how Linus had thrown himself into the work that day and had formed a new respect for him. "Maybe we could rota in a night-time vigil for those of us willing and able."

"That's not a bad idea," agreed Arlo. "For the time being, anyway."

And so finally, the day drew to a close and people began to drift back to their homes. Arlo was the last to go. He looked up at the sky as though searching for answers. There was a strange muddiness about its colour, he thought, as though it was echoing the disturbed soil beneath. They had patched, repaired and renewed and gone away a little more positive than when they started. But Arlo felt uneasy and suspected the months ahead could well hold more challenges.

Chapter 5

ROSE MADDER

Finn rolled onto his back and put his hands behind his head. He tried to regulate his breathing and calm himself. This had nothing to do with his recent activity which had resulted in Barbara laying pink-faced and smiling next to him. No, that was just to keep her quiet until he could gather up the courage to tell her that their time together was coming to an end. It had only been a month but it was a month in which so much had happened and most of that in the form of newcomer, Daisy. Finn had always been the type of man to whom, as he'd once said, "it didn't matter what the fireplace looked like when you were poking the fire". He was a good-looking, full-blooded male and his philosophy, mostly gleaned from his father, was to enjoy himself to the max while he could. He knew these times wouldn't last forever and he didn't mean to waste one precious minute of all the enjoyment life could offer a young, attractive man.

Daisy, or Marguerite Henshaw-May to give her full title, had turned all that on its head. For a start, she didn't swoon at first sight of him. She treated him much like she treated everyone, respectfully but with a twinkle in her eye and a kind way about her. He'd just watched her at first, noticing how she was with customers. She stayed the same no matter who they were, what they looked like or how they behaved. She listened to people intently. She had a ready smile and a gentle way with banter. If someone was disgruntled or looked fed-up, she would have them opening up to her in a matter of minutes. And of course, she was very, very pretty.

Finn didn't know when he fell for her - really fell for her, that is -

in a way he'd never before experienced. It was far more than mere sexual attraction. He expected to feel that. But there was something else; a new vibe that made him not want to let her out of his sight. In fact, he found himself pining for her when she wasn't around. When she was, he couldn't tear his eyes from her face; something else that was different. Before, it would have been other parts of the female anatomy drawing his attention. But now, he just wanted to look into her eyes; to smell her skin and to hear every opinion she'd ever had. He wanted to know every last thing about her.

He'd told her, a few nights before the barbecue, on another evening when he'd had too much to drink thus fuelling his courage.

"I think I might be falling in love with you," he'd said. "And I'm not even joking."

"Yes," she'd replied, laughing gently. "I think you could be right."

"So what are you going to do about it?"

"Nothing I can do apart from advise you against it. If only it were that easy."

"I don't know what you mean." he'd replied, sliding his hand under her hair and round her neck.

She'd let him kiss her briefly and then pulled away, saying, "You have a lot to sort out in your life, I think, Finn. Certainly before you start complicating it with adding me to your list."

And with that, he'd had to be satisfied but, as time went on, he knew she was right. There were a lot of changes to be made, especially with regard to how casually he treated the opposite sex. There was the kiss with Trish at the barbecue for a start. If truth were known, Trish had caught him by surprise and he'd gone into automatic pilot in kissing her back. It had meant nothing. If he hadn't been so sloshed, he may have been able to dodge the situation but it high-lighted how much work he had to do if he wanted to make those changes. If he was serious about Daisy, he had to clean up his act, which was why he was with Barbara, hoping above hope that she'd be so grateful for his recent attentions, she'd release him from any further involvement. Some hope!

* * *

Patrick Baxter was feeling a whole lot better, mainly due to the fact he'd managed to persuade Giselle to have dinner with him. He'd booked a swanky French place and ordered cabs to take them to and from the restaurant. He couldn't help glancing up from the menu every few seconds, just to make sure he wasn't dreaming. She was one gorgeous woman, dressed to perfection in a rosy pink dress, her hair piled on her head with the odd tendril caressing her softly blushing cheek and she was with him. He'd noticed how heads turned and eyes lingered when they'd entered 'Le Mange Tout' and his ego liked that very much indeed.

After they'd given the waiter their order, Patrick stretched out and took hold of her hand. It was incredibly smooth and golden in colour.

"I'm so glad you agreed to come, Giselle. I really feel I want to get to know you better."

She smiled and slid her hand gently out of his.

"Yes, Patrick, getting to know one another is the first step. You may find once you do know me, you won't want to take things any further."

He laughed then, his eyes crinkling, adding to his attractiveness.

"As if! Really, don't you ever look in the mirror? You must know what a stunner you are."

"If that's all you're looking for, then maybe I fit the bill."

"Well, you're obviously a lovely person as well."

"Am I though, Patrick? I don't know what you do for a living but do you deal with business people on face value, as you've just done with me?"

He laughed again and saw her face darken.

"No, good point," he added hurriedly. "But I have instincts and when it comes to relationships, that's what I usually go on. Besides, that's why we've got together tonight, isn't it? To learn a bit more about each other and to see if we get on?"

The first course arrived and Giselle made an effort to lighten her mood. Patrick was, without doubt, an attractive and charming man and he'd really done nothing wrong. His attempt to take her hand had been, she was sure, an affectionate gesture and nothing more. If she didn't want to see him again, she was confident he wouldn't try and force the issue. Why then, did she find it so difficult to just relax and enjoy herself? She already knew the answer but really didn't want to open that box. It had been closed for too long.

* * *

Harry Footlik was worried about Anya. She was repeating herself rather too often. Of course, all the older members of the community had that tendency, of forgetting a subject had been mentioned and discussed before, but Anya's repetitions sometimes came within a few seconds. He started calling on her more often. Not just because he was worried about her but rather because he liked being in her company. Ever since she'd invited him to tea and he'd sampled an hour or two of the nurturing, female ambience of her home, he'd yearned for more. Now she seemed more used to his presence, prompting him to find out a bit more about her and the sort of life she'd led. One day, he went in and found a huge pile of paraphernalia on her living room floor.

"What's all this, Anya? Having a clear out?"

"What, dear? Oh that. Yes, I vas looking for something. I can't remember vhat. In the end, I had to pull the whole drawer out, so there it is. Don't vorry, I'll sort it later. Tea, dear?"

"That would be more than acceptable," said Harry, with a little bow. He knew she liked elegant manners. As she became less guarded, he learned she was rather partial to a world where everything was soft, genteel and filled with flowers, sweet music and people who were always charming to each other. He still hadn't worked out the Russian connection but felt confident he would hear more as time went on.

Anya disappeared into the kitchen, having instructed Harry to take a seat. Instead, he chose to lower his cumbersome body to the floor and begin gathering up the bits and pieces he found there. He couldn't help but glance at some photographs and a smile broke out on his face as he recognised what he thought was a very young Anya. And then, miracle of miracles, there she was in a tutu posing beautifully on points, her head gracefully inclined to one side. So, she'd been telling the truth all along.

The sound of china rattling on a carefully laid tray drew Harry's attention away from the photograph and he turned to smile at Anya. But she wasn't smiling back. She was shaking and the tray was beginning to tilt in her hands.

Harry moved as quickly as he could, rolling over to his side and then, onto all-fours before grabbing the arm of a chair to haul himself to his feet. Panting with the effort, he reached the tray just in time and took it from her grasp.

"How dare... how dare you pry into my things," she said haltingly and to Harry's horror, he saw tears running down her cheeks.

* * *

Finn disentangled himself from Barbara's grasp. She pawed at him a lot. It was something he didn't like. He preferred to do the chasing and found her fawning and clinging extremely irritating. He pushed the covers back and pulled on his pants, socks and jeans.

"Going so soon?" said Barbara, lowering her voice sexily and stroking his back.

He actually felt his skin crawl. He had to tell her.

"Well, yes but there's something I wanted to talk to you about first."

Her eyes darted across his face, darkening with suspicion.

"Really? Well, I have something I want to tell you too."

Finn was to regret his next words for a very long time.

"Go on then. You first."

If only he'd just told her before she'd had the chance to plant those next words on him. Words that made his own unsayable; that threw an invisible net over him and captured him, sticking him to her as tight as any glue. But he hadn't. He'd said, 'Go on then. You first'.

"You're going to be a daddy."

She didn't say, 'I'm pregnant'; she placed the accusation on him straight away. "You're going to be a daddy." He was the father. No room for doubt. He was it. She was going to have his child. His legs gave way and he sat down heavily on the bed.

"Bit of a shock, I know, but you'll get used to the idea. It'll be fine."

He wasn't sure who she was trying to convince. He moved away from her hands which were again stroking his back. He couldn't speak - could barely breathe. The absence of response from him clanged around the room and he knew she was reading the vibrations of horror emanating from his skin. She never did ask him what it was he'd wanted to tell her. He suspected she already had a very good idea of what he'd been going to say and that it was no longer an option. She had null and voided his comment and ensnared him completely.

He pulled on his shirt and then his shoes. He took his wallet and phone from the bedside table, his jacket from the back of a chair and made for the door. Only then, did he turn and look at her. For a second, he felt a twinge of pity at the concern on her face, so he smiled briefly.

"It'll be fine," he said. "Talk to you later." And was gone.

* * *

Giselle loved food. The meal she shared with Patrick was so delicious she managed to regain a positive mood and held onto it.

"How did you find this place, Patrick?" she asked, cracking the dark, sugary lid of her crème caramel.

"Oh, it's run by a friend of a friend of a friend," he replied, sounding slightly bored. "I use the place and introduce others to its delights and, in return, I get very good service and a small discount. You know how these things work."

Gisellle didn't and looked at him blankly.

"Anyway," he went on. "I want to talk about you. I can't believe we've never really met before. Not properly anyway."

"I think I may have left before you turned up at the last Christmas do," said Giselle. She was savouring the vanilla creaminess of her dessert and had been hoping he would do the talking. "I had a bit of a cold and wasn't really up for socialising. I love all that mulled wine and carol singing around the tree though, don't you?"

Patrick shrugged. "Yeah, sure. Doesn't everybody?"

Her eyes shot up and she could tell by his expression he really wasn't moved by such things. For her, the gap between them widened.

"So, what do you do for a living?"

There it was. The Big Question! It always came. It was bound to. But it never failed to make her heart miss a beat.

"Guess," she said and licked the last dregs of creamy sweetness from her spoon.

* * *

Harry Footlik managed to get Anya to sit down. She was very shaky but then, he felt none too steady himself.

"I wasn't prying, Anya. Really, I wasn't. I was merely trying to help by picking up some of the stuff you'd dropped on the floor."

"You vere staring at my photographs. I saw you."

"Well, yes. I did catch sight of a couple," he admitted. "But you should be proud of them, not hide them away. I'd love to see pictures of you in your ballerina days."

For a moment, Anya looked puzzled and then, she held out her hand. Harry guessed she wanted to see the photos he'd looked at and gave them to her.

"These are not of me," she said, after a while. "They are my mother – Irina Petrovka."

"Well, so what? You can be proud of her, can't you?"

Anya's face began to crumple and so he quickly added, "She must have been a great dancer, Anya."

His ploy worked. Anya's eyes grew misty.

"Oh, yes. She trained vith the best. She vould have outshone them all if-"

"Here, have some tea," said Harry, grabbing the pot and pouring. "Tea always helps when you're telling a story, don't you think?"

Somehow, he'd found the right words. She seemed to perk up after sipping the tea and clung to the fact that she was just, as Harry had said, telling a story.

"So what happened," said Harry cunningly. "To the beautiful ballerina who danced with the best in the world?"

"She fell in love," replied Anya, beaming like a child. "She fell in love vith the handsome prince."

"Oh my goodness, really?" breathed Harry. "And did they run away together?"

"Yes... no... I think they did. I can't remember."

"Have another sip of tea. That will help," Harry advised.

She did so and, with a little more prompting, she continued. It was as though a blockage was beginning to dissolve and the memories came tumbling out.

"Yes, she did go vith him... to his country. The Englishman, that's vhat she called him... but she missed her dancing so much, she begged to go back home. By then, she vas having his child and time vent on and still, she mourned her lost career. Eventually, she did go back... but vith her daughter. Of course, vith her daughter."

"When you say, go back home, Anya, what do you mean?"

"To Russia, of course. *Her* home. But there had been the var and terrible things happening. Terrible! I can't speak of this, Mr Footlik. I can't..."

Harry took her frail little hand, losing it in his own large paw.

"There now, Anya, don't upset yourself. It was such a long time ago. Just tell me the story, eh? It will do you good, I think. Yes, just tell me the story."

Again, the word, story, seemed to put things into a perspective with which Anya could work.

"Things had changed so much, Irina said, and now, she had her daughter to cope vith as vell as everything else. She vas no longer in good shape so, I suppose, she couldn't get back into the dance company." Anya paused to take a deep, calming breath and dab at her eyes. "I don't know... They became so poor. Destitute? Is that the vord? She did everything she could to keep them alive."

"But what about the Englishman?" asked Harry. "Didn't he come after them?"

"No, he had to go to fight, I think. Yes, he left them to go and fight in the var vith Germany."

"Yes, of course. That would make sense. But your m... I mean, the ballerina, Irina? What happened to her?"

"She never danced again. Never. She kept vorking so she could feed her child and eventually, they managed to get back to England."

"To look for the Englishman?"

"Yes, but she didn't find him because he never came back. Missing in action. Isn't that vhat they call it?"

Harry nodded gravely.

"And his family didn't vant to know her. I don't know vhy."

"Perhaps, if they weren't married," mused Harry. "Do you know if they ever married, the Englishman and the ballerina?"

"Perhaps, not... No, I don't think they did. Do you think that's vhy they didn't like her?"

Anya's eyes had a faraway sort of look about them and Harry, confused, was concerned he was going to lose her. He gave her hand a little squeeze.

"So what happened next to Irina and her daughter?" he prompted.

"Oh, didn't I say?" Anya looked at him with wide-eyed surprise. "She died. TB I think it was."

"And what happened to the poor little girl?"

"She... I don't know! How should I know? Vhy are you asking me?" said Anya crossly. Her anger seemed to flare up from nowhere.

"But you must know," said Harry gently. "Otherwise you can't finish the story."

"Oh yes. Finish the story. Of course." Anya's eyes darted about the room and for a moment, Harry thought he wasn't going to get the ending he wanted. Her anger dissipated as suddenly as it had arisen but, in its place, a worrying blankness. Then, her eyes alighted on the small pile of photos now on the coffee table in front of her. Slowly, she leant forward, picked them up and pulled out one of a family group. In the middle, was a little girl who could quite easily have been Anya. The adults in the picture were not smiling. Their faces were stiff and grim and unyielding.

"Here, you see," said Anya. "She got a new mummy and daddy and two brothers and a granny and cousins so she vas a very lucky girl, vasn't she? Because, even though the Englishman's family didn't vant her, they still gave her a home, didn't they? And no, they couldn't let her dance because there wasn't the money for that sort of thing. No, she had to do something sensible, like shorthand and typing so she could get work as soon as possible. Of course, then she could get her own home and leave them all in peace. They vouldn't have to listen to all her silly stories about her mother dancing with the best because... that couldn't possibly be true, could it?"

"But of course, it was true," said Harry firmly. "The ballerina wouldn't have made that all up. She wouldn't have told her little girl such lies."

"No, no she vouldn't! She taught her daughter so much. All the dance moves, the steps. Vhen they vere living in the horrible places, they pretended they vere on a big stage with all the lights and the other dancers and the orchestra playing..."

And suddenly, Anya was up on her feet, moving gracefully around the room to some music that played in her head, her thin body seeming to lose all its stiffness. Harry watched her, tears in his eyes, and wished he'd met her when they were young, so he could have dissolved her pain and loved her and looked after her forever.

* * *

Echoes of the strange phenomenon called love, landed its rose madder glow on various residents from around the Harlequin triangle during the last weeks of summer, albeit in different guises.

One of those was Frances Arbuthnot, who had a conversation with her sister which shed some light on her continuous bad attitude. It came about because, for once, she lost her temper with Valerie and snapped at her.

"I don't want to sit indoors all day, Valerie," she said. "I know it's a bit chilly but I do possess jackets. Besides, I'm not ill. My problem is my joints and sitting still for too long doesn't help. So, will you just let me make my own decisions!"

Valerie's face fell. The thin line of her mouth turned down at the corners and her sparse eyebrows came together. She stared down at the floor, her whole body seeming to droop.

"Valerie? Are you alright?"

Valerie Figgis straightened herself and put her face back to its normal hard expression.

"Me? Of course, I'm alright. I apologise for caring about you. You wouldn't understand that though, would you? You've never had to care for anyone else. No, you just selfishly kept yourself to yourself, so you don't know what it's like to try and give yourself to someone and have it ignored or thrown back in your face."

"But I-"

"Oh yes, you get all the sympathy because you never married but I'll tell you something, sister dear." Valerie leant forward and pushed her face at Frances so she could smell the recently drunk coffee on her sister's breath. "You were the lucky one. A million times over, you were lucky. So do what you want, I'm past caring."

Frances watched as her sister marched out of the room and wondered. She'd seen very little of Valerie and her husband, Hugh, when they were married. They'd had the occasional phone call and exchanged birthday and Christmas cards but, other than that, she had no knowledge of what her sister's life had been like, except for what Valerie had chosen to tell her and she'd barely mentioned it. Now, it became blindingly obvious she'd been deeply unhappy and Frances was filled with compassion. She hoped she would learn a little more as time went on but, meanwhile, Frances decided she would open her own heart and pour some much needed love on her sad, hopeless little sister.

* * *

Then, there was Benson, who'd been to the hospital for treatment for a deep cut on his foot which happened when he came into sharp contact with a rusty nail sticking out of a skirting board. Nurse Florence Ntombe had treated the wound and teased him unmercifully when he winced and whimpered through it all. Somehow, this led to a sudden realisation they rather liked each other and they agreed to meet for a drink at The Bee's. This was nothing unusual but in arranging to go together at a specific time, made them ridiculously excited and walk around with stupid grins on their faces.

* * *

And Hilary. She'd always kept an eye open for large sized outfits of the kind Reg Prodger liked but since his dramatic appearance at the barbecue, she was even more vigilant. She now arrived at his flat quite regularly, handing over things for "his mother" to try. She was particularly delighted when a pair of bright pink stilettos had turned up in a size twelve and had hurried over with them as soon as she shut the shop. Reg was beside himself with delight and, in an unguarded moment, his mother forgotten, began talking as though the shoes would be just perfect for Reg himself. It wasn't long before realisation hit them both and Reg's face turned a very similar colour to the coveted shoes.

After a brief moment of panic, Hilary spoke up.

"Podge dear, I think they'll look great on you and they will certainly go with the flowery dress you penchased the other week. And before you say anything, I've always believed in the freedom of suppression. For people to be who they are and to be cepted for that, no matter if it's unusual or different or what. Oh, you know what I mean! So I'd be obligated if you'd let me carry on supplying you and enjoying the happiness you get from your penchases. Cos, believe me, it gives me great pleasureness too."

Reg's blue eyes glistened when he finally managed to raise his large, round head and look her in the eye. He smiled and whispered his thanks and their friendship was cemented forever.

* * *

Some of the roses in the triangular shaped garden had reached their blousy fullness and petals were starting to fade in readiness for dropping. In a couple of the households around the courtyard, love was doing the same thing. Tom was hanging on by the narrowest of threads, while Catriona tightened her hold on that thread. Trevor also, was questioning his relationship with Bryce on a daily basis. But, as in nature, everything has its time and everything comes to a natural end, whether it be by death or another form of separation. The trouble is, when it comes to love, most people find it very difficult to let go.

Chapter 6

YELLOW OCHRE

There was unrest at number four Grenville Row. On the one hand, Benson was full of joy, laughter and bonhomie whilst at the other end of the scale, Finn barely spoke and spent most of his time glowering at no one in particular or sitting, head in hands, emitting huge troubled sighs. Linus, whose life was a straight, boring line of dullness, didn't know who he envied more.

"At least you two seem to have a life," he bemoaned one Saturday afternoon, as they sprawled on sofas watching football. "All I have is work and this." He indicated the room with hands outstretched. "What are you so bloody cheerful about anyway, Ben?"

"Me? I'm happy I was lucky enough to injure my foot recently." Benson chuckled and shook his head as if he found such good fortune extremely hard to believe.

"Oh, very cryptic," snarled Linus. "Just answer the question, why don't you?"

"You don't really want to know, Li," said Benson. "It'll only make you envious."

"Derr, I'm already envious," replied his friend, glaring at him. "I might as well know why."

"Okay, you asked for it. When I hurt my foot, I was treated by the lovely Florence and since then, we've been seeing each other."

Even Finn looked up at this.

"But you've known each other for ages," he said.

"So? We've always got on well, too. And now, there's new growth in our relationship. What's so strange?"

"Is that how it happens?" said Linus, with a sigh.

"Well not always-"

"No," Finn butted in. "Sometimes it hits you like a ton of bricks and is just as painful."

"Ah, is that what's wrong with you?" said Benson, smiling sagely. "You've finally fallen in love."

"Oh God, not you as well." Linus slumped back into his chair, deflated. "Why does it never happen to me?"

"Don't count yourself unlucky, Wanks," said Finn bitterly. "You wouldn't want to change places with me, I promise you that."

Something about him halted the usual flow of banter that took place around Finn's love life. There was a catch in his voice and his eyes darted about the room in a desperate manner.

"Tell us," said Benson gently.

"No, no I can't. I really can't."

"Finn, for God's sake, we're your mates. You obviously need to talk to someone." Linus was genuinely concerned, all feelings of envy wiped away by his friend's obvious distress.

Finn closed his eyes, and sighed deeply. Finally, he looked at them, a wry smile on his face.

"You're just gonna say it was bound to happen and serves me right," he said.

"Well, maybe we will," said Linus. "But that doesn't mean we won't have sympathy or that we can't help."

"I'm not sure anyone can help. I've looked at it in so many ways and I'm fucked."

"Just tell us, mate." Benson's huge, brown eyes were full of compassion.

So, Finn told them, from the moment he'd taken Linus's joke suggestion on board, to when Barbara Harris had told him she was pregnant.

"The thing is, even if I tell her I'm not interested in a lasting relationship, if she decides to keep the baby, I'll have to pay maintenance. I mean, I wouldn't want not to but that'll finish me financially. So, what do I have to offer Daisy then? Anyway, when she finds out, she's not going to want to have anything to do with me.

After all, I only went with Barbara to keep her sweet with the job and everything. It's not going to look good. Fuck, it's not good. I must have been mad. And, apart from anything else, that's my baby."

His words rang out like the tolling of a bell; a declaration of truth. A mistake had been made and had to be paid for. There was no point in saying anything to Finn. He already knew what the lesson was and what he had to do about it. They had to agree, he was in the brown stuff right up to his neck. Their silence spoke volumes.

* * *

Tom had rehearsed his leaving speech so many times but when it came to it, he bottled every time. He didn't love Catriona. He doubted he'd ever loved her. They had fallen in with each other rather than fallen in love. They had, as a friend had remarked, just seemed to fit. And Catriona was a force to be reckoned with once she had made up her mind about something. He remembered her planning their future together, even before he had thought of asking her to marry him. Then, suddenly, it seemed to have become accepted amongst their friends and families that they'd be tying the knot. He remembered her saying to him they really ought to set the date and asking him if he would prefer summer or autumn. Other friends were marrying and so he'd allowed himself to be swept along with it all. He supposed he must have thought himself in love at the time but he couldn't, for the life of him, remember what being in love with Catriona felt like.

She'd always been a highly strung person, making it even more difficult to go against her wishes for fear of the consequences being explosive. She was clever, academically, and very good at manipulating life to go her way in general but her most brilliant achievement was in the field of guilt-tripping.

Tom knew what he would get if he told her he was leaving. She would make him feel like the biggest bastard that ever lived. And while he could put up with that being her opinion, he didn't want his children having that view of him.

Tom loved his children but he didn't like them very much. Besides which, he had no aptitude for fatherhood. He wouldn't have chosen to have children, had he been given a choice. But, like everything else, it was Catriona who dictated how their family was to be shaped, although even she was thwarted when nature decided not to give her what she wanted. Her determination for them to go through the IVF programme was, to say the least, monumental and Tom had, once again, caved in the face of it. In truth, he hadn't believed it would work for them and was knocked for six when she'd first broken the news of her pregnancy. He'd somehow come to terms with it and, looking back, had it just been Sonia in their lives, it may have been slightly easier to cope. But the arrival of Nigel, after his redundancy, when they were trying to get back on track with their finances, had been disastrous. Apart from anything else, Sonia was instantly and violently jealous of her baby brother and the fact that he was so bright, made matters a million times worse.

To Tom, who was an only child, sibling rivalry was a mystery and he didn't begin to know how to handle it. Sonia had been daddy's little princess for a while and morphed overnight into a miniature replica of her mother, prone to violent mood swings and making everyone around her feel like they'd dealt her enormous and unjust amounts of pain. She became ugly in his eyes, just as his wife had done, and the distress it caused him made him want to avoid her.

And Nigel, with his brain the size of a planet, was a mystery to everyone, including his mother. Most of the time, it felt like he was the adult and everyone around him, a half-witted child. Tom didn't have a clue how to deal with him although, to give him his dues, he did try. After failing miserably on more than one occasion, his son became the third member of the family, Tom avoided.

Ever since the embarrassing brawl between his wife and their neighbour at the barbecue, Tom had been bracing himself to announce his opinion that he and Catriona should split. He planned to tell her he would move out of the family home and that she could stay on until the children were of an age to look after themselves. He couldn't say fairer than that, surely? He hoped she wouldn't ask where he would be going. He really hoped she wouldn't ask that.

The door slammed. It was the same Saturday afternoon that Finn had come clean to his friends in the house next door. Like the boys at number four, Tom was sitting in the front room watching football, bizarre in itself since he wasn't a fan. Catriona poked her head around the door and her face darkened.

"Oh, it's alright for some," she scoffed. "You could've gone to the supermarket and given me a break. Did you think of that?"

"Yes, I told you," Tom replied, with a sigh. "I had one humungous migraine this morning, remember?"

"Oh, yes. The convenient migraine. Hangover more like. Where were you last night until God knows what time?"

"With friends from work and yes, I had a drink. One drink. That's all. Okay?"

"Am I expected to believe that? D'you really think I'm that stupid?"

"Believe what you like. I no longer care. Because, you know what? It wouldn't matter what I did or didn't do, you'd find a reason to have a go at me."

There was a slight pause. He could almost imagine her testing the atmosphere, like a snake feeling the vibes with a flick of its sensitive tongue. Silently, he cursed the pause, knowing what he'd been building up to was about to be cleverly turned around and avoided once more.

"Oh dear, Tom, if you're in one of those 'poor me' moods, I'll have to leave you to get on with it. I've too much to do to indulge you at the moment. I've got to unload the shopping and get on with dinner."

And there it was; she'd gone, leaving him wriggling on the end of her line once again. No chance for him to spew out all the things he'd so carefully planned to say; no chance to defend himself, let alone point out a few of her own short-comings which might, in the end, actually make *her* want to break up with *him*. He slumped back in his chair, exhausted and frustrated as always, wondering when he would next get the opportunity to engineer a discussion finally leading to the crux of the matter. And, of course, whether he would pluck up the courage.

* * *

The blue window frame of Trevor and Bryce's flat was pulled firmly shut on that very same Saturday afternoon. Bryce had already raised his voice several decibels and Trevor was not a fan of airing his dirty linen in public.

"Would you please keep your voice down, Bryce," he pleaded.

"Why? Who d'you think would be interested in what we have to say to each other. It's supremely boring, I can assure you, mate!"

Trevor shuddered and drew the back of his hand across his eyes. Bryce, in this mood, was not easily persuaded to do anything, let alone lower his volume.

"I'm not going to have a conversation with you if you're going to shout," Trevor stated. "I'm really not."

"We don't have to speak at all if it comes to that."

"No, well, maybe that would be for the best."

"What's your problem, Trev? D'you wanna get rid of me or what?"

That was the question. Trevor's heart skipped a beat at the audaciousness of Bryce's words. But then, Bryce knew him so well; knew if he threw the whole thing right in Trev's face with all his might, Trev would duck. And duck, he did. The image that flashed through his mind of life without Bryce was so desolate and miserable, he couldn't help but want to avoid its close examination. Silently, he cursed his lover's cleverness and knew he couldn't do it; not at this precise moment anyway.

"Don't be ridiculous," he said and opened the window again.

* * *

"Giselle, thank you. They're lovely." Marsha Malloy took the bouquet of flowers, popped them in the sink and carefully removed three, deep yellow blooms from the otherwise cream and pink creation. "I'll find a vase presently," she said, with an apologetic glance at the discarded flowers. "I've made tea. Would you be so kind as to bring the tray through?"

Giselle, who was used to Marsha's idiosyncrasies, did as she was bid and walked into the pastel palace that was Marsha's living room. She set the tray on the coffee table before sitting down.

"It's been a while since you visited, dear," said Marsha, pouring. "I do hope everything's alright."

"Yes, it's... it's fine."

Marsha carefully replaced the tea-pot on its stand and pulled an embroidered cosy firmly down over the top.

"Hmm. You don't sound too sure," she said, her eyes narrowing.

Giselle took a cup and saucer from the tray and sipped her tea. She seemed to be preparing herself to say something unpleasant.

"Well, I... it's the body in the alley, you know..."

"Yes, of course I know. What about it?"

"They haven't caught anyone, have they? And I'm worried that..." Giselle's words trailed off and she seemed to be having difficulty finding the words for what she wanted to discuss.

"Giselle, dear. You really mustn't worry so much. I'm sure we're quite safe now. It wasn't some serial killer or anything like that, you know."

Giselle scanned the other woman's face. Marsha's eyes were boring into her, her head nodding just slightly. Everything about her said she didn't want to discuss the subject further. Giselle let out a slow breath and did her best to relax a little.

"It's not like you to be so jumpy," said Marsha. "Is everything alright? Nothing else worrying you?"

Giselle dropped her gaze and wriggled in her seat a little. "No, no. Everything's fine. I went out with Patrick Baxter recently."

"Oh, did you? Well, he's a nice enough man, I suppose. How did you find him?"

"Shallow." Giselle pressed her lips together, a replication of what she'd done when he'd tried to take more from her than she wanted to give.

"Really, dear? But he was so generous when the garden was trashed. Buying all those plants for us."

"Yes, but it's all for show. You know what I mean, the sort of person whose motive in giving a tip has nothing to do with their satisfaction for service received but everything to do with a desire to be admired for their generosity. It's-"

"Hollow and egotistical." Marsha was nodding, sympathetically. "You didn't get along with him then?"

"Well, I wouldn't say that. He's interesting, charming, intelligent. He buys and sells properties abroad and he has that sort of relaxed worldliness about him. I suppose lots of women would find him extremely attractive but..."

"Not for you?"

"No, I don't think so. It's the arrogance. The assumption that he's irresistible. Not my type at all. But then I'm not sure what is. I don't think I've met anyone who's my type. Not since..."

"I see. Still no Prince Charming to rescue you from your present situation?"

"I never said I wanted to be rescued, Marsha. It's just the murdered councillor that bothers me."

"Giselle, leave it! Forget about it. If there's one thing I've learned in life, it's that worrying about stuff never makes it better. It'll get sorted or it'll fade into the past like other unsolved crimes. Just concentrate on your life and all the good that you do. How's your portrait coming on, by the way?"

Giselle's train of thought was redirected without her even noticing and her smile appeared automatically.

"Well, it's not exactly a portrait. Arlo's got me as a sort of elemental, growing out of the soil with the rest of the foliage. You can see it's me but that's not really the point. It's all ethereal and magical. Different to what he's done before. But we haven't worked on it lately because of the rubbish weather."

"Is that how Arlo makes his living, selling his paintings?"

"No, he does book covers as well and I think he's designed posters for films and stuff. I'm not too sure."

They chatted on and eventually, Giselle left.

"Thanks for visiting!" Marsha called out from her kitchen door, as Giselle made her way across the yard and into the gardens. Giselle turned and waved, smiling broadly.

Marsha paused and glanced up at a sky that had gone a dull yellow as the sun was disappearing behind heavy grey clouds. She hated the colour as, to her, it represented jealousy, anxiety and foreboding. It was illogical, she knew, but it was a colour worn by someone who had stirred up those exact emotions at the most traumatic time of her life. Impatiently, she pushed the thoughts away and went inside, reflecting on how she cherished Giselle's visits and how she would miss her, if she did meet someone special and move away.

Chapter 7

COBALT

Linda Pugh stared at Freddie and shook her head.

"You're not helping yourself, Freddie," she sighed. "You're just getting a reputation as a bad boy. What good's that gonna do you?"

Freddie shrugged and looked off into the distance, his eyes a startling blue against the swarthiness of his skin. Then, dropping his head, he allowed dark waves of hair to swing forward, shielding their owner from giving away any emotions.

"I'm wasting my time, aren't I?" Linda turned back to the sink and began to scrub furiously at a pan. "You don't give a toss about me and Baz, do you?"

She didn't see it but rather felt this had caught Freddie's attention. It wasn't surprising as it was the sort of thing *he* usually said to wind her up. '*No one cares about me. Why should I worry about anyone else?*'

"D'you know, I think you can have the satisfaction of being the one child who broke me. Because I give up. I really do. I had such high hopes for you, Freddie. You're bright and intelligent and... well, yes, I admit it, I absolutely love you to bits. But you don't want that, do you? You're so used to feeling unloved and useless and bad that you've got addicted to it and you don't want to let go. And d'you know why?"

Even a cool kid like Freddie was helpless in the face of Linda on a roll and he gave an involuntary shake of his head.

"Well, I'll tell you! Because you're scared, that's why."

Freddie's mouth tightened into a thin line of anger.

"I ain't scared of nothing."

"Exactly! If you're not scared of nothing then you must be scared of something! Do your English homework, boy!" Linda was not the best example of expertise in English grammar but she did know about the double negative. She smiled triumphantly and continued, "You're scared of being decent and clever and lovable because you don't think you'll be able to keep it up. You think it would be too difficult and you might fail, so it's easier to be a pain in the arse."

Here, she paused and let her words sink in. She could see, by the look on the boy's face, he was thinking hard. There was no sign of the usual backchat. She went in for the kill!

"Freddie, if there's one thing I believe in, it's freedom of choice so you go ahead and be who you want to be. But I'm telling you now, I'm not going to waste my time on someone who doesn't want what I'm offering. There are kids out there who would bite my hand off for it; kids with enough guts to make changes for a better life. But maybe, you're not one of them. Whatever you choose, remember I believed in you, will you? Just do that much for me."

And Linda Pugh wiped her hands on the tea towel, threw it on the table and walked out of the room.

* * *

Finn wiped down the last of the tables in The Bee's and put some chairs upside down on its surface. His face showed no expression, his actions robotic. He was trying hard to think of nothing but the job in hand. It was the only way he was going to get through the mess his life was in. But inevitably, thoughts came, slowly, insidiously, worming their way in.

Barbara was a difficult woman to get out of your mind or to avoid at all, once she had her claws into you. She'd quickly become aware of his attempts to stay out of her way.

"I think we need to have a little talk," she'd hissed in his ear, a few days after she'd revealed her condition to him.

He'd looked at her, his eyes full of despair infuriating her even more.

"What's there to say?" he'd muttered. "What's done is done. The consequences have to be faced."

She'd grabbed him then as he tried to leave; taken hold of an area of his shirt - the thick talons that were her nails, scouring his flesh - and pulled him into the back room.

"What sort of attitude's that?" she'd demanded.

"It's the only one I have," Finn had replied. "Take it or leave it."

And he'd yanked his shirt from her hand and walked away from her, once again.

And now, he had to speak to Daisy; to come clean and watch as any affection she may have had for him, slid from her eyes and ended up in a pool at their feet.

* * *

Trish couldn't bring herself to open the bank statement that nestled in the envelope, still laying on the mat from the morning. She wouldn't allow herself to dwell upon such negative information. It would all come right. She just needed to reign herself in for a few weeks and her finances would sort themselves, ready for the next round of spending and worrying and spending again to compensate for the awful feeling of panic that having no money gave her. Even as she thought about it, her desire to nip to the market and see what new bargains were on offer was mounting; or, worse still, to go on to the shopping mall and check out all the designer stuff.

Trish felt her stomach constrict and the first trickle of tears made their way down her cheeks. Was it always going to be this way for her, she wondered? She remembered her mother working two jobs, hairdressing during the day and waitressing in the evening, just to 'keep the wolf from the door'. Trisha had spent a lot of time at her aunt's house or with friends. Her clothes and toys mostly consisted of hand-me-downs, for which she'd endured a great deal of teasing. She felt the fury at that treatment rising in her until it reached her throat and forced its way out in a scream of indignation. Then, grabbing her bag, she left the flat to do the only thing she knew would ease the pain.

* * *

Valerie stood by the window and stared out at her sister who she could just see on one of the benches – the turquoise one by the apple tree. She'd insisted on struggling out there with her sticks, a determined little figure refusing to give up on life however uncomfortable it sometimes felt. Frances had always been an inspirational sort of person, a fact which only served to irritate her younger sister even more.

Valerie shook her head as though trying to dislodge a wasp that had somehow managed to penetrate her ear. Her thoughts about Frances felt just like that - an angry buzzing sensation that she knew, in the end, would sting only her and no one else. Except, if she was hurt, she knew Frances would feel it too. That was the thing about Frances; however much you upset her, she kept loving you and forgiving all your nasty, little ways which, of course, only made you feel worse.

To her surprise, Valerie felt a moistness around her eyes and something dripped off her chin. Why, oh why had she been born the evil sister? And hadn't she paid for it by now? All those years of being married to a man who treated her with contempt, wasn't that payment enough to atone for the badness in her? Apparently not. And really, had she been that bad? She'd just enjoyed being the sister with whom everyone wanted to hang out. She'd only teased Frances a little bit for her quietness. *'Girly swat, girly swat! Come and show us what you've got!'* She didn't want to remember the tears that had welled in her sister's eyes at being taunted or how it had become worse when her friends joined in and made Frances the butt of all their jokes. The wasp buzzed loudly with remembering! Frances, with her spectacles, plain clothes and bulging satchel, scuttling out of school to avoid the bullying and get home as quickly as she could, to open her books and study. Frances, who left school with flying colours but halted her studies to look after their sick mother. How noble! Frances, who'd never had a boyfriend but landed a series of really good jobs which paid well and, once again, earned her respect and admiration. Valerie's mouth twisted. How come her mousey, quiet, boring sister was so content? Was it because she'd made all the right choices whilst she, Valerie, had chosen foolishly? Had it really been so wrong to just want to have a good time? She'd been the better looking of the two; a handsome girl with an outgoing personality, always chasing the next thrill. She was never at home and spent her money as soon as she'd earned it. Valerie had been an emancipated woman of the new age and she'd wanted it all.

And then, Hugh Figgis had come along; strong, opinionated and attractive. Valerie had been captivated; captivated by the thought of a man who would put her on a pedestal; who would keep her and look after her and occasionally, spoil her. She'd gone all out to get him, with not one iota of realisation of who he really was. A shuddering sigh left her as she remembered her late husband, controlling, short-tempered, unfeeling and with one foot back in the forties. He'd demanded complete obedience from her. She'd had to put him first at all times. When she didn't, the consequences were dire. He didn't like her going out with her friends so gradually, she'd lost them all. The only friends they had were his and associated with his work; who came for dinner and were not interested in getting to know Valerie for herself.

He wasn't a wife-beater as such but he wasn't above lashing out at her if she pushed him. It had only happened half a dozen times as far as she could remember. One of those had been after a discussion about children. Valerie had always assumed she would become a mother. She was rather good with kids, her exuberance and enthusiasm for finding exciting things to do appealed to the youngsters with whom she'd had contact. But Hugh Figgis was adamant he didn't want babies cluttering up his well-ordered life. He was totally unsympathetic to her distress at his declaration of leading a child-free life and finally, when she refused to stop pleading and crying, he had slapped her across the face, claiming the necessity of such action was due to hysteria on her part.

Her husband was a clever man and, for some time after that incident, he'd treated her like a queen and made her fall in love with him all over again. And so her life had gone on with periods of peace, living well in a lovely home, nice holidays and no financial worries and then, when he became dissatisfied and angry, crumbling into an abyss of loneliness, anxiety and regret. Valerie would find herself wondering why she'd never found the courage to leave and, as always, the same answer presented itself. Time and again, she'd convince herself, it was just about to get better.

The sunshine was hazy over the garden area and a few clouds gathered in the distance, crouching like a pack of wolves ready to swallow up the cobalt blue expanse above. Valerie's mood echoed the blueness but, looking over at her sister's curly, grey head, she felt her heart open a little. She was lucky to have Frances; in so many ways, she was lucky to have her but the sadness came because she knew the same could not be said of the other way around.

* * *

"The reason I've got you all here, is to post the question of what we're going to do about Anya?"

Hilary looked around her sitting room at the people present. Their eyes stared back at her, some questioning, some understanding. Outside, the rain tapped insistently against the windows, like a ghost begging to be let back into the real world.

"Hilary's noticed... that Anya... is not herself," explained Reg Prodger, in his halting, apologetic way.

"I think we've all noticed that," snapped Harry Footlik irascibly. "It's getting more obvious by the day."

"Florence and some of the other younger people have been popping in on her but, you know, they have their own lives to lead. They can't be expected to give up all their time to keep an eye on us oldies," Marsha stated, hoping the others would agree with her sentiment.

"I don't think there's a lot anyone can do," said Hilary. "If it's Allzimmers, she's going to need proper help."

"Exactly," said Marsha. "That's why I thought we could try and contact her family. She's probably got some, somewhere."

"Alzheimer's!" roared Harry, having finally worked out Hilary's word for the disease. "Who said anything about Alzheimer's?"

"Calm down, Harry," urged Reg. "It has to be taken into consideration, that's all."

"Well, I'm sorry but I don't think she has that. She's a bit forgetful, yes, but you don't know her. She's been through a lot."

"All of us have been through a lot," said Reg, with feeling. "I don't see what bearing that has on memory loss."

"Well, I s'pose if one has a lot of traumatics in life, you might be declined to bury things which could set up a precipice... in the subscious, I mean," retorted Hilary, again struggling to express herself.

"Good Lord, woman! Can't you keep it simple for once," snapped Harry, glaring at Hilary.

Fortunately, she was spared the trouble of replying as there was a knock on the door. She hurried to open it, to find Valerie Figgis standing there, an expression of resignation on her face.

"Hope I haven't kept you all waiting," Valerie said, stepping into the sitting room and taking Hilary's chair. "Frances insisted I come although I really don't see what I can do. I've enough on my plate seeing to her."

"It's a disgustion as much as anything," said Hilary, bringing in a stool from the kitchen. "To see if anyone had any ideas or info that could help us help Anya."

"Well, for my part, I think dealing with those sort of problems should be left to the experts." Valerie shrugged her jacket back on, as though that was all that needed to be said and she could now go home.

"So, if it happens to you, you'd be happy to be shuntered off to some home and forgotten about, would you?" Hilary was quite pink with indignation.

"I'm sure Valerie didn't mean it to sound like that," said Marsha hurriedly, stepping in before war broke out. "But we do have to consider just how much we're capable of handling, ourselves."

"Surely, we should contact her relatives," began Valerie.

"Yes, we were just about to disgust that when you turned up," said Hilary snippily.

"If you would just let me get a word in," roared Harry, "I could have told you she doesn't have relatives. At least, not any who would give a damn."

There was a stunned silence.

"But how do you know that, Harry dear?" asked Marsha gently.

"Because I've been visiting, haven't I?" Here, he made a great show of huffing and puffing, as though the truth were there for all to see if they'd only taken the trouble to look.

"Oh, well," said Hilary, looking round to see if anyone was as flummoxed as she was. "That's very good of you, Harry. So you've had a chance to watch Anya and learn more about her, have you?"

"Yes! That's what I've been trying to tell you," said Harry triumphantly. "I know she's forgetful. I can see that but she's a long way from Alzheimer's, I'm sure."

And Harry proceeded to tell them what he'd recently learned of Anya's life, taking particular care to explain how her father's family had wanted to rid themselves of her as quickly as possible.

"Oh, poor Anya," breathed Hilary, when he'd finished. "So all that stuff about the ballot was true."

"That's why she's always so elegant and graceful," sighed Reg. "Her mother must have taught her everything she knew, even when they were struggling to survive." He wiped his eye surreptitiously.

"Yes, exactly," said Harry. "She's not had it easy at all."

"But what about the rest of her life?" asked Valerie. "For all we know, she could have had a good marriage and there may be children somewhere. They should be made to take some responsibility, if you ask me."

"In my experience, no one can be *made* to do anything they don't want to," said Marsha. "But you're right, we should find out if Anya does have family who, for all we know, may want to help."

"That seems like the place to start," said Hilary, pleased. "We could have a go at getting her to talk more about her life. Harry, p'raps you're the best person to take that on, as you seem to have won her over. Anyway, have a chat about it while I go and make us some tea."

She left them talking animatedly as she went into her kitchen to switch on the kettle. When she walked back, a few minutes later, carrying a plateful of cakes made by Marsha, Hilary noticed that even Valerie seemed to be enjoying herself for once. Wonders would never cease!

Chapter 8

AMBER

Trish stared at herself in the mirror, turning her head this way and that and moving her body so she could see her reflection over her shoulder. She pulled her hair from its pony tail and fluffed it round her face. Finally, she realised that whatever she did, she couldn't hide what she had done. Her upper lip protruded from her face like an enormous inner tube distorting her looks and making it appear like she'd been in some horrific accident. She had never been a beauty but she had, at least, been reasonably attractive. Now, she had destroyed what nature had given her in a few short minutes, by giving in to the craving for the excitement that something new brought her. Why, oh why, had she not stopped to think about what she was doing? Why could she never seem to exercise a bit of caution? If only she'd waited; thought about it for a while; discussed it with someone. She leant back against the wall and slid slowly down, watching her reflection disappear and wishing she could disappear with it.

* * *

Linus Swankey squeezed himself through the sardine can that was the London Tube, battling with the hordes trying to get into the carriage. Gritting his teeth, he stuck out his elbows and, surging forward, had the satisfaction of seeing people fall aside in the wake of his determination. His triumphant mood wavered however, when he realised a young woman had lost her balance and stumbled back onto the platform. His shame worsened when a small child grabbed her hand and began crying with alarm.

"I'm so sorry. Are you alright?" said Linus, raising his voice as the doors shut and the train rattled off down the tunnel. He reached down and took her arm to help her up.

"Yeah, I think so." She looked pale and shaken. "It wasn't your fault."

"I think it probably was," said Linus guiltily. "I was pushing hard to get out."

"Well, you have to, don't you?" she said, with a little smile. "It's such a nightmare at this time of day."

"It is, absolutely," agreed Linus wholeheartedly. "But I didn't need to get quite so aggressive."

"You think that was aggressive?" murmured the young woman, picking up the child tugging at her sleeve. "It's alright, Megan. Mummy's not hurt."

The little girl put her arms around her mother's neck and squeezed tightly. Linus felt terrible.

"Where were you trying to get to?" he asked.

"Oh, just one stop," she replied. "We were going to look at a maisonette for rent, just off Beresford Road."

"Yes, I know the road. Near the new shopping mall." Linus scratched his chin and threw caution to the wind. "Look, I know this is probably going to sound bizarre but I live quite near here. I have a car and I could give you a lift, if you like... to make up for you missing your train. I'm not a serial killer or anything, I promise you. S-sorry, that was a bit bizarre. One of my neighbours is bound to be in and would vouch for me anyway. It's up to you, of course-"

"Okay! Okay," she laughed, holding up her free hand. "I'll take a chance. You don't look dodgy to me. What do you think, Meggie? Do you think this gentleman's a nice person?"

Megan's eyes wandered over his face momentarily and she nodded, smiling. Then, shyness overcame her and she nestled back into her mother's neck.

"I think that's a 'yes', don't you? I'm Sally, by the way. And thank you. I appreciate this, er...?"

"Linus. I'm only too glad to be able to make amends," replied Linus with a grin and led the way out of the station.

***

Benson watched Florence as she took her knife and chopped an onion before scooping it into the saucepan.

"Ooh, me eyes," she gasped and stretched out her hand for the kitchen roll.

He moved forward swiftly, tore off a piece for her and watched sympathetically as she dabbed the paper over her eyes. He crossed to her and taking her in his arms, held her so close she couldn't move. Finally, she managed to raise her head and look up at him. His eyes were shut tight and he had such an expression on his face - one she couldn't fathom.

"Benson, what the matter with you?" she asked. "I can't get me breath, you squeezin' so hard."

He broke into a smile and loosened his grip. Looking down at her he said, "I just realised something, Flo."

"Oh yeah, what that then?"

"I can't bear to see you in pain or discomfort."

"What you talking about, you big lummox?" She pushed at him but was laughing at the same time.

"It hurt me to see you with your eyes all sore. I just wanted to make it better for you." He gently smoothed his thumb over her eyelids. "So, what d'you think that's all about, eh?"

"Don't aks me. You losing your marbles, man." She pushed him away, still chuckling, and turned back to her chopping board.

"I want to ask you to marry me, Flo. What d'you think of that?"

She stopped what she was doing. She was very still; her back rigid and not even a hair of her head moving.

"Flo?"

Finally, she turned round. Her eyes were moist but the expression on her face was deadly serious.

"Benson, we only been out a few times. We don't proper know each other..."

"But we do. We've known each other for ages. We've been neighbours for, what – four years?"

"Just have a bit o' patience, Benson man, an' do this right. I enjoying this datin' ting. I don't wanna rush it. It too easy, you know, get carried away. You got my full attention right now, so don't spoil it, eh?"

He chuckled and took her face in his big hands to plant a kiss on it.

"Whatever you say, my flower. You can have it any way you want."

She pulled away, a haughty expression on her face, and gave a satisfied nod before attending again to the meal. But he saw she was soon smiling and, after a short while, humming happily over her work.

He could wait. If necessary, he told himself grandly, he would wait forever.

* * *

Hilary Scantleberry was perturbed. A youngish man had come into the charity shop on several occasions, unremarkable in itself, but there was something in his manner that puzzled her.

"Did you notice anything?" she asked Pam, one of the other volunteers.

Pam shook her head and shrugged. "Can't say I did. P'raps he's new to the area and feeling his feet so to speak. You know how it is."

This was one of Pam's favourite expressions, used when she didn't really know how it was, herself. Pam didn't like not having answers. She was one of those people who wanted to give the impression she knew everything there was to know about anything.

"You didn't feel there was something furtive about him? As though he was checking to see if you were watching him?"

"No, dear." Pam shook her head. "Perhaps he felt you *were* watching him – which you obviously were – and that made him feel furtive."

"Sorry? You've lost me," said Hilary and then realised Pam didn't really know what 'furtive' meant. Sympathetic as she was, knowing how often her own mind played tricks when it came to words, Hilary allowed herself a second of superiority. The word had recently come up in a conversation with Reg who'd gone to the trouble of explaining its meaning. Rather proud of her newly acquired knowledge, she'd been pleased to have the opportunity to use it. She was about to explain its meaning when she remembered Pam would only get defensive and sniffy if her ignorance was highlighted and decided against it.

"Oh well, not to worry. I expect it's just me suffering from a bit of paranoiamal. Happens a lot since the body in the alley. Just ignore me."

"I'm sorry to hear you're not well, dear. Should you be working, do you think? I mean, I can't afford to go down with anything at the moment. I've got Eileen's wedding to sort out, you know."

And so she went on. But Hilary, now befuddled as to why Pam thought she was unwell, turned her thoughts to the man again and decided not to over-react - for the time being, anyway.

* * *

"Just gonna scratch my nose," said Giselle, out of the corner of her mouth.

Arlo gave an exaggerated sigh and put the back of his hand to his forehead in a dramatic gesture of extreme frustration.

"How is an artist expected to work in such circumstances?" he declared and broke into laughter. "Really, you don't have to act like a ventriloquist. I told you, if you want to say something, just go ahead. Anyway, let's have a break and get some coffee."

Giselle grinned and stretched luxuriously. "Aha, my ploy worked. Coffee is indeed what's needed."

There was silence as Arlo poured strong black coffee from the insulated jug he'd brought from his flat. Silences were not a problem between them. Both were comfortable just listening to the sounds around them without having to comment. The autumn sun was low in the sky, still producing some warmth, its light enhancing the rich amber of the turning leaves. There was a fair amount of insect activity going on, made evident by the soft buzzing around the buddleia and birds, too, chirruped busily in the apple tree; all seeming to indicate that nothing had quite given up on summer. The dull roar of traffic appeared far distant in the peace of the Harlequin gardens that morning and Arlo and Giselle sighed in simultaneous satisfaction.

"We're in perfect harmony, aren't we?" Giselle smiled at Arlo over her coffee cup.

"Hmm, getting there," replied Arlo. "Perhaps it happens with artist and model. I know Jess and I became very tuned in to each other. Knew what the other was going to say."

"Was she one of your models?"

"To start with and then, she became my wife."

"Oh." Giselle hadn't expected that. "I didn't know you were married. Or did I? I must have done but she's not-"

"She died. Jess died." It was as though he had to say it twice to make himself believe it. "Cancer. It was a while ago."

The pain etched on Arlo's face was raw. It made Giselle suck in her breath and hold it until the vibrations of the pain of his loss stopped banging into her. She noticed him taking deep breaths of his own and gradually, things settled again.

"I'm so sorry, Arlo," she said softly. "I didn't mean to bring up..."

"It's alright. They say time heals but not for me. Not yet anyway. I have to make sure I count my blessings. Twenty years I had. Twenty years of absolute bliss of being totally loved and in love with the most wonderful human being you could wish to meet. How lucky is that? Some people never even have a second of that feeling. So! So, I'm not complaining you understand. Not at all..."

He took a sip of his coffee and leant back on the bench, his eyes closed. Giselle stood quietly by, watching him and remembering what it was like to be loved that much by someone you, in turn, loved. For a split second, she nearly said something but realised, just in time, it wasn't an appropriate moment to be making declarations. And maybe, as far as Arlo was concerned, that moment would never come.

* * *

Finn finally approached Daisy, one Thursday afternoon, after their lunchtime shift at the pub. They were growing closer by the day and had fallen into an easy camaraderie, him constantly telling her he was falling for her whilst she countered by saying he was making a big mistake. But whatever they said or didn't say, their feelings for each other were obvious; a beam of light in the darkness, impossible not to spot.

Finn had no idea how it was going to pan out. He was desperately hoping that somehow they would be able to get past the ridiculous mess he'd made of his life; a bit of an understatement, he knew, for fathering a child with a woman for whom you had no physical attraction or feelings whatsoever! He could have, and at times was tempted, to just tell Barbara that he couldn't be with her; that he would support their child but that was it. He didn't know how to begin to admit that finding money for that support was going to be extremely difficult, as he barely had enough to pay his share of the rent. He'd even swapped rooms with Linus, taking the tiny box-room in exchange for paying a little less. But Barbara was a vindictive vixen of a female who would, he was certain, think up plenty of ways of getting at him. It was driving him mad with worry. He had to tell Daisy before they got any closer and then, at least, if she dumped him, he could re-assess the situation. But he knew if she did that, he would no longer care what happened to him.

"I need to talk to you," he said, as they walked into the Harlequin gardens. "I've been putting this on hold for too long and I-"

"Same," Daisy interrupted. "Something I need to tell you."

That was a curve ball for Finn. It hadn't occurred to him she might have secrets too.

"Look," he said. "Before you go saying things you might regret, you should hear what I've got to say because you may not want to be with me after you hear-"

"Same," she said again.

He reached out then and put his fingers on her mouth. "D'you know what, I don't want to know. I don't care what you've done, it won't make any difference to the way I feel about you."

"It's not what I've done," she began.

"No!" He shook his head. "Please, just let me get this off my chest and then decide whether or not, you want to say whatever it is. Please."

Daisy looked worried but nodded, her violet blue eyes full of concern. And so he told her. He'd thought about embellishing the story with a few things that would excuse his behaviour but, in the end, he just said it exactly as it had happened, his head hung down and his hands twisting with anxiety.

"It's my own fault," he said finally. "My arrogance, thinking I could manipulate things. I don't even like the woman but that was no reason to treat her that way and now, I've created a new life and..." His voice caught in his throat and he bit down hard on his lower lip, hoping the pain would dull his emotions.

There was silence. Finally, Finn lifted his head, hardly daring to look. Daisy's face was a blank canvas. She was so still, she seemed to be barely breathing.

"I'm so sorry, Daisy," he said.

"I don't think it's me you should be apologising to," she said, at last. "I'm not one of those people who think you shouldn't have had a life before I came along."

Finn felt his spirits lift a little.

"But where does that leave us?" he asked anxiously. "And it has overlapped - her and me - and me and you."

"Look, Finn, I get it. You did something for which you're rightly ashamed. I believe whether I'd come along or not, you'd still have regretted your actions and needed to do something about them. So, I think you should sort that out yourself. It has nothing to do with me."

Finn looked at her, his eyes wide with anxiety. "Does that mean it won't affect our relationship?"

She looked down at her hands and, after a few seconds, raised her eyes to his.

"I know it doesn't seem like it to you but this is a very small incident in the greater scheme of things. From what I've heard today, I don't think you're a terrible person. You know you've been stupid and irresponsible but now, you're prepared to take responsibility. I like that. Of course, if you were to decide to make an honest woman of Barbara, I would no longer be dating you or having any expectations."

"Of course. That goes without saying," cried Finn, unable to believe how reasonable she was being.

"But I warn you, it won't be long before all this will seem like nothing in comparison to-"

Finn didn't wait for her to finish. He rushed to envelope her in a bear hug.

"I don't care, I don't care!" he yelled. "As long as you can still care for me, after all I've done, then I can put up with anything."

Daisy hugged him back but her eyes were dark and troubled. He'd quite forgotten she had something to tell him and part of her gave a sigh of relief. Another time would do. For now, she would let things lie and enjoy the man she was beginning to love deeply.

* * *

Amber, the colour of caution. An amber light can be ignored, of course, and some do just that; taking a chance, racing forward and to hell with the consequences. Others hold back and wait. Both ways have 'fors' and 'againsts' hence the early bird catching worms and conversely, fools rushing in where angels fear to tread. But, decisions have to be made in life and it's pretty much a waste of time and energy to look back with regret and wish things had been done differently.

Chapter 9

IRON GREY

Sally had been so taken with the Harlequin triangle that Linus had felt confident in inviting her and Megan back to have a proper look. She'd refused to allow him to take her home after she'd viewed the grotty, little maisonette in Beresford Street so he had dropped her off at the tube station with an invitation to have tea at the weekend; in the gardens, if the Indian summer continued. Her ensuing delight with the whole place and to his growing astonishment, him, had fired up a long-awaited dream that there was, after all, someone in the world who could care for him. Since then, he'd spent so much time in his room pondering blissful outcomes to this new relationship, his house mates had started to become suspicious. He made the excuse of having a hard time at work and needing some space.

This wasn't entirely untrue. It wasn't the work as a systems analyst that bothered him, it was more about the people with whom he spent his working hours. Compared to his friends in the house, they seemed such a materialistic, back-stabbing bunch. Linus had grown up in quite a modest home, the son of a working-class family blessed with a high degree of intelligence. He'd been encouraged to make the most of his brain but no one had told him he might have to change his outlook on life as well. He was sick of hearing about his colleagues' latest purchases whether it was a car, a holiday or a meal in a flashy restaurant. He just wasn't interested in how much money they spent, especially as their satisfaction with their purchases seemed to wear off so quickly. No, Linus was much happier slobbing about with Benson and Finn, despite his constant moaning regarding beer cans and wrappings from takeaways having been left about instead of being deposited in the bin or the odd items of clothing draped over furniture for days. He was happier with them, he acknowledged, because they cared about him. They might tease and laugh at him but, when push came to shove, they would stand up for him without hesitation. And he loved them for it.

He wondered what they would think of Sally. She was an ordinary sort of girl; attractive but not a head-turner. Straight, brown hair cut in a bob to her jaw, framing a pleasant face with pretty but rather anxious hazel eyes. She had rather a good figure; he'd noticed that. The clothes she wore were plain, mainly jeans, tee-shirts and long cardigans. He'd also noticed a small tattoo on the back of her wrist. He didn't normally go for girls with tattoos but then, he wasn't exactly *going* for her. She'd turned up in his life and, for once, Linus allowed his instincts to take over. It felt good, comfortable and what would be, would be. Linus decided he was going along with what life was offering and see where it took him.

* * *

Tom had come home to a house full of screaming. Sonia was railing at her mother; something about stopping her doing stuff because she was old and jealous. Catriona was demanding respect and shrieking a request for a lower volume. Nigel was drumming on something and chanting words which Tom couldn't decipher. He stood in the hall and took a few deep breaths wondering how, in God's name, it had come to this. He took another deep breath, made a decision and entered the kitchen. He stood there, waiting for the noise to die down. His wife stopped first and then, Sonia. Nigel stopped chanting but the drumming of his fist on the biscuit tin continued for a few more times. Tom looked around the kitchen.

"It's a nice room, isn't it?" he said finally. "We put a lot of effort into making it look good. D'you remember how we scrubbed the cupboards out with bleach and bought new doors. It looked like a different kitchen after that. The table we got from a boot fare, remember? And we scrubbed that and painted the legs. Oh and then, we found those chairs in that Emporium place. More scrubbing and painting and, okay, they don't quite match but it all looks very vintage, don't you think? And that's very *in*, at the moment. And we've done much the same in the other rooms, haven't we? In fact, we're very lucky. We have a lovely home. Oh, and we have food on the table and clothes on our backs. And then, we have each other. I wonder how many people would kill for the lifestyle we enjoy? And yet, all we seem to want to do is kill each other. I don't want to leave the home I've helped to build and the family I've created but I can't live like this. I don't know what else I can do so I'm leaving. I hope you sort out your differences. I'll be in touch."

And Tom walked out and away from his family. His heart was thudding in his chest and there were tears in his eyes but he felt lighter than he had done for a very long time. Until, for some reason, it came to him what Nigel had been chanting - 'Help, help me, help'.

* * *

Frances lay at the bottom of the stairs. As she came round, she registered the rough feeling of carpet beneath her fingers and her cheek. She tried to move and became aware of a new sensation. Pain! From the lower part of her body right up to her neck. She tried to call out but, as in a dream, her voice seemed to have no strength to it. Where was Valerie? Then, she remembered her sister had gone to the market to get supplies. But would she go for coffee somewhere first? And hadn't she mentioned she was calling in at the library? She could be gone ages. Then again, Frances had no idea how long she'd been laying there or what time it was now. She couldn't even move to a position where she could see her watch. She closed her eyes again and silently sent up a prayer.

* * *

It was Reg's turn to visit Anya. He ambled over to her flat, a small package in his hand. He didn't feel confident about offering someone else support but was too kind-hearted to refuse his help. Her door was on the latch although they'd had keys cut just in case. Harry Footlik had removed the door chain, worried that she might put it on without thinking and make entry to her place nigh on impossible. They'd had to get her into the gardens to give him a chance to do the job. It had been rather tense as she hadn't been very responsive to their ministrations that morning. Hilary had done her best to get her to talk further about her past but Anya was not interested. Nor was she interested in giving her opinion on new plants for the garden and eventually, insisted on returning to her home. Fortunately, Harry had finished just in time and, apart from a bit of sawdust on the floor, there was no sign of him or his recent activity. Reg had chuckled with the others later but had to admit, he could do without that sort of excitement at his time of life.

Anya seemed pleased to see him. She was childishly excited when he offered her the small package. She opened it slowly and carefully, savouring the anticipation.

"Oh, how beautiful," she sighed, holding up the scarf he'd brought her.

Reg thought so too. It was one of his favourites and had cost him dear to part with it. But he knew her taste and that she would like it and it seemed a small price to pay if it gave her some pleasure.

"Put it on, Anya," he said, smiling at her delight.

The soft turquoise and sea green of the scarf brought out the aqua of Anya's eyes as she curled it around her neck. Her skin appeared pinker and more vibrant. Reg noticed these things. He moved forward and tied it for her and told her how attractive it made her look. She laughed softly at first but then, her face clouded and she sat back in her chair, looking down at her hands.

"What is it, Anya?" asked Reg. "Why are you upset?"

"Ptolemy, he bought me a scarf once. Very similar colours. Vent vith an outfit, I had. Beautiful."

"Ptolemy?" queried Reg, remembering what Harry had advised about getting her to say things as though they were just part of some fiction. "That's an unusual name. Where does he fit into the story, I wonder?"

It worked. Anya's head came up, her eyes shining.

"Oh, it vasn't his real name. He vas a professor of history. That vas his subject and he specialised in ancient Egypt so he got that nickname because Ptolemy vas one of the pharaohs, I think. His real name was... Jeremy? No, it vas Peter Jeremy and ve all called him Ptolemy. Aah, my Ptolemy..."

Anya's eyes had misted over and Reg hesitated, in two minds whether to continue. But instinct drove him on.

"So, the professor, Ptolemy, did he marry the ballet dancer's daughter?"

She slowly turned her gaze on him, a look of confusion crossing her eyes. Reg smiled encouragingly but jumped in alarm when she barked her answer at him.

"NO! No, they never married. How could they? *She* vouldn't divorce him. She hated him but she vouldn't let me have him. She vas a first class BITCH!"

Reg was off his seat and at her side in an instant. He took her hand and put his other arm around her trembling shoulders.

"There, it's alright," he gasped. "Don't think about it anymore now. We'll finish the story another time."

Reg held her until she stopped shaking. He didn't feel able to cope with this level of emotion. His own life had been full to the brim with anxiety, confusion and sadness. He'd have to let one of the others carry on but at least he'd gleaned a little more of her story which, maybe, could lead them to someone from her past.

* * *

"How much?" asked the man, taking out his wallet, his hand twitching as he scrabbled to open it.

There was no reply and when he looked up, she was shaking her head.

"Thank you," he said, disbelief flooding his features. "Thank you, so much. I'll see you soon. Next month."

Giselle nodded and smiled. She went to the door, held it open and waited patiently for him to make his way awkwardly past her.

"You'll be okay?"

"Thank you. Yes."

She knew he wouldn't.

* * *

The ambulance screamed to a halt by the entrance to the Harlequin triangle and two paramedics leapt out. Linda Pugh appeared in the alleyway, waving frantically to attract their attention. Even in emergencies, the back entrance was preferred and they all raced to the purple door through which Frances and Valerie resided. Sometime later, the paramedics appeared with Frances on a stretcher and Linda Pugh, leading a very distressed Valerie, after them.

Linus, who was just coming into the gardens to meet Sally, was shocked at the scene that met his eyes and hurried across to join them.

"What on earth...? Miss Arbuthnot! Are you alright?" he called.

Linda took his arm solicitously.

"Frances has had a fall. They're not sure if she's broken anything but she's in a state of shock." She paused, giving Valerie a worried glance. "She'll be fine, I'm sure. I'm going with Valerie to the hospital so when we know Frances is settled, I can bring her back."

"Oh yes, good idea. I'm so sorry, Valerie. Try to keep calm. I'm sure Frances will be fine."

Valerie looked grey but rallied to give a half smile before Linda ushered her away.

"If you see, Freddie, will you explain for me, Linus?" Linda called over her shoulder. "He should be home from school in a while."

"Of course." Linus held up his hand with a raised thumb to reassure her. So much for a peaceful afternoon in the garden with his new friend. He glanced at his watch, noticing Sally was due any minute. He wandered over to one of the benches. It was a lovely warm afternoon despite the onset of autumn and he was determined to make the most of it. He would bring the tray out when she arrived. He'd bought iced buns and chocolate biscuits to have with their tea, hoping it suited her taste. Time went on and Linus started to have doubts Sally was going to turn up. He sighed deeply. What did he expect? He was no catch. He was a thin man; thin and beige, some spiteful woman had once called him. His hair was a non-descript colour and lay flat on his head. He had a long, skinny body, most suited for a picture in the before category of a muscle-building advert.

His face was pale with a few acne scars dotted about. He used contact lenses when socialising but the rest of the time, it was spectacles. Linus had no illusions about his looks and, if he was honest, about the likelihood of his ever attracting a mate.

He saw movement out of the corner of his eye and spun round to joyfully welcome his visitor.

"Sally, I'm so glad you could make it. But, where's Megan?"

"Well, I wasn't sure the invite was for Megan as well," she replied. "I've left her with a friend."

"Okay but don't ever feel you have to leave her out, please."

"That's really nice of you but it'll be easier for us to talk without a child around. Children are very demanding, you know."

They smiled at each other until Linus remembered the purpose of the meeting and darted off to get the tea tray, leaving Sally instructions to have a look around and choose a bench on which to sit.

"It's so beautiful," Sally breathed, when he came back. "I just love all the colours on the fire escapes and the artwork on the back of the flats and this garden is amazing."

"I know," said Linus, pouring the tea. "We're very blessed but then again, the residents put in a lot of effort to create and maintain it. They're a pretty decent bunch. We get together, here in the gardens, for celebrations. It's a great bonding exercise, if you know what I mean."

Sally nodded but there was a sadness in her eyes that puzzled him.

"Where do... I mean, you have family, don't you? Where were you brought up? Sorry, don't mean to cross-examine you." Linus suddenly felt like he was prying, although he wasn't sure why.

"Oh, it's alright. Erm, nothing very... children's home and then a couple of foster homes."

Linus knew why, now. He'd sensed she was reluctant to talk about her background.

"To be honest, it wasn't great. I don't like thinking about it," she admitted. "I guess I try and compensate by giving Megan the sort of life I wanted. She's so precious to me. It's the first time I've had someone to call my own - my own little family. But it's tough, you know, in the position I'm now in."

Sally bit down on her lip and stared hard at a butterfly that had landed on a last spear of buddleia. Linus's heart went out to her and, feeling extremely inadequate, he struggled to find something to say.

"She's got you," he said finally and, in a bold move for him, took her hand and squeezed it. "That's a great start for her. Now, help yourself to some cake. Whatever's left, you can take home for Megan."

Sally seemed to relax and they chatted on until the early evening, their flow broken only by the appearance of Freddie. Freddie agreed to phone Baz to let him know Linda wasn't around and inform Linus, if and when his foster-father could get back. Sally's look of admiration for the way Linus was dealing with things was payment enough for the interruption to his plans.

Later, it occurred to Linus that he'd instigated most of the topics they'd discussed. Sally still seemed reluctant to talk about her life, unless it was her plans for the future. He was pleased when it transpired they had similar tastes in several areas and she agreed there was plenty of scope for meeting up again. Finally, Sally announced she would have to get back to Megan but once again, refused when Linus offered to drop her back home.

"Look, I'm driving over to the hospital to see how Frances is, so it would be no bother to-"

"Well, drop me off at the hospital then. It's not far from there." Sally had a stubborn look on her face and Linus didn't want to argue with her when they were getting along so well. He gave in, grateful that she had, at least, agreed to see him again.

* * *

It hadn't helped that Daisy had stared, open-mouthed, for several seconds before speaking and then, all she'd said was, "Jeeeez!" Trish, now convinced she'd ruined her looks for life, felt she would never be able to be in anyone's company again, let alone attract a member of the opposite sex. To add to that, her finances had reached crisis point so it wasn't surprising she'd downed a bottle of wine and several glasses of vodka before passing out on the living room floor. She awoke the next morning to find a pillow had been pushed under her head, a blanket tucked around her and a bowl placed by her side. For Trish, it seemed as though things couldn't get any worse and the thought crossed her mind that maybe she needed to leave the planet – permanently!

* * *

At number three, Grenville Row, Catriona Penworthy was having similar thoughts but, because she had two children depending on her, she dismissed such action as swiftly as it occurred to her. She was reeling from Tom's announcement and the realisation he'd actually left. Her emotions had gone from shock to anger to despair and then, extreme fury. It was this last emotion that had driven her to an, 'I'll show him' moment.

Sonia had started wailing as soon as he'd left, blaming her mother for the mess in which they now found themselves. For once, Catriona wasn't cowed by the violence of her daughter's emotional attack.

"That's fine, Sonia," she stated firmly. "When your father lets us know where he's staying, I'll arrange for you to go to him. I've enough on my plate without you whingeing on and blaming me for everything. No! I'm not discussing it. Just get out of my sight and leave me to think things through."

And Sonia went. Catriona had heard her stomping up the stairs, still wailing and moaning like some aggrieved banshee. Nigel, on the other hand, had started banging on the tin again but this time it was softer and more rhythmic. He stared into the distance and was humming quietly to himself. Catriona took hold of his hand and moved the biscuit tin away.

"It'll be alright, Nigel, you'll see. Mummies and daddies have fights just the same as children do but we'll work it out, don't you worry."

But Nigel's face was a mask of stone and Catriona had no idea what he was thinking.

* * *

Valerie sat by the bedside looking down at her sister's familiar face and made a promise to whoever was in charge of such things that if

Frances could be allowed to survive, she would become a changed woman.

* * *

A couple of weeks later, Linus made his way to the gardens, the smile on his face stretching from ear to ear, despite the dark metallic gloom of a sky that threatened to put an end to mellow autumn days. After meeting up a few times, usually over coffee somewhere, Sally had agreed on an outing to the Tate Modern. She wanted to improve her knowledge she said so, when Megan was a little older, she could take her to all the different places of culture and be able to explain and discuss things with her. As usual, she'd refused to let Linus pick her up but agreed to meet him in the Harlequin courtyard. She told him she wanted to enjoy the beauty of the place once again.

But his happiness was short-lived for no young woman appeared. Instead, a man made his way from the alley to the garden area.

"You Linus?" he rasped.

"Y-yes..." replied Linus, his guts churning with the certainty he was not about to receive good news. To make matters worse, the man snorted, obviously thinking to be called Linus was a huge joke.

"Sal ain't coming. She ain't ever comin', buster, and if you try it on wiv her again, you'll regret it! D'you understand me?"

The man now had hold of Linus's shirt and pulled him close. He was shorter than Linus but thick-set and muscley. Linus got a whiff of stale sweat and tobacco, making him want to retch, while the look in the man's eyes turned his blood to ice. But, at the same time, a bolt of anger exploded inside him, fuelling his courage.

"What's the matter with you?" he demanded, pulling his shirt from the man's grasp. "I've done nothing wrong. Why are you threatening me?"

"She's not free to see other men, yeah? She's spoken for. Out of the game. Not available. Get it? So keep the fuck away, right?"

"Oh! Really? She didn't say. I mean, I know she has a child. Anyway, what's it to do with you? Are you her husband or something?" Linus was smoothing down his clothes, trying to shake himself into some semblance of dignity.

"In a manner o' speaking." The man was starting to move towards him again. "You just keep away. Leave her alone, understand? Or there will be serious consequences. You get me, buster?"

And he drew back his fist and lamped Linus in the solar plexus. Devoid of all breath, Linus crumpled and fell to the ground, helpless. He felt another blow and saw several stars as the man's boot connected with his head and then, all went black.

Chapter 10

MAROON

Linus was found by Florence on her way across the courtyard to Benson's place. She later declared she was utterly sick and tired of being the only one to come across all the traumatic situations in the world. She was inclined to exaggerate which was one of the things Benson loved about her. It amused him highly. He wasn't amused, however, at the state of his friend when he joined Florence after her frantic call for help. For once, Florence had her mobile phone with her, both charged and topped up. Before Benson, she'd been very bad at remembering her phone, let alone dealing with it. Now, there was a lot more incentive for her to be contactable.

"Give me a hand here, Benson," she said and together they got Linus to his feet and headed to the bright, green door of number four, Grenville Row.

"He say he kicked in the head by some thug," explained Florence who, once indoors, began expertly examining Linus's head. "There no skin broken but you gonna have some fine ole bruise there, Linus."

"Thug?" said Benson. "What thug?"

"I was supposed to be meeting this girl..." muttered Linus groggily.

"Oh, the one you finally mentioned the other day - with a little daughter, yeah?"

"Yes, only she didn't show up. This ape appeared instead and threatened me to keep away from her. And then, punched me in the stomach and kicked me in the head. Next thing I remember is Flo on the phone."

"Okay, honey, take it easy," said Florence soothingly. "You gonna have to chill for couple o' days to get over this. We get you checked out at hospital."

"No, I'm okay. I need to get in touch with Sally and find out what's going on."

"What's going on?" Finn appeared, his face draining of colour when he saw the state of his friend.

So, of course, Finn had to be filled in on everything and was vehement in his agreement that Linus should do nothing, at least until he'd recovered from the attack.

"Oh and you'd do nothing if you thought Daisy was in danger, would you?" demanded Linus angrily.

"Probably not but then you and Benson would be saying the same things to me," began Finn.

"Look, we're going round in circles here," said Benson. "You need to recover properly, Linus." He held up his hand as Linus opened his mouth to protest. "In the meantime, we can make some plans about how we're going to deal with this situation."

So, they sat down in the living room, Linus on the sofa with his feet up, covered with a blanket and the pillow from his bed behind his head. Florence put a large glass of water next to him, which slightly ruined the feeling of being spoiled and cared for, as the others had cans of lager.

They went through everything Linus knew about Sally, which didn't appear to be a whole lot. He had a mobile number for her but admitted he'd never been allowed to pick her up from her home so had no idea where she lived.

"It has to be somewhere near the hospital because she let me drop her off there when I visited Frances," mused Linus. "Said she could walk home from there."

"But you said she was looking to move," said Benson. "So how do you know she's still there."

"I did take her to see a maisonette in Beresford Street," said Linus, rubbing his eyes wearily. "But it was awful. I can't believe she would've taken that."

"Well, it's something to go on," said Finn. "We could check it out. And you could try phoning her."

"Yes but what if whoever he is, is monitoring her calls and takes it out on her?" cried Linus, becoming agitated.

"You're right but look, stop fretting, Li. We'll just take it one step at a time and make a few discreet enquiries. We'll get to the bottom of this, you'll see." Benson put a large, gentle hand on his friend's shoulder.

"Absolutely," agreed Finn. "I'm not having some bastard attack a friend of mine and get away with it."

"Okay now," said Florence, flapping her hands to quieten everyone down. "Linus need to rest. No, not sleep, we have to keep an eye on him for concussion."

It was hard not to talk about it. They were indignant and angry that anyone should enter the hallowed grounds of the Harlequin triangle with violent intentions, let alone actually carry them out.

* * *

Frances Arbuthnot opened her eyes, just a crack. Yes, she'd been right the first time. It *was* the Reverend Tiplady sitting next to her sister, whispering to her, his hands hanging in front of his chest in that ridiculous way he had. She decided to stay asleep and ignore her visitors but she was suffering a lot of pain around her lower back and, in the end, she had to give in, open her eyes and ask for a nurse to be found. Valerie looked genuinely overjoyed that she was compos mentis enough to make the request and rushed forward to take her sister's hand. Ernest flapped around like a trapped moth for a while but eventually made it out of the room in search of assistance.

"I can't tell you how relieved I am you're awake," whispered Valerie. "I'm so sorry this has happened and that you were left so long on your own. Truly, I am."

"Not your fault," said Frances hoarsely. She couldn't get over the anxiety in Valerie's voice, nor the affection in her eyes. "These things happen."

"Yes, you're right." This was another first. Frances had never been told she was right before. "And you're going to be fine. A hairline fracture and some bruising, they said. Once you're better and back at home, things will be different. I promise."

Valerie was actually smiling and Frances felt herself smile back. She hadn't expected her accident to end like this. In fact, she hadn't expected to still be around. The veil between life and death was a lot thinner than she'd realised and it now felt like there was a substantial tear in it. Then again, Frances told herself, it may be a bit drastic but, if falling down and damaging yourself, changed your relationship with your sour-faced cow of a sister, then so be it. What was the expression they used these days? Ah yes, bring it on!

* * *

Patrick Baxter hadn't given up on Giselle. Back from one of his trips abroad and looking tanned and toned, he looked up her phone number and dialled it with confidence. There was no reply and, to his irritation, she didn't appear to have an answer service - or, at least, hadn't bothered to switch it on. This was an annoyance to Patrick who embraced all things technical and expected others to do the same. To be available and contactable at all times was the least a person could do, in his opinion. Surely, the world now ran on that premise, didn't it? Knowledge, communication, information - Patrick was hooked on the buzz of that sort of high octane life and sadly, couldn't understand anyone who wasn't. In his travels, he'd come across people who embraced yoga, Tai Chi and meditation but those foolish enough to recommend such pursuits to him, received intense mockery for their trouble. No, Patrick wanted wheeling, dealing and success during the day and fine dining and a compliant female companion at night. He insisted on the best restaurants and his women had to be clean, healthy and classy although the last category had been let slip on rare occasions when lust overcame every other consideration. The one thing that had never occurred, was lack of interest from the opposite sex and yet, Patrick had noticed a distinct coolness from Giselle when he'd wined and dined her. This was compacted when she'd neglected to invite him into her flat on their return home.

Grinding his teeth in frustration at being unable to leave a message, Patrick shrugged on a Burberry trench coat and braved the rain to walk across the courtyard to Giselle's flat. He stomped up the stairs to the cherry-red door and pushed on the bell, leaving his finger there a tad longer than acceptable. Nothing. He tried again but still, no reply. Finally, he pushed it several times in succession and was about to walk away, unusually defeated, when he heard the lock click and the door opened.

She looked unbelievably ravishing, her thick, burnished locks all tousled and tumbling around her pretty face. Her long-lashed eyes were half-closed but he could just see the smoky, green hue of the irises glinting through. She wore a short robe the colour of red wine, tied carelessly around her trim waist and giving a flattering view of smooth, tanned legs. She was shorter than he remembered but then, her feet were devoid of the high-heeled shoe she'd favoured on their night out. They were bare and perfectly shaped, each toe being tipped by pearly, pink nails, glistening like little seashells. He caught his breath and stood gazing at her open-mouthed, like some inarticulate idiot.

"What is it? What's happened?" Giselle's eyes were wide open now, as though anticipating bad news.

"What? Oh no, nothing. It's just, I couldn't get hold of you on the phone and I wondered if you were okay so I thought I'd better call round and make sure." It sounded lame even to his ears. He didn't expect to be greeted with anything other than sheer delight so hadn't bothered thinking of an excuse.

"What? Because I didn't answer the phone? Are you mad?"

"No but... well, I- I was concerned!" His voice rose indignantly.

"Patrick, I'm thirty six years old and much of that time, I've lived on my own. Never have I needed anyone to check up on me because I've failed to answer my phone."

"But don't you have an answering service? I could have left a message."

"Are you in trouble?"

"Well, no. I just wanted to ask you-"

"So, you've come round here and woken me up, just because you couldn't wait to say whatever to me, other than at a time that suited you?"

"Well, I-"

"Do you know why I have a phone, Patrick? Do you? No, don't answer that because it's obvious you don't. I have a phone for my convenience. Not yours or anybody else's. MINE! When I don't answer my phone, it is because I'm tired – if I've been working late, for example – or, for that matter, if I don't feel like talking to anyone!" Her eyes blazing, she started to close the cherry-red door but suddenly, it flew open again.

"And I don't use a messaging service because I don't like them. It doesn't suit my philosophy of life! Okay?"

And this time, the door did slam shut and it stood there in front of Patrick, both defiant and triumphant in its redness. He felt like kicking it. He couldn't believe she'd just spoken to him like that. What made it worse was there was a ring of truth in her words. He *had* tried to control the situation and he hadn't respected her privacy. But still, you'd think the girl would be grateful he'd cared enough to check she was okay. Deep down, he knew his motivation for finding her was somewhat different. He brushed the thought aside as he stomped back to his own flat. He wanted her now more than ever. On their date, he'd made a couple of wild guesses at what job she did and, eventually, she'd told him she was a therapist. Well, *she* would come crawling to him for his kind of therapy before long. He would see to it.

From one of the benches, her face streaming from the rain and her tears, Sonia sat and watched his progression round the path, a plan forming insidiously in her confused, young mind.

* * *

Linda Pugh told Baz she would be supporting Valerie in caring for Frances and that he might have to fend for himself a little more than usual. Baz was a simple man with no complications, as his wife was the first to point out, but even he could see that her presence would be missed by their foster-child and, honest as always, he wasted no time in confiding his fears to her.

"I know what you mean, Baz," Linda replied. "But it will do him good to spend time with you and to see you supporting me in my choices." Linda was always quick to pick up jargon from social services and any other authority. She'd learned that using the right phraseology went down well and got you places, you wouldn't otherwise have reached; a bit like having the right combination for a safe. She wasn't a highly educated woman but she was a quick learner and would have achieved an 'A' in common sense, had there ever been such an exam. Baz was looking puzzled.

"Whoa! Sorry, love. Your choices?"

"Yes," said Linda patiently. "I'm *choosing* to help a neighbour in trouble. I don't *have* to help her and, by looking after Freddie more, you're supporting me. And that's a good example for him, eh?"

"Hey, yeah!" Baz had a habit of starting all his conversations with exclamatory phrases. "Of course. I never thought of it that way." He nodded his closely shaved head slowly. "Don't you worry, my love, I'll keep an eye on the boy. We'll be fine."

And Linda knew they would. Baz might not be the sharpest tool in the box but he was solid and capable and, unless *she* was threatened, a calm, level-headed sort. And Freddie seemed to be settling of late. His attempts at shocking the world and its mother were less. He was responding to the rhythm of the routines she'd established. One of her methods, which had always worked well in the past, was to ask his opinion on things. He'd been openly surprised the first time she'd put something to him.

"What do you think about junk food, Freddie? D'you think we should just eat what we want and be damned?"

Freddie had opened and shut his mouth, frowned, bitten his lip, shrugged and finally, come up with an answer.

"Yeah, course. Why not? I mean, why eat stuff you don't much like?"

"Well, because the good stuff is better for you. You're likely to live longer."

He'd shrugged again at that. "Why'd you wanna live longer? Life sucks for most people."

"Life's what you make it, boy," she'd said, angry with herself for reminding him of the life he'd had before. Freddie had never known his father. His mother, now deceased, had been addicted to drugs, alcohol and a succession of violent and abusive lovers, all of whom seemed to want to take their anger out on him. "Lots of people have rubbish lives but there are still choices to be made. You're not going to let your past hold you back, are you? I don't see you as a weak person who'd do that."

He looked at her then. Part of them both knew she was manipulating him, daring him not to succeed but he also knew she cared. A little smile crept over his face.

"Well, I'm still not giving up burgers," he said.

"No, well," Linda countered. "I'd rather you concentrated on giving up the fags first."

And she walked out of the room leaving him open-mouthed, wondering how she'd found out.

* * *

Daisy was beginning to realise that there was more to Trish than just being a silly cow. The girl had been off work for a week now and there were a lot of scary, windowed envelopes on the hall table. She didn't really want to confront her as she had troubles enough of her own to deal with. Finn had so far bottled dealing with Barbara and her pregnancy but she could hardly complain, as she still hadn't hit him with her own confessions. Daisy sincerely wished she'd come out with them as soon as he'd shown interest in her but the longer it went on, the harder it was to tell him. She knew what she had to tell him was going to devastate him and, despite having come to terms with what was happening in her life, she was finding it difficult to share her story with someone to whom it would deeply affect.

Daisy picked up the pile of envelopes with a sigh and went in search of her flatmate. Trish was in a familiar position, wrapped in a fleece blanket on her bed, staring unseeing at daytime telly blaring out from the corner of her room.

Daisy went over and turned it off.

"Trish, we have to talk," she said firmly.

"Don't tell me - you've had enough and you're moving out. That's all I need."

"No, that's not what I was going to say," Daisy replied, holding her temper in check. "Look, I'm seriously worried about you. I think you're depressed."

"Depressed, huh?" shrieked Trish contemptuously, her eyes filling with tears. "You don't say!"

She looked so utterly lost, her newly plumped lip making her look like a little duck, that Daisy's heart went out to her. Sitting down next to her, she pulled her close, saying, "You need to share this with someone, sweetheart, and that someone might as well be me."

And then, Trish broke down; broke down so completely that she sobbed solidly for five minutes. She sobbed until there were no tears left in her to cry and Daisy held her, knowing that soon everything would come out and she would have to find solutions to help her friend.

* * *

The rain was still streaking down relentlessly but Patrick's spirits lifted when he heard a knock on the door. He was convinced Giselle had come to apologise and, no doubt, offer herself to him in compensation for having offended him earlier. He was, therefore, extremely disappointed when he saw Sonia standing there. She was dripping wet, her dark hair hanging in rats' tails around her face. Her eyes looked puffy and bore the remnants of black mascara.

"I need to speak to you," she croaked and pushed past him, into his sitting room.

Patrick stood at the door still, his mouth open to speak, hardly able to believe the girl's audacity. After a few seconds, he shook his head and shut the door, an action he was later to regret.

"Sonia, look, what do you want? I'm busy. I don't really have time... What are you doing?"

"I have to get out of these wet things." Sonia was unbuttoning her blouse. "I'll catch a chill if I-"

"No!" Patrick put both hands out in an effort to stop the girl in her tracks. "You can't do that here. You go home and get yourself sorted out, d'you hear?"

"But it's started raining again and I'll get even wetter." She began to unzip her jeans.

"No! Stop!" Patrick grabbed her arm and tried to turn her round to face the route out of his flat. "You only live a minute across the courtyard. That's not going to make any difference. Please, just go home."

He gave her a little shove but she swivelled around to face him.

"What's the matter, Patrick? Are you afraid a younger girl would be too much for you?"

She was laughing, her left hand going back to the buttons on her top while her right came up to his face and stroked it. "Come on, Patrick, you know you want to. I won't tell anyone. Not that they'd care anyway. It'll just be our little secret. I know that skank, Giselle, has blown you out. You looked so pissed off when you left there earlier. She only does it for money anyway. You can have me for nothing."

She tried to pull his head down to hers, her eyes closing and her mouth opening as she did so. Patrick was never quite sure what triggered his next actions but certainly, for a few seconds, he was in a state of shock, trying to decipher Sonia's words. He felt a rush of humiliation that she'd somehow witnessed the scene with Giselle and that took all his focus. And, for a second, she won and got his face near enough to lock her lips onto his. Triumphant, she stuck her tongue into his mouth and he came back to reality with a shock. He pushed her away from him as hard as he could. She fell back against the wall but far from being dismayed, she recovered herself and looked ready to spring again; a cat, ready to leap on its prey. He felt himself gather up in preparation to defend his position... against a fifteen year old girl? What was he doing? Patrick stopped and drew himself up to his full height. He pulled the back of his hand across his mouth, glaring at her.

"I don't know what the hell you think you're playing at but you better leave. Right now!"

A little shadow of doubt crossed the girl's face but she quickly exchanged it for a seductive smile. "Sorry, darling, d'you like to do all the running? Don't worry, I can be very dismissive."

Her use of the wrong word reminded him of her age but somehow, didn't induce any sympathy.

"I think you mean, submissive," he said, his voice heavy with contempt. "Look, there's nothing you can offer that would tempt me, not now, nor in ten years time when you might, at least, have grown up a bit. I want you out of here or I'll call your parents."

Sonia's face darkened. "No, you won't. I promise you, you will not do that."

"Oh for God's sake, will you just go away, you silly little girl. I've had enough of your games, do you understand me? I AM NOT INTERESTED IN YOU!" Patrick grabbed hold of her arm and propelled her towards the front door, wishing he hadn't closed it. As he reached for the handle, she wrenched herself away and turned to him again, a look of pure hatred on her face.

"You'll regret this, PRICK Baxter. Yes, that's what we call you cos that's what you are, isn't it? A stuck up, arrogant tosser. Sorry to have wasted your time. You obviously prefer the whore over the road. Well, be my guest-"

"Don't call her that, you evil little bitch," Patrick was incandescent by this time, no longer caring that he was talking to a child.

"Oh, didn't you know?" laughed Sonia gleefully. "Well, I tell you what, just ask her. Go on, I dare you!"

Pushing her out of the way, Patrick tried to get to the door to open it. Sonia had other ideas however and, slipping under his arms, threw herself at the door, shutting it with a bang that echoed through the building. He shoved her away again and yanked the door back but, to his frustration, she hurled herself forward again and the crash of it closing with such force was deafening. Patrick lost his temper and, gripping her arm, hauled her back so he could open the door and lean upon it himself to hold it there.

"Go!" he barked, pulling at her arm until she was through. "And don't come back. I *will* be telling your parents, you can be sure of that."

"Oh, no need," she hissed, like the venomous, little snake she was. "I'll be doing that myself."

Patrick shut the door and putting his forehead on it, let out a shuddering sigh. An icy cold hit his stomach as he thought about why she'd said such a thing. He wondered who was at home in the other flats and wished he'd kept his voice down. He knew with chilling certainty he hadn't heard the end of this.

* * *

New wounds had been inflicted and had barely dried, before the dark maroon of old blood resurfaced and began to seep out once again. It all started to feel a bit chaotic.

Chapter 11

BURNT ORANGE

It was becoming one of those autumns which prompts poets to pick up their pens and wax lyrical. Mornings, often crisp and misty, would open into warm softness produced by a fat, orange sun sitting low in the sky, bathing everything in its golden glow as the day wore on. The residents around the Harlequin triangle dutifully gathered up fallen leaves and deposited their rich treasure in the compost bin for the magic to occur. The few apples that remained were left for insects and birds to feast upon at their leisure. There was a sense of preparation, of bedding down to sit out the coming months in anticipation of new results, rewards and beginnings. This was a cocooning time and many were anxiously awaiting the emergence of the next stage.

* * *

Valerie had prepared the house for when Frances returned. She had her sister's bed brought down to the lounge with a commode placed in the corner. She'd looked forward to Frances coming home so she could put into practise her promise of a serious change in behaviour. Nothing would be too much trouble, she vowed; even indulging Frances in her favourite TV programmes or topics of conversation. She, Valerie Figgis, would sit, like 'patience on a monument', smiling and content just as long as her dear sister was happy. The only trouble was, she soon realised it wasn't all that easy to change the habits of a lifetime. She was already feeling little prickles of irritation when Frances changed subject mid-conversation and neglected to inform her what the new topic concerned. But the point was, Valerie was going to try her hardest to be kind. And surely, the longer she tried, the easier it would become.

* * *

Anya Petrovka did not appreciate what a loving group of friends she had around her but it wasn't her fault. Her life was losing meaning and felt as though it was going in and out of focus from moment to moment. The visits, mainly from Marsha, Reg, Hilary and Harry, actually provided a bit of an anchor for her and on their visits, her mind appeared to recognise it was required to go back in time and find the stories that existed there. She no longer remembered wanting to keep her past to herself for she'd lost some of the bad memories along with the good. She was also losing the sense of shame her father's family had instilled in her, all because she was his illegitimate child and her mother, theatrical rather than academic. She started to talk about her affair with Ptolemy, the professor of history she'd met when she lived in Oxford. The story came out sporadically and took many hours of painful prompting from her friends but gradually, they began to piece it all together.

* * *

The man who'd come into the charity shop and given Hilary 'fizzes round the head' did not appear for some time. She found herself looking out for him every day and feeling quite deflated when he didn't show. She'd promised herself, the next time she saw him, she was going to approach him and let him know she was getting psychic vibes about him. Hilary had experienced such feelings before when she had 'a message from spirit' for someone. She pictured the meeting with a mixture of excitement and anxiety and didn't want to wait any longer for it to take place.

* * *

Reg was happier than he'd ever been. Hilary's kindness in finding new outfits for him and her acceptance of how he chose to live had brought a new joy to his life. Their friendship grew and it was rare for a week to go by without them spending an evening together, sharing a bottle of wine and the occasional meal, discussing all and sundry and laughing a lot over nothing in particular.

* * *

Daisy had found the problems of her flatmate a welcome distraction from her own worries about her relationship with Finn. It became horribly apparent that Trish had an addiction to spending and whenever even slightly unhappy or stressed, she would look for something new and shiny to take her mind off her problems.

"Do you have any idea why you do it?" she asked Trish gently.

"No, not really. I just know it makes me feel better – for a while anyway. Like everything is alright with the world. I guess I need to see a shrink, don't I?"

"Well, I started a degree in psychology, specializing in addiction, so I might be able to help a little."

"Started? Why didn't you finish then?" Trish's voice held an accusatory tone, almost as though she was jumping on the chance to find a flaw in Daisy's otherwise perfect character.

"Lots of reasons," said Daisy, with a shrug. "But this isn't about me. Let's concentrate on you, shall we?"

That sounded good to Trish. It wasn't something that had been said to her before and made her feel suddenly optimistic. She acquiesced and mopped her face in anticipation of being indulged in a heavy whingefest. It didn't go quite like that.

Two hours later, Daisy had drawn from Trish many of the traumas and disappointments of her childhood. She had cried a good deal more and remembered stuff she thought was dead and buried. Not only had she been the child of a single parent family, they'd been extremely poor. Despite that, her mother had insisted on Trish having a good education and spent most of her life working to make that possible. The trouble was, Trish wasn't academic and knew she'd disappointed her self-sacrificing parent. All the hard work, the scrimping and saving and making do had culminated in a daughter who, like many girls, was only interested in fashion, hair and make-up.

"She wanted me to go to university and be a lawyer or a doctor or something that would ensure I always had plenty of money coming in," sobbed Trish. "But I just couldn't do it. I wasn't clever enough so I enrolled in a hairdressing course but that made her ill so I left. Now, I just work in a horrible office. It's a solicitor's because at least that pleased her but it's just a clerk's job and I hate it and I don't earn enough to..."

"To go out and buy all the pretty stuff that makes you feel better about your life and helps you feel you have the sort of salary your mum wanted for you?"

Trish nodded and scrubbed at her face with an already sodden tissue.

"Hmm, well I think we've established what the problem is," said Daisy. "Wait here."

She disappeared off to her bedroom, leaving Trish limp and exhausted and wondering what her flatmate was going to do next. Daisy soon re-appeared, holding a bottle of wine.

"I was taking this over to Finn's this evening," she said, setting it onto the table and going in search of some glasses. "But I think we need it more here."

Trish was too tired to argue although her head was already aching and she didn't think alcohol would help. She watched wearily as Daisy poured the wine, the friendly, glugging sound, familiar as it left the bottle.

"You're a good friend, Daisy," she sighed. "But I really don't know what you can do to help."

"You might not, Trish, but trust me, I do. Drink some wine and try to relax. I promise that you can, and will, get over your problems. Just breathe and be glad you can breathe. I'm going to get some nibbles for us."

Trish was still sceptical but before long before she began to realise her good fortune in meeting Daisy.

"If you knew you didn't have too long to live and you could choose exactly what you wanted to do for your last years on this planet – I mean, work-wise, leisure, relationships – what would you choose?" asked Daisy suddenly. "Don't think, just say the first things that come into your head. Go!"

Trish opened and shut her mouth and then, prompted by a sharp nudge from Daisy's elbow, launched into a list of things, some of which she had no idea would be there.

"I'd like to do something creative - hairdressing, beautician, that sort of thing. Making people look and feel better about themselves. And of course, I'd want to be debt free. Actually, I don't really need a lot. I love living here. I like a holiday each year but perhaps, I'd try something different, away from the tourist spots. Somewhere peaceful with beautiful scenery and lovely food and maybe experience some new things like - I dunno – listening to opera in Italy, seeing some wonderful art in Paris, the tulip fields in Holland, that sort of thing. I'm sick of all the sex, sun and sangria stuff."

"Stick to what you do want, not what you don't," instructed Daisy firmly.

"Well, of course, I'd like a relationship with someone and share all that stuff. And maybe a family. But I'd like to find a man who would accept and love me for who I am. He doesn't have to be minted or good-looking although that would be great too. But accepting of me, that's the important bit." Trish had a faraway look in her eyes as she painted the picture, happily discarding all the things about herself she knew weren't that great.

"Yes," said Daisy. "I can see that's terribly important to you. So now, we're going to work out how you can get the things you most desire or, at least, go towards them."

By the time they dragged themselves off to bed, Trish felt some real optimism for the first time in her life. Daisy had a way of convincing you that anything was possible and Trish was ready to take some advice. She might be stuck with a fat lip – Daisy hadn't offered a way round that – but she now knew she wasn't stuck in her job nor to her addiction of spending money she didn't have.

* * *

Giselle continued to sit for Arlo, this time for a poster for a fantasy film that required a central female character. They both knew he didn't really need her for that but they'd grown fond of each other's company, enjoying their time together, laughing at the ridiculous and putting the world to rights. She was also one of the few people who visited Marsha Malloy on a regular basis, a practise that puzzled a lot of the locals although no one had yet had the courage to question her on it. Of course, it was no one's business but that doesn't often stop those of a curious nature. Conversely, Giselle avoided Patrick Baxter until, that is, she heard the terrible news.

* * *

Sonia had gone straight home after her attempt at seducing Patrick had gone so monumentally wrong. She was seething with anger and indignation. She'd misjudged him. She'd been quite sure he was one of those men she'd overheard her mother describe "would do anything as long as it had a pulse". Sonia had been surprised to hear such words coming from her mother's mouth regarding Patrick's sex life but worked out, as she'd also been referring to his apparent attraction for Giselle, she was actually jealous. Her mother seemed to begrudge anyone a little happiness and now Tom had left, perhaps she'd been hoping for solace from other areas. Catriona had always been rather enamoured of Patrick, disappointed if he didn't show up at Harlequin parties and full of smiles and banter when he did. Sonia couldn't imagine Patrick preferring her mother to Giselle. There was simply no comparison. She thought of Catriona's lean, curveless body next to Giselle's voluptuous flesh, Giselle's ready smile as opposed to her mother's constant complaining and knew Catriona didn't stand a chance. And now, it seemed, neither did she. So, she too hated Giselle and her composure and alluring beauty. She was one of those smug bitches who had life sown up and Sonia, having inherited her mother's bitterness, wanted to mess that up and make sure that Patrick and Giselle would never be together. Having decided she would "fuck them right over", Sonia went home and stewed on it. The next day, she told her mother that Patrick had lured her into his flat and tried to have his way with her.

* * *

Finn had begun to hint to Barbara that he was not intending to create a family unit with her and their baby. However, whenever he tried explain his involvement with Daisy, Barbara would resort to histrionics and floor him. She would wail about how ill she felt and how she was so prepared to put up with that for his and the baby's sake. She said, over and over again, that she knew he wasn't in love with her but his decency as a human being would get them through all that and, once the baby had arrived, things would look different. She hinted strongly that, if he wasn't there for her, she wouldn't be able to bear having him around at all. She hadn't, as yet, told her parents, she said; something Finn found rather strange in view of her assumption they would be together. However, she was quick to point out, if things didn't work out, she would persuade them they needed to find a new barman. This stumped Finn most of all as he desperately needed his wages - even just pay to his rent - and there was little other work around. But fate was waiting in the wings and Finn was about to receive a positive outcome from his audition.

* * *

"She's fine. Yes, I'm fine too. Stop worrying. It'll die down soon enough. As long as you're sure there'll be no repercussions..."

Hilary looked up in surprise at the Marshmallow's anxious tone. Marsha felt her scrutiny and smiled apologetically before turning back to her mobile phone.

"Anyway, can't talk now. I'll ring you later," she said, and picking up a book from the shelf, moved to the counter to pay.

"Trouble?" asked Hilary, never backward in coming forward.

"Oh no, it's nothing." Marsha shook her head. "How much do I owe you?"

Hilary, unsatisfied, glanced at the book and was highly puzzled. Marsha didn't seem the type to be reading about vampires.

"This for you?" she queried.

"What?" Marsha grabbed the book. "Oh! I must have picked up the wrong one. Not paying attention because of that stupid phone call. Damned mobiles. I used to manage perfectly well without one but, you feel you have to keep up with the times..."

She stopped, knowing she was over-explaining. For once, she cursed Hilary's perceptiveness and her ability to worm information out of people. She took the book back to the shelf and began looking again, although her mind wasn't really on what she was doing.

"Think I've gotta ghost," said Hilary unexpectedly.

"You what, dear?"

"A ghost. I keep hearing things go bump in the night but nothing ever seems to go missing, so it's not a burgular."

Marsha would normally have found Hilary's mispronunciation amusing but now, her mood dictated otherwise.

"You've not investigated then? But no, that would be foolish. You should call the police next time."

"Well, no dear. You can't arrest a ghost. It feels a friendly energy anyway so I'm not too bothered. I just wish it would come upstairs and say hello. But there, I've never been blessed with actual infestations from the other side."

She sighed mournfully and Marsha, unable to think of a suitable response, decided it was time to leave.

"I can't find the book I saw so I'll leave it for now," she said briskly. "I'm calling on Anya later so I'd better crack on. Take care of yourself, Hilary."

And she hurried out of the shop, leaving Hilary with the usual impression of there being a lot more to Marsha than met the eye.

* * *

Linus took a chance and contacted Sally but to his dismay, was told in no uncertain terms that he must leave her alone.

"But you gave me this number and said to call you," he countered. "What did I do wrong? And why did you send that big ape round?"

"Oh no! I didn't, I promise. But Linus, just leave it. You did nothing but I can't - I can't see you. I'm so sorry."

The phone went dead but Linus didn't move for a long time while he tried to digest what she'd said. Finally, he put the phone down, grabbed a jacket and went to his car. He drove to the maisonette he'd taken Sally and Megan to see and sat outside, pondering on his next move. It occurred to him, if she was living there, he may well be putting her in danger. Part of him hoped she hadn't moved to such an awful dump. On the other hand, knowing where she was, meant he could get to her when the time came. And come it would, of that he was sure. He hadn't known her long but there had been a connection and, more than that, he had a strong feeling they'd been meant to meet that day. Linus wasn't a particularly brave man and certainly wasn't built for heroics but there was a stubbornness in him that dictated he wasn't going to give up easily.

His patience was finally rewarded and Sally came out of the maisonette holding a bag of rubbish. There was a heaviness to her step and her head was down as she descended the concrete staircase, deposited the bag in the bin and climbed back up. Linus stopped himself from leaping out of the car and calling to her. He had to be careful and think things through but, at least now, he knew where she was.

* * *

Freddie nipped over the fence into number two and leant over the hedge to speak to Sonia.

"D'you wanna do it with me then?" he asked pleasantly.

Sonia jumped and glared at him.

"What? Fuck off! What are you doing in Frances's garden? Just go away!"

"Oh, come on. You must want it. You wouldn't have gone chasing after old Baxter, if you didn't."

"I *didn't*! He grabbed me."

"As if. Nobody in their right mind is gonna believe that shit."

Sonia stared at him, opening and shutting her mouth, hating the look of amusement on his face. Finally, she said, "I don't give a fuck what you think. I know the truth."

"Yeah and so do the rest of us," smirked Freddie. "Look, don't be embarrassed. I understand those urges and I'm prepared to help you out. In fact, there's a few of us who would do the honours. We've talked about it at school. You know, to help – despite the moustache – we're there for you."

Sonia was knocked for six. All the breath left her body in one enormous gasp. The bag of scraps her mother had given her to put on the bird table, dropped from her hand and she grabbed at her solar plexus as she felt it twist. Never in a million years had she envisaged such consequences from her actions. Freddie was grinning inanely at her. He turned and climbed back over the fence to his own garden, calling over his shoulder as he went.

"I'll leave it with you. Just let me know what you decide."

* * *

Giselle was horrified when she heard what had happened and was one of the first to visit Patrick. He looked grey and deflated when he opened the door, as though the life had been sucked out of him. He regarded her suspiciously which she ignored and put her arms around him.

"I know she's lying, Patrick. I would know if you were that sort of man."

She felt him relax inside her hug and, letting him go, she pushed him gently through to his lounge.

"Wow, this is gorgeous," she breathed, as she took in the cool, contemporary decor. "You have really good taste, Patrick. I want to get a look at your kitchen. May I make us a cuppa?"

He nodded, relieved to be taken over and not having to think. He sat down and listened as she enthused over the kitchen whilst busying herself making tea.

"Even your mugs are cool," Giselle laughed, as she carried through a stainless steel tray and placed it on a side table.

"I've brought the sugar in as I couldn't remember how you took it. Patrick, are you alright?"

"Yes. No... I can't believe you're here. I thought everyone would ostracize me, hate me."

"No, they won't. Anyone with half a brain would know you wouldn't go after a kid, especially a kid like Sonia. You're just not the type. Yes, you like women and you're probably quite fickle but I seriously doubt you have the need, or inclination, to risk your reputation on a silly, little bitch like Sonia."

A slight smile lifted the corners of Patrick's mouth and he shook his head.

"No, of course I wouldn't but there's no proof. I mean it looks like... oh, God." Patrick put his head in his hands, the picture of despair. Giselle's heart melted with pity.

"So what did happen?" she asked gently. "Obviously something. She's not so stupid to make all that up completely out of the blue."

"She came on to me!" shouted Patrick, all the frustration of the situation coming out in one burst. "I told the police, she came here soaking wet and started to undress. They asked me why she didn't go straight home, WHICH is the whole, bloody point! She came with the specific intention of getting me into bed. Her body language, the things she said... I knew what she was trying to do. After a struggle, I managed to get her out. I had to take hold of her arm to get the door open. There may have been bruising. She fought me. People must have heard the doors slamming. God, Giselle, it looks so bad."

"Ah, the woman scorned, the teenager rejected," said Giselle, nodding knowingly. "Classic. She was never going to let you get away with that."

"To have police come, the humiliation... and, of course, it'll go to court. I can't even talk to her and beg her to tell the truth." He leant forward, his eyes wild with desperation. "This is the most awful thing, I can't tell you. I feel completely disempowered. Nobody will believe me. It'll go in her favour, of course it will. Men who are accused of this are reviled, even by other criminals. My life is ruined. In just few sentences, she's ruined me!"

Patrick's head dropped into his hands again and his shoulders began to shake. Giselle was on her feet and over to him, taking him in her arms.

"No, Patrick, you mustn't give in so easily. Hold your head up. Show people you're not afraid of these lies. I know it won't be easy but you can do it. You'll be surprised how many people will be on your side. Really, you will. You can come through this."

Eventually, she calmed him. He was surprised how he felt. His eagerness for her sexually had abated – perhaps not surprising in the circumstances – but still, with that proximity and her show of affection, he might easily have jumped to certain conclusions. Instead, he was soothed and reassured. He was happy just to be held and to listen to her voice. He knew she would champion him and that, for now, was all he needed.

* * *

Arlo listened carefully to what Giselle had to say on the subject. He didn't know Patrick that well but he didn't strike him as being the kind of bloke who would go after a kid. He was too smooth, too sophisticated a character; not really Arlo's cup of tea but certainly not someone he would label a child molester. Still, you never knew. He was aware that, like most people, he probably had a picture in his mind of how a paedophile looked and, maybe, that was instrumental in helping real criminals get away with stuff. Didn't someone once say, the greatest trick the devil ever played was to convince man he didn't exist? It was food for thought. These days, the most unlikely people were being whisked away to face similar allegations. However, after Giselle had her say, he was mostly convinced the man was innocent.

Finn, Benson and Linus were hugely shocked, although their own little dramas tended to take priority. Plus, they all knew Sonia and were immediately sceptical of the allegations. They certainly had no intentions of withdrawing their friendship from Patrick, should they bump into him. Sonia, however, would be given a very wide berth.

Hilary, who only ever listened to her own 'tuitions', was more than happy to voice her opinion. To her, Patrick was a charming gentleman and any suggestions of a darker side were dismissed with a wave of her hand and a contemptuous, 'pwuaff!'.

Reg was sympathetic. He, alone, knew what it was like to fear people getting the wrong impression. Patrick had always been courteous and friendly towards him whereas the Penworthy girl would stare at him, looking him up and down and then, smirk rudely. Two such differing behaviours definitely coloured Reg's views – although, he did remember hearing doors banging on the night in question. This, he told himself, could just as easily have been one of Trevor and Bryce's domestics which occurred on a regular basis.

Harry's opinion seemed to fluctuate. One minute, he would condemn the entirety of the population for their lack of decency and morals and the next, he would bang on about the fuss people made about nothing. No one was quite sure where he stood, so most just let him ramble until his spleen was vented. Harry was another resident of the flats who could easily have heard the commotion but, as he was in the habit of having his TV turned up due to a hearing problem he refused to acknowledge, it was unsurprising he had nothing to report.

In fact, the majority of people were rather doubtful that Patrick had tried to molest the vile and obnoxious, attention-seeking teenager that was Sonia Penworthy. Even Valerie Figgis snorted derisively when she heard but Frances cautioned against making premature judgements, thus testing her sister's newly-found patience. With some effort, Valerie managed a brief nod of her head, saying it was probably good advice. She later repeated Frances' opinion - as her own - to Mrs Kshatryia at the shop and was hugely gratified when Prithyma thanked her, acknowledging that she, herself, had been too quick to judge.

Florence, who'd been at work on the fateful evening, was strangely condemning of Patrick, who lived in the flat above her. She would, she said, have been down there like a shot, had she been home to hear any disturbance. It caused the first big argument between her and Benson. As compassionate and caring as she was, Florence was quick to spot what she thought of as sin. And she believed that the world was full of sinners. Benson, on the other hand, was the optimistic type and tended to see the good in people. Working with deprived young people in his spare time, he knew how easy it was to get a jaded view of the world and would always try to redress the balance in those situations. Benson believed if you looked for the good in people, you would find it. And the same, if you looked for the bad.

"Yes but you gotta be so careful," argued Florence. "People very tricky, you know. They fool you and rip you off and worse."

"Yes, of course. I know," Benson replied. "But you get back what you put out and if someone is desperate enough to want to behave in that way, I'm not going to change them by being the same. You have to teach by example, Flo. That's the only way it works."

Florence huffed and puffed and gave him daggers but he just grinned, so she couldn't stay mad at him for long. Sometimes, his views were in direct opposition to what her religion taught and this concerned her a great deal. Her parents hadn't been impressed that the new boyfriend was not a church-goer and challenged her on her choice of partner. But so far, Flo was too much in love to take much notice of their opinions.

It was Linda Pugh's views that caused the greatest friction.

"I knew that girl would do something like this one day," she said, as she stood by the counter in the Kshatryia's general store. "She's been like a coiled spring for months and no one's been paying any attention to it. Girls like that are extremely dangerous."

"Girls like what?" asked Daisy, pausing in her examination of the spices section.

"Well, you know, they get to puberty and sometimes their sexuality kicks in big time. It's very confusing for them because they have these huge grown-up urges and yet, their minds haven't matured enough to meet that level of desire. I'm telling you, they need an awful lot of love and attention and understanding."

"Well, I don't remember being like that," said Daisy.

"No, I don't suppose it's across the board but we fostered a girl very similar and we really had to work hard on keeping her active, having lots of fun and giving her all our attention."

"Well, I expect it helps if you're a decent sort of kid to begin with," said Trish, coming out from another section. She was wearing sunglasses and a peaked cap to avoid being readily recognised and having remarks made about her 'trout pout' but had quite forgotten when she became interested in the conversation.

"I don't like speaking ill of anyone," said Prithyma. "But she's not a pleasant girl. Very rude whenever she comes in here and Prem caught her shoving something into her jacket once. I managed to persuade him to give her another chance and not report her but she's never shown any gratitude for that."

"I'm not surprised," said Linda, grabbing a chocolate bar and adding it to her basket. "She's only focused on herself at the moment. She won't see anyone else's point of view at all. And, of course, Tom's left so she's going to feel abandoned by the male of the species."

"Tom's left?" echoed Daisy.

"So I believe. It's been on the cards for ages. Obvious!" Linda added the last after seeing the expressions on their faces. It patently was not obvious.

"I had a feeling it wasn't all a bed of roses," said Trish.

"I didn't think they would separate," Prithyma added. "They have children to consider."

"Who separated?" Florence had come into the shop and joined in the gossip.

"Tom and Catriona," said Daisy. "I must admit I saw problems that needed addressing but I hadn't envisaged a split." She chewed her lip remembering what she had said to Tom about lancing the boil at the barbecue. Perhaps her metaphor had been too strong. "Maybe they just needed a break."

"It's Patrick who needs a break, if you ask me," said Linda. "He's the one who's copped the fallout from that situation."

They all nodded thoughtfully, considering whether there was any truth in what she said.

"Have you had a fall and bashed your mouth, Trish?" Florence asked, genuinely concerned.

Everyone stared in confusion at Trish's back as she made a hasty retreat from the shop, leaving her shopping trolley abandoned by the door.

* * *

Tom stared at his daughter as she sat moodily in the armchair, her legs curled underneath her and her thumbs flicking expertly around the keypad of her mobile phone. She didn't look like someone who'd recently been molested by a much older neighbour.

"Do you think you could give me your undivided attention for a while and put down that phone?"

She ignored him. He didn't even know if she'd heard him. Tom walked over to her and took the phone from her hand. Her head shot up and she looked at him with a shocked expression.

"What d'you do that for? Gimme my phone."

"No."

There was something different about him; no flicker of panic in his eyes that she was so used to seeing when she confronted him. It worried her.

"I'm here to talk to you about what happened," he continued. "And I'm not going anywhere until we have that conversation."

Sonia made her face screw up as though she was trying not to burst into tears. Tom's expression remained impassive. He sat down in the chair opposite her, keeping his eyes on her all the time. Sonia's gaze slid away to the side.

"So what were you doing in his place?" Tom kept his tone flat.

"He dragged me there. I already told the police."

"You didn't scream or struggle?"

"Well, erm... he said he wanted to speak to me but he took my arm and sort of pulled me."

"You didn't think to ask him why he couldn't speak to you there and then - why you had to go up to his flat?"

"Well, it was raining really hard."

"Why were you out in the rain in the first place?"

Sonia managed to squeeze out a few tears. "I was depressed. I wanted to die!"

Tom bit the inside of his cheeks so he wouldn't lose his rag. It was just the sort of emotional clap-trap his wife would dish out when her back was against the wall. He opened his mouth to ask another question but Sonia got in first.

"Why are you allowed to go on at me?" she said shrilly. "The police weren't allowed to. They were told it was too stressful for me. Emotionally damaging the social worker said and yet here you are, acting like you don't believe me."

The door burst open and Catriona came in with mugs of tea. She glared at Tom and, after placing the mugs on the table, put herself between her daughter and estranged husband.

"What on earth do you think you're playing at?" she said angrily. "Don't you think she's been through enough?"

"That remains to be seen," replied Tom firmly.

"Mu-um!" gasped Sonia, her hand held up to her mother in an appeal for support.

"Tom, I really think-"

"NO! You *rarely* think!" corrected Tom. "You're not looking at this dispassionately. This is serious. Either way, it's serious."

"You don't believe me. You don't believe me. You don't believe me!" Sonia carried on shrieking the words, pushing her mother away when she tried to hold and comfort her. Tom watched, momentarily stumped. Then, he dropped to his hunkers in front of her.

"Sh, sh, sh," he said softly. "Don't say that, Sonia. I'm here to help. But you have to tell me what happened. I need to know so I can defend you and we can get justice and get Baxter out of here. You have to help me to help you, however painful it may be."

His eyes never left her face and he watched a hundred emotions flicker across it. He noticed her breathing finally slow down and her hands unclench. His heart lurched. What a mess they'd made of their daughter. He couldn't blame it all on his wife. He'd stepped too far back and let her get on with it. He made a silent promise that when this was all over, he would find a way to make it up to both of them.

"So," he said and took her hand. "He found you in the gardens. Where had he come from? Home or had he been out?"

"No, he was coming from *her* flat," replied Sonia, her face darkening.

"Who?"

"The prostitute. Giselle. They must have had a row by the look of him. Perhaps, she over-charged him."

Tom refused to rise to that.

"So, did he come over to you or did you make the first move?"

Sonia swallowed. She'd managed to make such a fuss at the police station that they'd agreed to postpone the interview until she was less hysterical. She'd assured them she hadn't actually been raped but refused to go any further with her explanation. She hadn't thought to get her story detailed but then, she hadn't expected her father to act the way he was. However, it made sense to have him on side.

"Well, I er... I called out to him. Asked if he was okay. He said he wasn't and that he needed to talk to someone. I said he could talk to me so he grabbed my arm and pulled me up and I asked where we were going and he said we couldn't talk in the rain. Well, that made sense so I went with him."

"But why?" began Tom.

"I know what you're thinking but he's a neighbour. You and mum know him and you're friendly with him."

For a second, Tom started to believe her but in the back of his mind was a huge question. Why would an intelligent, successful man like Patrick suddenly make such a mistake in taking Sonia back to his flat for everyone to see. And why, when he was clearly not short of lady friends, would he choose to try and force himself on Sonia who was, at the very least, objectionable in most people's eyes.

"Did he leap on you as soon as he got you into the flat or did he ask if you were willing to... to sleep with him?"

Sonia licked her lips, her eyes darting back and forth as she tried to come to a decision as to what to say.

"No. He er... he tried to kiss me and I tried to get away. I got the door open and he slammed it shut and then I er... I knee-ed him – in the privates - and then I... I pushed him and got to the door again and I got out and just ran and ran!"

"So you came straight back home?"

"Umm..."

"And told your mother?"

"Yes. No. I can't remember exactly."

"She was upset, Tom. What do you expect?"

"Nothing. I don't expect anything. I'm just trying to help. Do you remember hearing her come in that evening?"

Catriona frowned, puzzled. Tom's tone was even and yet, he was most definitely interrogating them. She told herself, it was only natural he would want to find out what had happened.

"Actually, I didn't hear her come in," she admitted. "But then, as I hadn't realised she'd gone out, I wasn't really listening for her."

"Oh! I see. So, when did she tell you what had happened?"

"The next morning. She wouldn't get up for school. Said she wasn't feeling well. She'd obviously been crying so I sat with her and got out of her - what was wrong."

"And then, you called the police?"

"Well yes, of course but, by this time, she was hysterical and it was difficult to get much sense out of her. They'll interview her again when she's calmed down. You feel a bit calmer now, don't you darling?"

"I don't want to talk about it, ever. It was too horrible. I just want to forget it ever happened." Sonia's face crumpled and she began to wail again, drawing her knees up to her chest and burying her face in them. "And I want him - that man - to go away from here and never come back."

Tom straightened himself up and exchanged glances with Catriona. Her face was full of anxiety and she clearly didn't have a clue what to do. He made a decision.

"Right," he said. "I'm going over there."

Sonia's head shot up and he noticed her face was dry.

"No!" she cried. "You can't! You mustn't."

"Tom, really!" joined in Catriona. "That's madness. What could you do?"

Tom hadn't expected quite such a reaction. He carried on, following his instincts.

"I'm going to have it out with him. I'm not letting some sleaze get away with molesting my daughter. I'm going to punch the bastard's bloody lights out!"

"Don't be ridiculous," gasped his wife, grabbing his arm. "He's bigger than you and, by the looks of him, much fitter. And anyway, you could be done for assault. You have to leave these things to the police."

"Don't let him. Don't let him go!" wailed Sonia, real tears now springing into her eyes. "I don't want you to get hurt, Dad. I just wanna forget it!"

"Sorry," said Tom, dragging his arm away from Catriona's desperate grip. "I have to do this."

And he stormed out of the house, leaving the two of them sobbing in earnest.

* * *

The garden area had a deep orange glow about it; a golden palace, bedecked with fluttering leaves ranging from deep russet to yellow ochre, echoing the flames that would soon be licking around a pile of wood stacked on a concrete area to one side of the garden. All was set for Bonfire Night, with the barbecue making a second appearance that year. Arlo and Benson had set up some fireworks, ready for a nice, little display. They didn't go mad; it was more about the socialising than anything else but everyone enjoyed ten minutes of 'oohs' and 'aahs' before getting down to the more serious task of eating, drinking and chatting to their friends.

Catriona stared out of the kitchen window which overlooked their small back garden and the courtyard beyond. She'd always rather enjoyed this particular get-together; the air filled with a mixture of smoke from the bonfire and the acrid odour from the fireworks as they soared spectacularly into the air before exploding into a cacophony of crackles and colour. She loved the roast chestnuts and the dilemma of burning your fingers or delaying the gratification of their steamy, sweet, nutty taste in your mouth. Booze was always available of course but hot chocolate also on offer, even more delicious with a shot of rum and a squirt of cream on top. This was Benson's suggestion and had been enthusiastically adopted as part of bonfire night celebrations since its first appearance. Marsha always made bonfire toffee, a wonderful, burnt-treacle tasting sweet that somehow complimented the smokiness of the atmosphere and Hilary contributed slabs of parkin, an oaty, gingery cake from a recipe donated by an aunt in Yorkshire. Yes, it was all rather wonderful and yet, Catriona just didn't see how she could go out there after all that had happened. Another interview with the police had been unsatisfactory as Sonia's story seemed inconsistent but, when questioned, she became hysterical, claiming the trauma of it all was too much to go over. If only Tom had reported back on what had taken place when he went to confront Patrick. Part of her wondered if he'd chickened out. She could think of no other reason why he wasn't answering her calls.

"Can we go now, Mum?" Nigel was tugging at her sleeve. "They're all out there."

"I er... I'm not feeling too well," Catriona replied lamely.

"Don't be such a wimp!" Sonia appeared at her other side. "We've nothing to be ashamed of. I'm not going to let that vile man stop me living my life. And, if he has any sense, he won't be there."

"Who won't be there?" asked Nigel. He'd never quite got his head round what was supposed to have happened. But then, he never understood much about what went on in his sister's life so, most of the time, he tuned himself out when she was ranting on.

"Prick Baxter," snarled Sonia. "Molester of young girls and, for all we know, young boys too!"

The last was said right in Nigel's face so he drew back quickly, wiping the spittle from his skin. His eyes widened in alarm and Catriona rushed to his side to put an arm round him.

"Don't, Sonia," she yelled. "There's no need for that sort of behaviour!"

She stopped, seeing Sonia's expression darken and knew she had to divert the oncoming storm before it broke. "Right, let's go!" she said firmly. "Get your coats and wrap up warm. It's chilly out there."

Moments later, they stepped out into the night and tried, unsuccessfully, to melt into the groups unseen. There was no doubt looks were coming their way; puzzled, curious and suspicious. Catriona plastered a smile onto her face and chivvied her children over to the tables to pick up a bag of chestnuts and some hot drinks. She scoured the area for Patrick but there was no sign of him. Freddie was hovering nearby and seemed to be mouthing something at Sonia. Out of the corner of her eye, Catriona saw her daughter stick two, furious fingers up and wave them in his direction. Freddie grinned, nodded and made a lewd motion with his pelvis. Catriona's heart sank. Repercussions from Sonia's revelations were already beginning. Catriona was on the verge of confronting the boy but, before she came to a final decision, the firework display started and everyone gathered round to gaze in wonder and delight as though it was the first time they'd ever seen such a thing. It didn't escape Catriona's attention that there was a small space between them and the rest of the group and she raged internally at the unfairness of such behaviour.

Finally, the last display was set off and everyone began clapping and cheering. As the smoke cleared, two figures appeared, coming towards the garden area. Catriona gasped as she realised the one slightly behind was Tom. He was trying to grab the coat of the man in front and that man was Patrick.

"Dad!" cried Nigel, alerting anyone who might have missed it that something was going on.

Catriona grabbed the hood of his anorak to stop him from running forward and heard Sonia's gasp of fear. As the fizzle of fireworks died away and the smoke dissipated, it became easier to view the scene before them. All conversation died as everyone turned their attention to the two men.

"Stop and face me, you bastard!" This was Tom who now had hold of Patrick's coat and was hanging on to it for dear life, trying to stop the other man's progress.

"Get off me!" yelled Patrick. "I told you the truth. I never touched her!"

Tom finally managed to haul Patrick around to face him and grabbed hold of his collars. "Then why," he shouted, "has she got bruises on her arms?"

"Because I was trying to get her *out* of my flat," said Patrick furiously and, in turn, took hold of Tom's lapels. "She barged her way in. I'm sorry, Tom, but you have this all wrong and if you don't let go, I'm going to have to punch your-"

He got no further as Tom landed a blow to the side of his head. Patrick reeled slightly and then, retained his balance enough to come back at his attacker. Tom received the blow to his chin and found himself flying through the air to land with a thump on his back. Patrick was on top of him immediately and the crowd went into panic. Catriona screamed hysterically while nearby, Freddie started to laugh. It was Giselle's voice that came loud and clear over the growing shouts from everyone around.

"Oh my God, he'll kill him. He's a black belt. Tom doesn't stand a chance."

There were more screams and shouts for the men to stop. Arlo, Benson and Finn were already moving forward to wade in and break up the fight, when a figure from the crowd with flying dark hair and streaming eyes rushed into the fray. Simultaneously, Patrick raised his fist for his next punch when Sonia threw herself at him and grabbed his wrist.

"Stop," she screamed. "I'll tell the truth. Don't hurt my dad. Please, please, don't hurt my dad."

It was like someone had pressed the pause button. All fell silent and nothing moved. Even the crackling bonfire seemed to die down for a few seconds. Slowly, Patrick lowered his arm, wrenching his wrist from Sonia's grasp. He got to his feet and held out his hand to Tom, who allowed himself to be hauled up. Tom then took his daughter's shoulders, forcing her to look into his eyes.

"Just one word, Sonia," he said firmly but gently. "Did Patrick molest you or come on to you in any way? Yes or no?"

Tears sprang into Sonia's eyes as she shook her head but it wasn't enough for Tom.

"Yes or no?" he demanded.

"NO!"

The word rang out over the Harlequin triangle and echoed around the colourful buildings as though reiterating the truth. Patrick stared down at his hands for a second, gave a shuddering breath and walked back to his flat. Tom put his arm around his daughter and led her home, closely followed by his estranged wife and their bewildered son. Soon afterwards, the celebrations ended and everyone cleared off. No one felt in the mood to party any more.

Nothing remained except the deep orange embers of the bonfire, occasionally throwing up the odd flame as if trying to keep the drama alight. But, eventually, even those stopped and Arlo kicked over the burnt out wood. He stood silently contemplating the evening's events. Everything passes, he thought, but some things leave a much deeper mark than others. He noticed a small glow in a couple of embers, symbolising to him that both parties would continue to feel the burn from that situation for some time to come. Arlo sighed and shook his head sadly. Life could be very tough.

Chapter 12

SAGE GREEN

It was very Novemberish, someone had been heard to say; all mist and drizzle, with daylight barely putting in an appearance before night took over again. No one sauntered along the streets any more. Even the temptation to gossip about recent events wasn't enough. It was all rush, rush, rush to get inside whether that was home, work or the shops.

Hilary had barely been out of her shop two minutes so it was a stretch to work out how anyone had entered in that time. She'd come through from the back, opened up and noticed the rail containing sheets, blankets and throws appeared to be messed up. She'd glanced around the shop to see if anything else was out of order and, satisfying herself it wasn't, nipped back out to check the state of affairs in the store room. The usual pile of boxes and black bags were there, waiting to be sorted and tea, coffee, mugs and kettle in their position on the tray beneath the back window. Hilary moved to the fridge and pulled it open suddenly, as though expecting to catch someone hiding inside. Satisfied that everything was as it should be, she went back out to the main shop. She neither expected nor noticed a customer as her attention was once again drawn to the bedding rail. She remembered going round, last thing before closing, making sure everything was in its place, neat and tidy, just as she always did. As well as the bedding, the rail also held two, large Whitney blankets and several cushion pads. Hilary was quite sure they were no longer in the order she'd left them and were 'squew-wiff' on their hangers. She never left them like that.

"I think our ghost is back again," Hilary whispered to herself.

"Sorry?"

The unexpected response spooked Hilary to the point that she leapt a foot into the air, whilst emitting a bloodcurdling scream, prompting her customer to step back in fright and crash-land into a jeans and jackets display through which he'd been looking.

Hilary was still shaking as she moved, her heart thumping, towards the flailing figure on the floor.

"I'm so sorry," she gasped, holding out a hand to help. The figure pulled at his beanie hat which had slipped down his head and revealed a vaguely familiar face. Hilary dropped her hand and then, her jaw as she watched the man struggle to his feet.

"Oh, it's you," she said, in a bemused sort of way.

"Well, it was the last time I looked." The man, probably in his thirties, finally made it to standing position and brushed himself down. "I'm sorry if I startled you but I thought you said something and, as there was no one else in the shop, I assumed you were speaking to me."

"Oh, of course, you would do. I'm afraid I have this habit of talking to myself, you see. I noticed the bedding rail was in dismay and I can't think why..." And she was off again, puzzling and wondering, trying to work it all out and momentarily forgetting that someone was standing next to her. After a while, her mind clicked into the present moment and she turned back to the man. He was staring at her closely, watching her every expression, as though trying to commit it all to memory.

"Can I help you with anything?" asked Hilary, feeling slightly disconcerted.

The man shook his head. "No, just browsing. It's just erm... you seem familiar."

"Well, it's probably because you've been in the shop before," said Hilary, in her no-nonsense way.

He looked surprised, opening his mouth and shutting it again, as though not sure what to say.

"Oh yes, I've spotted you several times."

He began to look worried, she noticed, and wondered why.

"In fact, I'm very glad you've come back," she pressed on. "Because I wanted to speak to you and then, you disappeared. You see every time I saw you, I started to get the fizzes."

"The f-fizzes?" Now he looked really worried.

"Oh, it's just an expression. I'm a bit psycho. I get vibes and there is something about you that really makes me want to– Hey! Where are you going?"

The man's eyes had widened and he was backing out of the shop. Hilary marched to the door and stood with her arm across it to discourage him from leaving.

"Please! What have I said? I don't want you to go. I want to talk to you. Won't you have a cup of tea with me? I can't help being clearvoyant, you know. It's nothing to be scared of."

"Clearvoyant?" he replied faintly. "Oh... oh! Psychic! You meant psychic!"

"Of course," Hilary smiled and moved away from the door, sensing relaxation in his energy. "That's what I said. I'll go and put the kettle on."

* * *

"Hey, Benson! Ignatius back. You see him? He sittin' on the blue bench. Eatin' somethin' disgustin', I bet."

Benson wandered over to the window and flung an arm over Florence's shoulders.

"Ignatius! What kind of name is that?"

"Ha ha! You can talk, man. I mean – *Benson*! Where they get that from, eh?"

"Actually Flo, it was from an American TV series about a black butler called Benson. My parents favourite show, see?"

"Mmm," murmured Florence, obviously no longer interested. She stretched her neck trying to get a clearer view. "He got something. Hey, I think Ignatius got a dog, Ben. Let's go say hello."

The two wandered over, hand in hand, to where the tramp sat in the soft light of late afternoon. He'd been coming to the courtyard, on and off, for many years. Florence vividly remembered the war between the neighbours, some wanting to turf him out and others determined he should be allowed to stay and sleep on the benches whenever he wanted. Nothing had really been resolved and things always got rather tense whenever Ignatius turned up.

"Hey, Ignatius! How you doin', my man?" Benson greeted him.

"Ooh, you got a little dog. Just look at him." Florence put out a tentative hand, much to Benson's concern. But the scruffy little terrier just sniffed her and gave her fingers a lick. "What you call him?"

"That's Mr Soames," replied Ignatius, in his gravelly voice.

"He adorable," smiled Florence. "We get him some food. Would you like some shepherd's pie? I got some cooking right now."

Ignatius nodded, his face showing no emotion at all.

"How are you, Ignatius? We not seen you for a while," said Florence.

Ignatius just nodded.

"Did you hear we had a murder?" asked Benson, watching him closely. Again, the tramp's face didn't change but his eyes moved to meet Benson's.

"Who?" Ignatius was a man of few words.

"We don't know. The enquiry is ongoing."

Ignatius shook his head, an impatient gesture for him.

"Oh, you mean, who was killed," said Benson, catching on. "No one from the Harly. It was a local councillor. Poor Flo found him in our alley, bleeding from a stab wound."

"Upset someone, huh?" said Ignatius, carefully rolling a cigarette.

"Dunno," said Benson. "It's certainly a possibility. He wasn't Mr Popular, that's for sure."

"Suppose there no point aksin' if you want come in for a cuppa?" said Florence.

Ignatius shook his head. He never accepted invites into anyone's abode but Florence was rewarded with the hint of a smile from the old man.

"I bring you somethin' then," she said. "And for Mr Soames."

Benson sat down on the bench next to Ignatius and absently scratched Mr Soames' head as he watched Florence's retreating figure.

"Would you ever be likely to hear anything - on your travels, I mean - about the death of Councillor Lowdon?" he asked tentatively.

Ignatius put the thin roll-up between his lips and stared straight ahead, his face expressionless.

"I wouldn't ask, only Flo's still very unsettled about it all. She has difficulty sleeping and stuff. If it were all resolved, it would really make a difference to her."

"You together?" Ignatius hadn't moved a muscle and still stared ahead.

"Yes, we are." A huge, beaming smile crept over Benson's face. "I want to marry her but she says it's too soon."

Ignatius sniffed. It was not a pleasant sound and Benson expected a hawk and spit to follow. Mercifully, it didn't come but the man turned his head very slightly in Benson's direction.

"Marriage," he said. "Man-made crap."

"I'm sure you're right, Ignatius," said Benson. "But Florence isn't the sort of girl who would live in sin, if you know what I mean. Her faith doesn't allow-"

Benson stopped as Ignatius had held up his hand.

"Explanation not needed," said Ignatius. "'S'why I opted out – all the crap."

Florence appeared with a tray and Ignatius simply said, "I'll ask around."

* * *

Trish was getting used to her protruding upper lip. However, in a certain light, the area of filler just above her lip was all too visible. She'd foolishly presumed it would look quite natural and no one would know what she'd done. Silly really, because on the television, she often spotted those who'd had the surgery; the slight distortion when they tried to speak, as though they'd had a stroke or something; the awkwardness when they tried to rest their lips together and how many of them constantly tried to pull their lips in - subconsciously uncomfortable with the results of their choices. Had she really thought she'd look better? No, of course, she hadn't thought at all; at least, she hadn't thought any further than the feeling of empowerment purchasing anything gave her. The worse her financial situation became, the more she craved the feeling that spending money offered. She glanced at a photograph of her old self, sitting in a silver frame on the bookshelves and her eyes filled with tears of regret. Almost immediately, she started to think of what she could buy to take her mind off her anxiety and she hurriedly reached for the phone. Daisy's voice came floating across the airwaves.

"Hello, my love. D'you need me?"

"Y-yes," said Trish, her voice shaking. "I think I do."

* * *

Daisy kissed Finn on the forehead and rolled out of bed.

"She's having a bad time," she said. "I'll have to go."

"But you were going to tell me something," began Finn plaintively.

"It'll keep," Daisy replied, knowing it really wouldn't keep for much longer.

* * *

Barbara Harris couldn't believe what Finn had said to her; couldn't believe that she'd failed to ensnare him; that he could actually reject the mother of his unborn child. She had, she realised, misjudged him and yet, she could have sworn there was a certain degree of sentimentality and honour in him that would have assured his compliance to her wishes. All that trouble she'd gone to; telling him she was on the pill but insisting, of course, that he use a condom for her protection. After all, he had rather a reputation. He'd agreed, having been lulled into the false sense of security she'd planned. He would have agreed to almost anything at that time, just to get his life back on an even keel. Deep down, she'd never been in any doubt as to why he appeared to have developed a sudden passion for her but it had been nice to dream for a while. She'd supplied the condoms. The pub had to keep some for the machines in the toilets, she'd explained. She knew he wouldn't balk at this as he never had any money. So, of course, she'd been able to doctor them and put her plan into action.

And then, he'd sat there and told her he was in love with the barmaid and while he would, of course, help look after their child, he couldn't give up Daisy. It would never work, he'd said. He couldn't pretend to be in love with her as that would create a very bad atmosphere in which to bring up a child. Barbara had wanted to smash her fists into his face and see its handsomeness crumple into a bloody mess. As for Daisy, she couldn't wait to tell her what she thought of her. If she opened her mouth to say one word, she would slap that wide-eyed, petal-mouthed face and turn her blush-pink cheeks bright red. She was relishing telling her she was, 'soo fired' and that she needn't expect references. She looked forward to inventing the vilest titbits of gossip about her and spreading them throughout the community. Oh, she was so glad she lived in a pub – the best place to start a rumour.

Her mind turned back to Finn when she'd told him he could no longer expect to keep his job. He'd nodded and agreed as though taking his punishment nobly and then proceeded to tell her, he'd been given a small part in a soap and would be leaving anyway. At that point, Barbara had felt her humiliation was complete and there was no natural justice in the world. Since then, her every waking moment had been involved in plotting and scheming, trying to come up with a way to exact her revenge.

* * *

Those who cared for Anya Petrovka could see what was meant when someone was said to be fading away. She seemed to be disappearing before their eyes. Her skin no longer held any sort of colour and appeared to get a little thinner each day. Her hair, once a thick, strong bundle of iron grey grew whiter and more sparse; her eyes were losing their brightness, the rich brown of her irises paled by a milky film. Her body was becoming bird-like and her voice had no strength in it. When she spoke, the words came out in a tremulous whisper and, although she still managed to move around her home, keep herself clean and eat small amounts of food, it was as though her life force was leaving her bit by bit.

Her friends were anxious and did their best to help as much as they could. They had persuaded her to see a doctor and now she had regular visits from district nurses but she was quite adamant she would not leave her home. She couldn't understand why anyone would suggest such a thing although, in her more lucid moments, she would admit she was often muddled in her thinking.

Harry Footlik was the most distressed of Anya's caring neighbours. He'd never known what it was like to be really fond of anyone and wasn't quite sure how it had happened with Anya. There was such fragility about her and yet, at the same time, a core of courage and determination to stand up to all that life threw at her. One evening, Harry and the Marshmallow were sitting with Anya in her delightfully feminine front room. She'd been quiet for a while, seeming not to listen while they reminisced on the days before i-pads, games consoles and mobile phones.

"Ptolemny vas a very insightful person. He said things vould develop very fast and to lengths ve vouldn't believe."

Marsha grabbed Harry's hand and they stared at Anya, hardly daring to breathe. It was a while since she had mentioned him. Anya chewed at her lips, her mind fixed on scenes from long ago. After a while, they became aware of the ticking of the clock, the trill of a stray bird braving the oncoming chill of autumn and Harry's slightly wheezy breath, as they waited patiently.

"Yes, he must have been," said Marsha eventually, hoping to prompt more from her friend.

"He loved the ballerina's daughter," said Harry. "So, he must have been a very wise man."

Anya's head shot round and she threw him a baleful stare.

"That vasn't the opinion of many people," she said. "They thought he vas stupid to get involved, especially vhen his vife vas so clever and vell-to-do. Respected, rich and elegant."

"Which meant nothing if he didn't love her," ventured Marsha tentatively.

"She vas cold," said Anya. "A cold fish. All she cared about vas advancing her career. She didn't even care much about her children. She just vanted them to excel in their studies. But Ptolemy cared about them. He cared so much. He gave up everything for them."

Anya's face took on a haunted look and Harry put his hand on Marsha's arm to stop her saying anything. He had seen the look before. It was touch and go now as to whether she would continue or clam up.

"Had to let him go for their sake," said Anya wistfully. "But it vas a crying shame. Loved him so, so much."

"He must have loved her too," said Harry very softly. "How could he not?"

Marsha glanced sideways at Harry's face and saw someone she'd never seen before.

"But they had some time together," she said, using the same hushed tones as Harry. "And they had a great love. Some never have that, ever. Not even a tiny amount."

Anya turned her head very slowly and gazed, almost unseeing, into Marsha's face. "Yes, that is vhat he said. Had to be content vith that and live life. No regrets."

Anya started to smile. It was a smile that seemed to smooth the wrinkles from her skin and they could almost see what she'd looked like when young; strikingly beautiful and full of hope and happiness. The next few sentences came out brokenly but painted a vivid picture of a very precious time in Anya's life.

"People don't believe in love at first sight," she sighed. "But it happened to us. The first moment ve set eyes on each other - like a meeting of someone you knew long ago and thought vas lost forever. Of course, I got the job vorking in his department and I found out he vas married vith children. But you know, he vasn't in love with her. Vas he ever? He didn't know. Maybe, it vas wrong but it vould have been like trying to keep two magnets apart for us not to be together. And she was like the opposite – vhat's the vord? - pole! The side that repels. There vas nothing left betveen them."

Anya paused, her expression darkening but then she seemed to shrug off the bad thoughts and return to happier memories.

"Ve had such times," she said dreamily. "Ve loved the same things, you see. Books, music and theatre. Sometimes, ve vould manage to go to the same shows and pretend ve had bumped into each other. Ve never got seats next to each other because once, ve did see another professor and his vife at the ballet. Ve realised that ve should sit apart so no one vould think ve'd come together."

Anya giggled then, making her seem even more like her youthful self.

"It vas amazing how long ve actually did manage to keep up our relationship," she mused. "He vould come to my flat as often as possible vithout causing suspicion. But of course, his vife didn't think he vould ever prefer anyone to her. As long as he kept money coming in and they looked like a couple at University functions, vas all she cared about. Ptolemy's vife vorked as a researcher in another University and it kept her very busy. So, ve had lots of time together, cooking meals for each other, having great discussions, putting the vorld to rights, making love. All the things couples do, except, of course the holidays..."

Anya's face fell a little but soon, became cheerful again.

"But I could forgo those," she said brightly. "Because I had his love. But his children needed him too. *He* loved them, so I did. And vhen *she* found out and threatened to tell them and take them from him, I understood vhy he had to let me go." Anya gave a huge sigh before continuing. "He didn't *love* her. How could he, vhen he gave all his love to me," she said firmly. "Actually, it turned out that many people knew all along. A lady I vorked vith told me our love for each other shone out of us. Finally, somebody told his vife. Someone who vanted to hurt her, not get us into trouble. But of course, it doesn't vork out like that."

"And so the ballerina's child didn't live happily ever after?" Marsha regretted the words as soon as they had left her mouth.

"No!" There was sudden strength in Anya's voice that hadn't been there for a while and, following Marsha's lead, she slipped back into the third person. "She made the best of it. Got a new job and tried not to think of him or of his nasty vife who got to keep him. Only she didn't. No one did... no one..."

"Why, what happened?" Harry, eaten up with curiosity, threw caution to the wind.

"Car crash. Killed. Dead. Gone," whispered Anya. "My Ptolemy."

"What did she do then?" prompted Marsha, on the edge of her seat.

Anya gave a little shake of her head and sat up a bit straighter. She stared at them with a puzzled expression on her face. It was as though a different person had walked into the room.

"I left Oxford, of course. Couldn't bear to stay there any longer. I came here, bought this flat, got a reasonable job. I've enjoyed living around the Harlequin triangle, I really have. All the friends, the visits and gatherings."

"There was never anyone else then?" asked Marsha.

"Oh no, no. There could never be anyone after him. My mother said the same about the Englishman. He had every bit of love she could ever give anyone and Ptolemy had all mine. Every bit. You can't imagine vhat it vas like. He vas such a gentleman. You don't see it much these days – that's the downside of equality - but it shouldn't be. To have someone put you first in every vay, to hold the door, pull your chair out, ask if you need anything, it makes you feel so good about yourself, special. Love just shone out of his eyes, every moment I vas vith him."

Anya was smiling into the distance again. It was as though she could see him standing right there in front of her. In fact, her hand went up and stretched out as though to touch him but then dropped as she turned to look at her friends.

And the brightness faded from her eyes once more and they knew she was back in another time and place; back in the arms of the man she'd loved so completely and lost so sadly.

"I'm coming, my love," she whispered. "Be vith you soon."

* * *

Daisy threw her bag down on a chair and came over to Finn, putting her arms around his waist and resting her cheek on his back, as he stirred the pot on the stove.

"You were ages," he said sulkily. "What did she want this time?"

"I told you, she just needs support to get over a very bad habit. I promised I'd be there for her and I'm not going to let her down."

Finn put down the spoon and swivelled around in her arms. He buried his face in her shoulder so his words were muffled when he spoke.

"*I* have a very bad habit. Will you promise to be there for me?"

Daisy giggled and held him tight.

"And just what is this bad habit of yours?" she asked.

"I'm addicted to this girl. I have to be with her every minute of the day. I have to be able to smell her perfume, feel her soft skin, see her beautiful face, hear the melodic tones of her voice."

"Oh dear, that's bad. You need to break that habit immediately," she teased.

"Will you help me then? I'll need you with me all the time or I'll fail. I know I will."

"No!" said Daisy and pressed a kiss firmly on his cheek. "You need to grow a pair and do it yourself."

"What? You!"

She pushed him away, grinning.

"Nice try, Finn Hunt, but I can't be exclusive. It's not good. I don't want to hear, I complete you, or stuff like that. You need to be your own person as do I. That makes for a much healthier relationship."

Finn watched as she went to the cupboard and took out table mats and cutlery. She looked so cute and pretty as always but there was a change in her that he couldn't quite put his finger on. Perhaps, she was just tired. Her actions seemed a little slower than usual.

"You shouldn't let Trish tire you out," he remarked, keeping his voice casual. "She's rather a needy person and they can be draining."

"I know what you mean," agreed Daisy. "But she's my friend and she's doing really well. It was just a blip."

"What's her problem again?"

"There's no, again. I never told you the first time so don't get tricky with me. It's not my place to tell. Just wish her well, Finn. From your heart. That's all you need do."

"You're an angel. You know that, don't you?"

Daisy paused in what she was doing. It was an infinitesimal moment in time but it stood out for Finn and for some reason, he was always to remember it; Daisy stretching her hand out over the table to place a spoon down next to the mat; her slim, lithe body perfectly poised as if ready to take off and fly; her pale hair, silvery in the early evening light shining through the window, wispy strands framing her perfect face like a halo. A thought had passed through her mind; something profound and moving but he never had a chance to question her on it, as she spoke again and the moment passed.

"No, I don't know that. I just see things from a different perspective, that's all. We put so much meaning into everything - make it all so huge and none of it's real."

"How d'you mean, it's not real?" Finn always got a little wary when Daisy became philosophical.

"Well, Shakespeare had it right when he said that all the world is a stage and the men and women merely players. We're all just acting out these little dramas, making up the story of our lives. If you think about it, you can see none of it is real."

Finn shook his head, puzzled.

"Oh, I never know how to explain it," sighed Daisy. "But it's so clear to me. Take this house for example. It could be a place of tranquillity for a Buddhist monk or a prison for someone being held hostage. It could be a love-nest for a pair of newly-weds or a home for some poor tramp. It could be a place of torture for an abused child or sanctuary for an escaped asylum seeker. So, what is it? It's nothing until put into the context of someone's story. It's exactly the same with our bodies. They're nothing until put into a story."

"As far as I'm concerned, it's a love-nest," said Finn, putting his arms around her. "Until Benson and Linus come home, of course and then, it's bedlam. But thankfully, Benson is always at Flo's these days and Linus is constantly out stalking that girl so, most of the time, it's our love nest."

Daisy sighed and snuggled into him. Finn only wanted the basic pleasures of life and rarely thought beyond those things. But, perhaps that was just as well. One deep thinker in a relationship was enough. They balanced each other out. And, as she so often did these days, Daisy silently gave thanks for meeting Finn and that he'd finally had the courage to face up to Barbara. She'd yet to tell him that she'd been given the heave-ho from her job that day. Barbara had announced it with great relish.

"*You will no longer be required. You will leave at the end of the week. Your work is not really satisfactory. You're a bit too obvious. We don't want the pub getting a bad reputation.*"

And on and on, with each sentence becoming more and more insulting as Daisy had stood there smiling benignly, nodding understandingly and infuriating her attacker even more.

Eventually, she'd held up her hand to stop the flow of bile from Barbara's mouth.

"It's fine, Barbara. I completely understand. There are no hard feelings. None at all. I'll leave today if you like. No need to hold you to any notice."

And Barbara had opened and shut her tight little mouth, unable to say another word. Daisy had leant forward and kissed her on the cheek and whispered, "Be happy" in her ear and had gone. And Barbara had burst into tears but not at all for the reasons she expected.

* * *

Giselle was well aware that, despite Sonia's declaration at the bonfire party, Patrick was not over the trauma of what had happened. She could see the distress in his drawn, pale features every time she visited.

"It was the feeling of utter helplessness," he said, his eyes filling with tears which he dashed crossly away. "Totally disempowered. Of how much it was the truth had no weight at all. The lie was as powerful as the truth. Until you come across it, you don't realise that the truth doesn't always come out. And it didn't matter what I said, the suspicion was there and always would be - will be!"

Giselle opened her mouth to offer some soothing words but Patrick was on a roll.

"The pen is mightier than the sword. Oh yes. And I realised the other day that the word 'sword' is the same as 'words', just with the 's' in a different place. Because words can wound and ruin one's life just as sure as any sword."

"I know," she said soothingly. "But thank God for Tom, eh? I mean, doesn't that tell you anything; the fact that even he doubted his own daughter and gave you the chance to speak. A lot of men would just have waded straight in. But we all knew what she was like, Patrick."

Patrick nodded, remembering the night Tom had knocked on his door and how his heart had leapt into his mouth to see him there.

"How did he approach it?" asked Giselle. "I can't imagine what he would have said."

"It was amazing," said Patrick, with a sigh. "He really surprised me. He basically asked me what happened. And he really listened. He didn't take his eyes off mine all the time I was talking. It was like he was looking deep into my soul for some clue or something."

"He must have trusted what he saw. So, who came up with the plan?"

"Oh Tom, of course. He said it would bring out the truth. Thank you for agreeing to do your bit, by the way."

"No worries. As a matter of interest, are you a black belt?"

"No," A little smile appeared on Patrick's face, the first in a long time. "We just thought it would frighten Sonia more. And before you ask, the punches were real. They had to be. There's no way we could fake that."

"Oh, I know," laughed Giselle. "I've seen the bruise on Tom's face."

Patrick started to look serious again. "Rotten for them all really. I mean, there's something wrong there, for her to do what she did."

"They'll sort it. You have to concentrate on you."

* * *

And to be fair, Tom *was* doing his best to 'sort it'. Both Sonia and Catriona were deeply humiliated. Sonia wailed that it was hardly surprising she did what she did when she came from such a dysfunctional family, whilst Catriona was hell bent on laying the blame squarely at Tom's door. Tom wasn't really surprised as she always blamed him and he did have some feelings of guilt that he'd plotted, in the way that he had, to get his daughter to confess to the lie. He could never tell them, of course, but Catriona seemed to think he could have arranged things differently anyway.

"In front of all those people," she whined, as they stood in the kitchen of number three. "How could you, Tom?"

"I didn't have a lot of choice," he stammered, turning away so they wouldn't detect his lie. He took a glass, filled it with water and drank deeply.

"We'll never live it down," continued Catriona, trying to comfort Sonia but being pushed away for her trouble.

"Is that all you can think about? She's a kid and she made a mistake. Everyone will get over it."

Sonia wailed louder and Catriona continued to sniffle. Nigel had been sent to play computer games in his room and had escaped gratefully.

"Whatever the reason, Sonia, you told a terrible lie," Tom continued. "You could have ruined that man's life. You have to show you're sorry for that. And I don't mean pretending to be sorry to get you off the hook."

"Nooo," sobbed Sonia. "I c-can't."

"Of course you can. We'll let things die down for a couple of days and then, I'll come with you to see Patrick."

"Will you?" Sonia looked at him with bleary-eyed surprise.

"Yes, of course. But firstly, it's my turn to apologise to you." Tom swallowed and took a deep breath, well aware that both his daughter and his wife could hardly believe their ears. "Your mother and I haven't been happy for years. I'm not sure we were ever really suited. But, instead of facing up to that fact, we muddled along, had you children and tried to pretend it was all alright. But living under those sort of conditions does things to you. The unhappiness and falseness filters through to everyone and affects everything. It made me back away. I couldn't handle the fact I couldn't make you all happy, so I kept my distance. I neglected you. And I'm really, really sorry."

Catriona opened her mouth but Sonia got in first.

"It's not that you don't love me then, Dad? That I'm too awful?"

Appalled, Tom rushed forward and gathered her in his arms.

"No, no, no," he moaned, into her hair. "I just don't know you anymore and that's my fault, not yours."

She clung to him, his girl; his prickly, defensive, awkward teenage girl and over her shoulder, he saw his wife's face. It was a picture of misery. He might be able to make up lost ground with his kids but Catriona was quite a different problem. Her next words confirmed his worst fears.

"This is all very well. Don't get me wrong, I'm glad you've seen the mistakes you've made but you've spoken for me and I don't agree. I've never regretted marrying you, Tom, and I would still choose you today. Lots of couples have problems but they work at them and overcome them."

"Well, that's a conversation to have between us," said Tom, not meeting her eyes. "Right now, Sonia is the most important person. She needs our support and I, for one, am not going to let her down. Not anymore."

"Of course," agreed Catriona, her heart sinking. "But it needs sorting soon."

"I know," said Tom. "And I promise we will. I guess I'd better make my peace with Nige too."

The kitchen door opened and Nigel bounded in. He'd obviously been sitting on the stairs, listening. Tom held out his arms and, after a moment's hesitation and a puzzled look, Nigel threw himself into them. Tom held him tight and repeated his apology for neglecting his family and vowed he would never treat them that way again.

"Tho, we're all one big, happy family," said Nigel, beaming.

"Well..." began Tom but the little boy was soaking up the new attention.

"Tho ith Thonia thtill a virgin then?"

As always, Nigel had a way of getting to the nitty-gritty without really knowing it. There was a horrified silence.

"Do you even know what that means?" screamed Sonia. "What's the matter with him?"

For a moment, Tom felt like running again but knew, this time, he had to stand his ground and deal with all the discomforts family life could throw at you.

"That's not a question you should ask a lady, Nigel. Sonia is growing up and that can be a painful process as you will find out yourself before too long. Mistakes are made and lessons learnt but you have to be able to move on and face whatever comes along." He glanced at Catriona. "The main thing here is to remember to love each other whatever happens, to accept each other's choices and forgive the mistakes."

Soon after that, Tom kissed his children goodnight and pulled on his jacket to leave. Catriona followed him into the hall.

"You're with someone else, aren't you?" she said, her voice shaking.

Tom stopped, his hand on the front door. Then, he turned to face her.

"Yes, I am. I'm so sorry if that hurts you, Catriona but if I stay, that'll hurt you too. I do care about you. I always will. I'm going to do my best for you and our kids now. She's made me see where I went wrong. Please forgive me."

He held out his hand and touched her cheek briefly before disappearing out into the bleak November night. Catriona didn't move from her spot in the hall for a very long time. It was over. Now, she knew it was real. She experienced a sick feeling in her stomach she felt nothing would ever shift. She couldn't allow herself to cry or she would never, ever be able to stop. Her legs shook beneath her as though she were bearing a very heavy weight. Finally, she dragged herself to the stairs and sat down, resting her aching head in her hands, her elbows on her knees. Deep in her heart, she cried out for help and comfort and a small, still voice replied.

"Accept."

And she knew, wherever the voice had come from, accepting was her only choice. Fighting against it all would only make the pain worse. And, as she repeated the word over and over again in her mind, gradually she began to feel a small grain of peace creep in.

* * *

Anya Petrovka died on 26th November. Marsha had been with her most of the afternoon, doing a bit of tidying up and heating a casserole for her tea. Anya had not had much of an appetite of late and her body was becoming painfully fragile and thin. She managed to eat a little, however, and Marsha heaped plenty of praise on her for her efforts. Harry came to take over the evening shift and was happy to polish off the remains of the casserole, standing in the kitchen with the serving spoon.

Marsha laughed at his antics and told him it was the behaviour of a schoolboy.

"How's she been?" he asked, glancing through the door to the lounge where Anya sat watching the news.

"Very in and out, you know. She keeps talking to Ptolemy and then, all of a sudden, she's back to her normal self. Oh and she's mentioned the ballet a lot and the usual about her mother dancing with all the greats."

"Poor Anya. She's had a fascinating life in some ways, despite the sadness."

"Yes," Marsha nodded. "There's a lot to most people's lives that others never see. Every story has its triumphs and tragedies."

Harry glanced at Marsha and remembered how little they all knew about *her*. She was a strange woman. Her home, which he'd recently had occasion to visit, didn't seem to reflect her personality at all. There was a toughness about her which conflicted with the soft pastels of her decor. The steeliness in her eyes didn't match with the frilliness of her accessories. Her tone was mostly gentle but, like many others, he'd witnessed a cutting iciness which occasionally presented itself. There was a part of her he felt wasn't genuine but he couldn't fault her kindness when it came to Anya.

"Well," he said, in his gruff way. "At least, she's got friends to look out for her now. The Harly's a good place for friendship and people looking out for each other."

"Indeed it is, Harry," said Marsha, nodding. "And now you're here, I'll get off. I've business to attend to."

Harry grunted affably. Privately, he thought Marsha had delusions of grandeur about her "business to attend to". In Harry's world, women's business had been running the home, fiddling about in the kitchen or tidying something away they shouldn't and, however much time passed, he couldn't quite get his head around it being any different. He followed Marsha into the lounge as she went in to say goodbye.

"Alright, Anya. I'm off now. I'll see you..."

He knew as soon as she paused, her breath catching in her throat. With a moan, he pushed past her and dropped down next to the armchair, hardly noticing the pain in his knees as he did so. Anya's head had dropped and her chin was on her chest; a chest that was still and no longer moving gently up and down with each breath. He took her wrist and found no pulse.

"Should we...?" Harry looked up at Marsha, appealing for inspiration to bring Anya back to life.

"No, Harry. Leave her be. It was her time. She's gone. I'll phone the appropriate..." Marsha stopped, noticing the man's shoulders starting to shake. Quietly, she moved out of the room and left him to his grief while her thumb moved swiftly over the keypad on her phone.

* * *

The air was still in the Harlequin triangle garden, colours muted but still present as though, in dying, some growth remained. It seemed that everything had stopped, for a short moment in time, in order to let Anya's spirit leave her body and gently melt back into another dimension where all was peace and love; where she would be united with those whom she'd shared the closest of experiences. This sentiment was expressed by Daisy who, passing through the courtyard with a bag of shopping, met Arlo who'd just heard the news from Marsha. Arlo's eyes travelled over Daisy's face, examining it for expressions of guile or indulgent sentimentality but he saw only acceptance and a little wistfulness. He reached out and gave her a brief hug.

"We have to make the most of each other, don't we Daisy?" he sighed. "None of us knows how long we have."

Daisy hugged him back and went on her way leaving Arlo to gaze at the garden. He would plant something to commemorate Anya; a lovely white rose, perhaps. He noticed how everything looked muted and delicate, fading into soft sages and greys in the misty, autumnal air. Tiny drops of moisture hung from stalks and branches like precious jewels. They made Arlo think of a diamond coronet and, for a split second, he saw a ballerina in a pale tutu and sparkles in her hair, pirouetting across the lawn and then, fading into the distance.

"Goodnight, Anya," he whispered. "Safe journey home."

Ignatius, ambling back from picking up a mug of soup from Linda Pugh, saw it too and doffed his battered, old hat in respect.

Chapter 13

VIRIDIAN

Bryce was the only person living around the Harlequin triangle who didn't mourn Anya's passing. He had entirely forgotten the date of the funeral and had a good old moan when Trevor told him they either shut shop or he was on his own for the day.

'Vintage Treasures' sold a mixture of collectables and antiques and, mainly thanks to Trevor's pleasant manner, had built up a good reputation over the years, consequently doing reasonably well. Bryce preferred going off for the day and buying up stuff to sell. Trevor couldn't deny his partner had a very good eye for what would attract customers plus he'd done up their premises in bright, fifties-style pink and turquoise that made it almost impossible for anyone to walk by without at least a quick glance. The window display, which Bryce insisted on constantly changing, was always imaginative and colourful. His latest included a metal garden table and chairs looking fabulously 'shabby chic' in pale green with rust patches. A couple of ancient copies of classic books lay open and face down on the table next to a flowery tea set. A man's straw boater sat next to that whilst an old-fashioned lady's sun hat, adorned with a floaty chiffon scarf, hung carelessly off one of the chair backs. On the floor, various garden implements from the fifties were scattered amongst a collection of old terracotta pots, together with some children's toys and books illustrated by Mabel Lucy Atwell. Several streams of bunting set off the display and a faded union jack was draped across the back of the window. As pleased with it as he was, Bryce was itching to change it for something more appropriate to the season.

"It just happened to be what we had in," he explained, when Trevor looked sad at the news. "And I know it gives hope for sunny days to come but I just love a winter scene. We've got some great enamel cooking pots and that scrubbed pine table which I could turn into a Christmas preparations theme."

Trevor knew that would be beautiful too so he said no more. However, when he announced he wanted to shut up the shop on the very day that had been planned for working on the new window, Bryce stared at him aghast.

"Why on earth would you shut the shop...?" he began.

"Anya's funeral," Trevor said firmly.

"Oh God, you're joking. Really? Trev, seriously, what was she to us? Just a neighbour, some batty old girl we hardly had anything to do with. We can't shut shop just to go to the funeral of someone we had so little in common. I mean-"

"Just stop right there, Bryce," said Trevor, holding up his plump, immaculately manicured hands. "*You* hardly had anything to do with her but I knew her quite well and I was rather fond of her. I visited a few times when she was becoming ill and the others couldn't make it for one reason or another. AND...!" He raised his voice to stop Bryce from butting in. "She was part of the Harly. But you still don't seem to have quite understood the fellowship of the place though I'd have thought you would, by now. We've lived there long enough. So, what I'm saying is, I'm going to the funeral. You can open the shop if you like but I will not be there!"

"But how am I going to do my window, if I have to serve?" cried Bryce, pouting like a petulant child.

"Not my problem," said Trevor and swept away grandly, one hand in the air as if letting go of a balloon full of troubles to disperse where they would.

* * *

Frances Arbuthnot felt like she was the new project for the older members of the Harly, wanting to make themselves useful, now that Anya had gone and, in a way, that was true. But she came to realise those people actually craved someone to visit and fuss over and there was more of an excuse when that person was incapacitated as she was. It started at Anya's funeral and the gathering, thereafter. Frances was having a few challenging days as far as her health was concerned and was in her wheelchair. Valerie was being as patient as she could but was more than happy to hand over the responsibility of looking after her sister, so she could relax and mingle with their friends. Reg and Harry were first in the queue to take charge of the wheelchair and almost had a tussle over it.

"Just park her over here next to me," ordered the Marshmallow curtly, after watching the struggle for a few seconds. "And then, perhaps, you could get us some teas and a few sandwiches."

Frances, who felt all her powers of decision-making being taken from her, piped up loudly.

"Actually, I'd like some sherry first," she said. "I want to drink to Anya's life and tea just won't cut it."

Everyone looked rather taken aback but were soon rushing to fulfil Frances's wishes and join her in a toast to their dear, departed friend.

"I can feel her in this very room," said Hilary, looking around the rather garish function room at the Bee's Knees. "In fact, I feel closer to her now than I did when she was alive."

Harry Footlik was heard to mutter the word 'tosh' under his breath and Frances gave him a stern look.

"It may be, Harry," she said. "But let's face it, no one has yet proved beyond a shadow of doubt that death is the end. The end of the body, yes, but what of the soul?"

"Well, if there is such a thing," murmured Marsha, looking doubtful.

"Yes, that may be up for debate," continued Frances. "But for me, there is something that thinks my thoughts and that is the true me. It's my spirit which is sort of observing my actions. I believe that thought comes before everything. What is it now? Ah, yes, energy follows thought! So, thinking is the first port of call in creating everything that happens in our lives. D'you see? We think something and follow through on that thought with either words or actions so creating the next situation. Only sometimes, ego gets in the way and we ignore the original thought. But whatever, thought is an energy and energy doesn't just disappear."

"Ah yes, but-" began Harry Footlik, always up for a good debate.

"And if you're going to go all scientific on me, Harry, scientists have located the command post which is the brain but so far, they have failed to locate the commander - the one who gives the orders."

Everyone around Frances started to talk at once and she smiled to herself knowing, for a while at least, they'd forgotten their sadness. Presently, she felt a soft touch on her shoulder and Daisy crouched down next to her.

"I think we read the same books, Miss Arbuthnot," she said softly.

Frances took the young woman's hand. "I suspect we do, Daisy," she smiled. "And one thing I've learned is there's nothing about dying to be at all afraid of. Nothing."

"May I come and visit you sometime?" Daisy asked.

"Of course," Frances replied. "I shall look forward to it."

* * *

Once Bonfire night was over, it seemed to many of the residents around the Harlequin triangle that the weeks before Christmas gathered momentum and fairly raced by, bringing the holiday perilously close before they were anywhere near ready for the festivities.

The Bee's Knees had 'decked its halls with boughs of holly' almost as soon as the last rocket had released its popping candy stars to the skies and fallen to earth and Barbara finally had to admit to her condition as her abdomen, after a slow start, had risen to the occasion. Barbara's rather strange body shape had certainly helped to disguise the swelling of her belly but when Glenys Harris commented, for the third time in one morning, that Barbara needed to do less comfort eating and 'get out there' – whatever that meant – she snapped and announced it had nothing whatsoever to do with food consumption; although, if her mother didn't stop going on, she was more than ready to comfort herself by upping her intake.

"There's no need to be so nasty," admonished Glenys, a look of hurt on her over made-up face. "I'm sure you don't want to be overweight any more than the rest of us and it's such hell to get off once you've put it on."

"I don't have a lot of choice," stormed Barbara, spreading an inch of butter on her toast to annoy her mother even more. "But you needn't worry, once the baby is born..."

"Whaat?" Glenys dropped her own knife and halted the progress of her fork to her mouth. "What did you say? Once the baby is... Barbara! You're *not*!"

Dennis chose that moment to re-enter the breakfast room, having left some time earlier for his morning visit to the 'lavatorial facilities' - as he liked to announce it.

"She's not what?" he said, sitting down with a thump. It was an automatic response rather than genuine interest.

"Pregnant!" retorted Barbara and, objecting to the use of a pronoun instead of her name, added, "*She's* pregnant! Okay?"

This time, it was Dennis's turn to fail to get his food all the way to his mouth. He turned to Glenys with a look of pure horror. "But you can't... we... you... don't... I mean, haven't..."

"NOT ME!" shrieked Glenys, before he could give away any more details regarding their private life. "Barbara!"

"Oh." Dennis looked both relieved and puzzled. "Who... I mean, I didn't know you er... who er...?"

"Oh Dennis, for God's sake, will you just get with it! Tell him, Barbara."

Barbara couldn't help but admire her mother's manipulations and was tempted to call her on it by saying, 'who do you think is the father?' but she was too fed-up with it all.

"Finn Hunt is the father," she said wearily.

"But we just got rid of him," began Dennis.

"Yes!" yelled Barbara furiously. "Because he refused to stay with me and bring up the child. He's with that little blonde tart."

"But you told me... you know, the drugs and everything..." Dennis still appeared confused.

"Dad, I just wanted him gone so I said what I had to but anyway, it turns out he's got another job."

"Well, I don't see why Daisy had to go."

"Dennis, for God's sake! You'd keep her on and rub Barbara's nose in it, would you?" shrieked his wife.

Dennis looked round as though Glenys must be speaking to someone else a fair distance away.

"It would be untenable to expect Barbara to continue rubbing shoulders with a girl who has patently ruined her life," continued Glenys a little more quietly. She got to her feet and went to her daughter to put a supportive hand on her shoulder. "You should have said, dear. Fancy suffering on your own. Are you quite sure Finn doesn't want to be a part of all this?"

"Well, of course, I'm sure. Do you think I just casually asked him to let me know if and when he came to a decision about his child's future?"

"No, of course. Such a shame," mused Glenys. "Still, hopefully he'll be around to support the child."

Barbara shot a suspicious glance at her mother and accurately gleaned that the motive for her remark wasn't what it should have been.

"Well er... I'm not sure congratulations are in order," said Dennis in his usual flat, non-commital way. "But you are obviously dealing with it all very well. Good for you. That's my girl. I'd expect nothing less." He stopped, feeling the accusatory gaze of his family on him and got up from the table giving his mouth a perfunctory wipe with the serviette. He coughed nervously and moved swiftly to the door. "I'd better get on. Barrels to change and the like. Let me know if you need..." And he was gone.

"I don't want to talk about it," said Barbara swiftly, holding up her hand. "I am, as he said, dealing with it and yes, I'll let you know if I need anything."

Glenys watched her daughter disappear off to her room, with mixed feelings. She, herself, had never gained much pleasure from motherhood. In fact, Barbara was unplanned and brought little satisfaction, let alone joy, to her parents. She was bright enough and later, a huge help as far as the paperwork side of the business was concerned but her joyless attitude and spiky personality were not easy to live with. It didn't occur to Glenys that her own personality may have contributed to her daughter's behaviour but she did think perhaps a child would help to brighten Barbara's life and bring about some welcome changes. And now, of course, Finn would continue to be around, after all. She'd been ridiculously disappointed when Barbara had announced that Finn was involved in drug dealing and needed to be dismissed without delay to save the pub's reputation. The business being their number one priority, she and Dennis had agreed immediately and were grateful Barbara had offered to do the deed of sacking Finn, herself. Now Glenys knew the truth, she experienced a thrill of pleasure that she would be part of Finn's close family and have a certain amount of influence in his and the child's life. It didn't enter her thoughts just how far Barbara had gone with her lies in order to wreak revenge on him, or that she might find it somewhat horrific her own mother harboured rather a lot of fantasies about her former lover.

* * *

Daisy couldn't get over the amount of Christmas decorations Trish had collected over the years.

"It's due to my... you know, problem," began Trish apologetically.

"Now, what have we said?" said Daisy. "Out, loud and proud. You have an addiction to spending. Keeping it secret or feeling ashamed is only going to make it worse. It's no different to any other illness."

She stopped rather suddenly, making Trish look up from her job of untangling the lights but Daisy was concentrating hard on straightening out the wings of a small, pink and silver fairy. The room was cosy and warm with a comforting glow from the candles they'd lit and a soothing perfume from some spice scented joss-sticks. Daisy had insisted it was no use just keeping them in the drawer where they had, admittedly, lain for some years; things had to be used. They even had some festive music playing in the background. As Daisy said, it was cheesy but had to be done!

"I know. I keep forgetting," said Trish. "I'm so used to covering it up and making excuses. It feels odd but you're right. It's sort of liberating too. If it's out there in the open, it's easier because you're not having to watch your back all the time. Because you've admitted it, people are rather flattered you've told them and want to help."

Daisy looked up, pleased. "Exactly. You know Trish, I'm so proud of you. You've really done well and that makes me feel good too."

Trish glanced at her friend again. Something wasn't quite right with Daisy; hadn't been for a while now. It was as though she wanted to say something but kept stopping herself. She opened her mouth to ask her outright what was wrong but Daisy got in first, almost as though she knew what was coming and wanting to head her off before she could pose the question.

"D'you know, Trish, there's so much Christmas stuff here. It's almost too much for this room. You might want to have a colour theme perhaps. I mean, this pink fairy doesn't go with anything. Well, maybe that's just me. I can be a bit OCD sometimes. I love viridian." Daisy paused as Trish started to interrupt. "It's a rich green, Trish, like the colour of fir trees I think and, to me, silver and red look best against it. Anyway, I wonder, do you feel you could part with some of your old decorations. I think you might get as much of a buzz out of giving things away that you did from acquiring them in the first place."

Trish shifted her position on the rug as her legs were beginning to develop pins and needles. She bit her lip and gave Daisy a sideways glance.

"Well, maybe. If I could choose though."

"Oh, of course. It's your stuff but seriously, I think it could be quite cathartic. We could take it round to Hilary to sell for her animal charity."

"Oh, you didn't mean sell it on ebay then?" Trish was looking anxious.

"No, Trish. I just want you to experience letting go of stuff and giving joy to someone else." She stopped suddenly and looked a little sheepish. "Sorry, that was really patronising."

Trish grinned and shook her head to exonerate her friend. She'd learned to trust the other girl completely, mainly because Daisy was so quick to recognise her own shortcomings. Trish never felt judged by

Daisy. Her comments always seemed to be in the way of encouragement. They continued in amicable silence for a while until finally, Daisy said, "By the way, did you see the hairdressers is up for sale?"

"No, really? I'm not surprised. It's hardly ever open. Irene hasn't run it as a full time business for years and she's got to be getting on for - I dunno - seventy maybe? Rumour is, she drinks rather heavily."

"Hmm. The flat above is occupied, isn't it?"

"Yes, Giselle's there. Why? Oh, you're not planning on leaving me, are you?"

Daisy looked up, her eyes a little shiny. "No, Trish. But I might put in an offer and do it up. You see, I haven't been entirely honest with you."

* * *

Hilary was delighted with the box of Christmas decorations and it raised her spirits somewhat. The sadness that accompanied Anya's funeral had hung around in the misty Autumn air and refused to go away.

"Makes you reflect on your own life," Reg had commented at the gathering after the funeral and Hilary had realised how very true that statement was; especially when you reached your later years. Hilary had really lived when she was younger - as she'd so eloquently hinted during the summer barbecue - but a lot of those memories were unsurprisingly hazy. This she announced often and with pride.

"If you can remember the sixties, you weren't there, as the saying goes," she would state firmly.

The trouble was, Hilary had a horrible feeling there were some things it would have been rather useful to remember, just as there were others it was better to forget. She'd been crowing about her wild youth as she'd poured tea for her male visitor a few weeks before. She'd just been getting into the subject of her gift and how she felt she'd met him in another life, when he'd leapt to his feet, excused himself and hot-footed it out of the shop. Hilary had felt a ridiculously strong sense of loss and wished she would bear in mind that not everyone found her psychic abilities either interesting or acceptable. She would never have brought up the subject if she'd thought it would drive him away.

    She placed a small fir tree in the window of the charity shop. It was one she'd managed to keep alive for three whole years and a little sparse in places but the new baubles would soon hide that. She worked away happily until she suddenly realised she was being watched. A small boy had his face stuck to the window, his eyes following her every move. She winked at him and carried on but a short while later, she looked up again and watched as the child pressed his nose to the glass creating a horrible gargoyle face with pig nostrils. He moved his head slightly, making it look like his nose was moving on its own. She began to giggle. Her shoulders shook with laughter but to her horror, before long, her giggles turned into sobs and she had to rush off into the back room. There was no doubt about it, a memory had returned, brought back both by the cute kid at the window and the man who'd come into the shop and given her fizzes round her head. Years ago, she'd given birth to a baby boy; given birth and given away.

* * *

It had become an obsession with Linus. He had to rescue his damsel in distress before Christmas. He could no longer count how many times he'd parked near Sally's place, watching as she struggled home with bags of shopping, little Megan trotting obediently by her side. Sometimes, they pushed through driving rain, their hair stuck in sodden strands around their faces and, more recently, he'd seen Sally stop and take off her scarf to wrap around her daughter's head whilst shivering with cold, herself. It was almost more than he could bear and when, one day, she tripped and fell just a few yards away from him on the opposite side of the road, he could stand it no longer. He was out of his car, speeding across to her, before he had time to think.

    Grabbing her arm, he hauled Sally to her feet and pulled her close.

    "You're okay," he muttered, holding her head into his shoulder. He felt her beginning to struggle against him and, at the same time, became aware of Megan sobbing by their side. He let go immediately and turned his attention to the little girl, dropping onto his hunkers and taking her shoulders.

"Hey, Meggie. Look at you. You're getting such a big girl. You can't be crying now. You have to help look after Mummy."

"Linus! What are you doing here?" Sally's voice was sharp and clear in the cold evening air.

"I er- I just stopped to take a phone call," said Linus lamely.

Sally gave him a look and started to brush herself down. She leant down to gather her bag of shopping from the pavement, pulling in some of the items that had rolled out. Linus turned to her, urgently.

"Sally, please. I have to speak to you. Won't you get in the car? I'll drive us somewhere and we can talk. Please, just this once and after that, if you want, I'll leave you in peace."

Their eyes met, both acknowledging that peace was the last thing Sally would have. She glanced at her phone to check the time and then, back at Linus. He saw her expression soften and she began to punch in a message.

"What are you doing, Sal?"

"Don't worry, Linus. I'm saying I'm taking Megan to the cinema so I've got to turn off my phone. I think that will work."

Linus nodded and led the way to his car. When he got them both safely in, he breathed a sigh of relief and drove with silent determination towards the outskirts of London and the beginnings of the countryside.

* * *

Arlo and Benson were busy erecting a healthy-looking fir tree in the courtyard garden. It was a pleasant enough job although the air, which had been unseasonably mild, now had quite a nip in it and their breath surrounded them in ghostly clouds.

"We really should get some new decs," said Benson. "Flo was looking through them the other day and they're starting to look distinctly tatty."

Arlo was silent for a while and Benson began to wonder if something he'd said had offended his friend. On the other hand, he knew Arlo was a deep thinker so he let the silence lie. The older man stood very still, his eyes focused way into the distance seeing something that eluded Benson; something that only became visible with age and experience, perhaps. Finally, Arlo spoke.

"Things are changing, Ben. Have you noticed? I mean, they're always changing, of course. That's life - but somehow, I feel big shifts are starting to happen and I'm not sure how good they're going to be. I've never felt like that before... I don't think."

Benson stood up, mallet in his large hand, and stared at his neighbour. Arlo did indeed look troubled.

"Come on, man. This isn't like you," he said in his gentle way. "Perhaps, Miss Petrovka's passing has affected you more than you realised."

"Miss Petrovka," repeated Arlo, with a small smile. "That's nice."

"Yeah, I always called her that, never Anya. It somehow seemed to suit her more because to me she was like from another time, another place, where life was very genteel and elegant and people were respectful to each other. Not like now, with everyone effing and blinding all the time and having to express themselves whatever that might do to someone else. I like that old-fashioned stuff, you know."

"Yeah, maybe that's it," said Arlo, running a slim, brown hand through his hair. "The more people like Anya pass away, the more that old style of being gets lost. That's an old man's point of view, of course but I do get this feeling of foreboding sometimes - like the world has taken a few wrong turns."

"Well, it wouldn't be the first time," said Benson, giving Arlo a little pat on his back. "Meanwhile, we need to see to more important things, like decorating the Harly for the Christmas celebrations."

Arlo responded with a grateful smile and got stuck into securing the tree. A little stream of people visited while they worked, most offering to help decorate when the time came. Only Catriona hurried past, her arm around Sonia, sweeping her along to their back door in the hope no one would notice them, their hoods up against the chill of the winter air and the prying eyes of the curious. Arlo and Benson exchanged glances. There was nothing to say but both men were generous enough to feel some pity for their situation, despite the fact it was the consequences of their own actions that troubled the two females.

Finn and Daisy stayed to chat and Harry Footlik sidled up, looked the tree up and down and moved on with a shrug. Typical Harry; except in the past, he would have made some cryptic remark. It was as though he could no longer be bothered. Something of his former confident brusqueness had faded since Anya's passing and strangely, what had been irritating about it before, people now missed.

Freddie wandered by in typical schoolboy fashion, kicking a stone, which offered some explanation for his scuffed shoes. Part of his shirt hung out the front of his waistband and his hair was definitely a stranger to a comb. It looked like he'd been attempting to create guy-liner with felt tip pen around his left eye but he showed no sign of embarrassment about that as he wandered over to comment.

"Bit juvenile, innit, all this Christmas stuff? I mean, there ain't exactly hordes o' kids round here, are there? So why d'you wanna-?"

"Ever hear the word, tradition, Freddie?" interrupted Benson in a mild tone. "It's sort of what a lot of us like at this time of year, for whatever reason."

"No, really?" Freddie stood there, his mouth hanging open in blatant mockery of Benson's reply.

"Of course, the other reason is to give little, no-brain losers something to come in and destroy." Arlo made the remark quite casually and was interested to see a faint shadow of emotion flash across the boy's face. He'd long been convinced that Freddie had something to do with messing up the garden, back in the summer. He moved closer to the lad and bent forward so his face was on a level with Freddie's. "Nobody ever gets away with anything, mate. One day, you'll come to realise that but, until then, keep your juvenile remarks to yourself or someone will likely push them down your throat. Got it?"

It was difficult to tell who was the most surprised, Freddie or Benson. Freddie was certainly not expecting such a response from the normally placid Arlo and he nodded very hard before scampering off, his dignity between his legs.

"I won't be crossing you today, my friend," laughed Benson. "You weren't in the mood to take any nonsense from that young man, were you?"

Arlo shrugged and pulled a face.

"He's a little sod," he said. "I know he's had tough beginnings but that doesn't mean he should be allowed to get away with stuff. He tries it on, you know, like he's testing you to see how far you'll let him go."

"You think he was responsible for messing up the garden?"

"I dunno. I wouldn't put it past him. Did you see his face when I said about giving something for people to destroy?"

"Yeah, wasn't comfortable with that, was he? Like you said, it'll no doubt come out at some stage. Mind you, I can't believe they still haven't found the bloke who killed that councillor."

"Might not have been a bloke," said Arlo. "We tend to assume but you never know."

They finished securing the tree and went to tell Florence she could rally the troops to get the decorations and lights in place.

* * *

Megan had fallen asleep in the back of the car. They took off her seat belt and Linus got a blanket out of the boot with which to cover her.

"Are you warm enough, Sally?" he asked. "I can turn the engine on again if you get cold."

They had stopped in a parking area off an unlit country lane. Sally nodded.

"I'm okay for now. But look, Linus, this isn't going to work. You've seen what that man can do. I can't have you hurt again. I just can't."

"But don't you see?" pleaded Linus. "That's how I feel. I can't bear the thought of you being unhappy or bullied and under the thumb of that thug. What's he to you anyway? I need to understand, at the very least."

"Colm O'Leary? He's Megan's uncle. Mikey, her dad, was his half-brother. They had the same father. Colm reckons Mikey's death was my fault. They were on a job, robbing some warehouse. Mikey didn't want to do any of that stuff. He had a brain in his head and wanted to start his own business. He didn't want to be part of his brother's world but Colm kept finding ways to force him. It was always just one more job and he'd leave him in peace. Anyway, we'd had Megan by this time and I'd told him I wasn't having my child brought up in that sort of world so if he went on another job with Colm, that was us finished."

Sally took a deep, wavering breath as though to steady herself. Linus grabbed her hand and gave it an encouraging squeeze.

"Well, he promised he wouldn't," she continued. "I said he had to keep his mobile on at all times so I could always phone him and find out where he was. I reckoned if he was robbing somewhere, he wouldn't want his phone going off. He agreed to that. I suspect he didn't think I'd actually phone and check up on him once he'd promised but I did. It was my call that alerted someone passing the warehouse, who then phoned the police. When they turned up, Colm and Mikey and a couple of others who were with them, legged it. They all got away, except Mikey, who ran out in front of a car. They got him to hospital, Linus, but he was so badly injured. His back was broken and he never regained consciousness. If only I hadn't rung..."

Linus could feel her distress and gently squeezed her hand again.

"He wasn't really a bad person," she said, through her tears. "He was just born into that kind of family. Such a waste though. He had talent. He could design stuff and had great plans to build us a lovely family home - once he got his business up and running."

"A building business, was it?"

"Yes. But now, poor Megan will never know her father. She just knows his bastard of a brother and she's scared to death of him."

"There, you see. That's no good, Sally. You can't have her growing up under those conditions. We have to do something."

"But, you don't understand, I have to do what he says because he's threatened to get Megan away from me. I don't know how far he'd go."

"You're right, I don't understand. Why? Why does he want to keep control over you both?"

"Because he has to have control. He could never let Mikey lead his own life and now says he owes it to his brother to look after us. But he's not looking after us. We're just part of what he sees as belonging to him. He'll never let us go. I know he won't."

Linus turned away and was silent for a while, staring moodily into the distance. Sally began to shiver. Suddenly, he whirled round and took her hands again. Looking deeply into her eyes, he said, "I'm in love with you, Sally. I know that sounds mad. I mean, we haven't known each other that long but there it is. I may be a weedy looking specimen and not what you want in a man but I have a good brain and I'm going to find a way out of all this for you and Megan, whatever it takes and even if you don't want to be with me."

He got no further. With a moan, Sally pulled her hands away and threw them around his neck to draw him close so she could kiss him.

"I've caused the death of one man I loved," she said, when she finally drew back. "How could I bear it if it happened again?"

Linus, who was now in seventh heaven, donned a metaphorical suit of armour and climbed onto an imaginary white horse.

"My choice!" he cried. "And faint heart never won fair lady! Let battle commence!"

And Megan, rousing a little in her sleep, muttered, "Daddy" before settling down again. Linus turned the key and urged his trusty steed forward into the night. A dragon needed slaying and he was the one to do it.

Chapter 14

SILVER

Christmas was growing ever closer, some anticipating the event with pleasure and others, dreading it. The strange, warm weather earlier on in the month, had prompted a few to say it just didn't feel like Christmas. However, when one morning, a thick hoar frost turned the world into a crystalline fairyland, the general consensus was it was too cold to even think.

Despite being exonerated, Patrick Baxter disappeared off to warmer climes for the holiday season, claiming he had a lot of work on which to catch up. His friends and neighbours were hard pushed to know what to say. It was an uncomfortable, sticky sort of situation. People wanted to sympathise but it wasn't the sort of thing you brought up if you could help it. Apart from Tom, Giselle was still the only person with whom he'd discussed the incident, although Hilary had accosted him one day, loudly advising 'not to let the past steal his future' and to 'keep that chin up' and other encouraging phrases until, eventually, Patrick had turned tail and scuttled back to his flat without the provisions for which he had originally ventured out. Despite her concerns, Giselle had come to the conclusion that putting a bit of distance, both in time and space, between him and what had happened, could only be a good thing.

On hearing her opinion, Patrick suggested, in a roundabout way, that she would make him the happiest man alive if she would agree to accompany him and so forced her to tell him, as gently as possible, that she didn't think he was the man for her. Of course, then, the temptation to play the pity card was too much and he slid easily into how understandable it was and, considering he was a man accused of molesting a minor, she could not be blamed for her reluctance.

"Please, Patrick, don't do this," Giselle pleaded. "I just don't think you're the type of person I could spend my future with. You like the good life, jet setting, flashing the cash. Forgive me if I'm wrong, but I doubt you give a second's thought to those less fortunate than yourself. I'm sorry but that doesn't sit well with me. It never has."

Patrick stared at her long and hard and finally, he said, "You must know about the rumours about what you do at the massage parlour? I mean, how does that stand up against my life choices?"

"Patrick, you don't actually know what I do, do you? And even if what I suspect you're thinking were true, that would have no bearing on how I felt about what you prioritise in your life as opposed to what I prioritise in mine. Think about that."

And think about it, he did. In the end, Patrick knew she was right. There was something noble about her; something in her that could never be completely happy with a hedonistic lifestyle while there were others in need. Whereas he... well, she was spot on. As long as *he* was comfortable, happy and safe, that was all that mattered to him. But now his world had been rocked, he often felt a fluttering in his belly, realising just how tenuous his security was and how easily it could be removed. Reality had finally caught up with him. All he had to do was decide what to do with it.

* * *

"No wonder you weren't bothered about being kicked out of your job," gasped Trish, still not having come to terms with Daisy's revelations. "I mean, I don't understand why you bothered getting one in the first place if you're independently wealthy. God!"

"I told you, it's not that simple," sighed Daisy, already regretting sharing her situation with Trish.

"Really?" Trish's eyebrows disappeared under her hair line, she lifted them so high. "I mean, really? I'm sorry but it does seem a little bizarre to me. To have money and not to appreciate it and make the most of it and enjoy it."

"I know, it's totally bizarre! Not what you said but the fact that you and I should come together and have experienced the complete opposite ends of the financial scale."

"I know which I'd prefer," said Trish with some feeling.

"I'm not discounting the freedom that money gives you," replied Daisy. "And the choices you have. It's just that I chose not to have it all handed to me on a plate. I wanted to experience what it was like to have to make your own way in life. But, of course, I can never really have that because the money's always there if all went horribly wrong. But I've learnt so much, not least that there really are some things money can't buy and those things are far more precious."

Trish frowned and shook her head. Some of what Daisy said went too deep for her to comprehend. She was starting to get familiar feelings of being inferior, that she wouldn't be able to keep up with Daisy and be left behind on the scrap heap. She felt herself sliding down into panic and despair but Daisy began clicking her fingers in her face, hauling her back into the present.

"Hey, where did you go? I'm trying to give you something and you're miles away. Focus girl, this is important!"

"Sorry. I just... oh, I dunno. What're you saying?"

"I'm going to buy the hairdressers and do it up. I want you to enrol in a course or two and then get you to run it. It could offer all sorts of stuff. Beauty, nail bar, hair, complimentary therapies. What do you think?"

"What do I think?" Trish was flabbergasted. "I think I'm dreaming."

"Well, you're not. If it appeals to you, then hand in your notice and get training. I'll pay the bills for now and I'll get the place done up. I'll enjoy that. I don't know how long it'll take for you to get enough training so I'll maybe get a couple of people in to start work if necessary but you could be the manager in the long run. You could do that, couldn't you?"

"Ye-es, I suppose." Trish looked a little worried. "But you'll be there to steer me, won't you? While I'm learning the ropes."

"Well, yes. For a while anyway. Oh, just say 'yes', Trish. Give it a go, eh? Why not?"

Trish could have come up with several reasons but there was

something about the look on Daisy's face; something desperate and urgent. So, embracing the feeling that this was going to be the best Christmas ever, she said 'yes'.

* * *

Linus just didn't know what to do about Sally and little Megan. His first instinct had been to take them to a police station and get them to report everything that had happened but Sally was reluctant.

"What if they don't believe me?" she'd said, her eyes full of anxiety. "Or more likely, they need some sort of proof of his intimidation towards us? They'd be bound to question him and then, my life wouldn't be worth living. No, that's not going to work, Linus."

And so it had been left and Linus, despite his desperation to get her out of the situation, was forced to take his time and try to come up with a plan. Even his mates weren't around that often to talk things through with him, being too pre-occupied with their own love lives. One evening at the Bee's Knees, Linus, after one drink too many, found himself unburdening to Giselle Greene who turned up hoping for a quick word with Dennis regarding some sale or return booze for the new year's bash.

"I've got to find a way to stitch him up," he said, his hands twisting around each other in his stress. "I mean, he's a criminal, for God's sake. There must be a way to get him locked up."

"You know that for sure, do you?" asked Giselle, her face softening with sympathy for her neighbour.

"Well, yes. I can't see why Sally would lie about that. Her husband got killed whilst robbing some place with him."

"Do you know his name?" Giselle asked.

"Umm, yes... Now what was it? She did mention it, I'm sure. Colin something. Irish bloke."

Linus took another swig of his beer while staring hard at nothing in particular. His anxiety was plain to see and Giselle reached out and gave his back a rub.

"Leave it, Linus. It'll come back to you. What are you doing for Christmas?"

"Christmas?" Linus looked at her as though he'd never heard the word before. His gaze travelled around the pub, crowded with people looking forward to the coming festivities. Glenys's decorations, this year themed on regal purple, twinkled luridly from every corner. Favourite Christmas tunes blared out over the babble of laughter and conversation. The occasional festive hat appeared on heads – a pair of antlers, a green, pointed pixie cap and the obligatory scarlet Santa hat complete with white trimmings.

"It's cancelled," he said and then remembered the name of Sally's tormentor.

* * *

It was the 23rd of December. The wine was mulled and the brazier burned brightly, charring the outer layer of several fat chestnuts until they were ready for peeling and popping into eager mouths. A tray of spicily sweet mince pies nestled under layers of tinfoil to keep them warm. A similarly wrapped tray sat beside them, this time containing copious sausage rolls. Hilary and Reg were handing out song sheets while Benson, Trevor and Bryce lit lanterns.

"I'm only holding up a lantern," said Bryce moodily. "I'm not singing."

"You say that every year," sighed Trevor. "And you always end up joining in."

"Yeah, cos you keep giving me dirty looks but I'm only here for the grub and the booze and I don't care who knows it."

"And we don't care why you're here, Bryce," said Hilary a little tersely. "And despite your altitude, you're welcome anyway."

The generosity of her declaration suffered a little in the way she pushed past him so forcefully that he nearly overbalanced. Bryce glared after her and went to shout something cutting but Trevor grabbed a mince pie from under the tinfoil and shoved it in his open mouth.

"Here, chew on that, sweetheart," he said with false brightness. "That'll keep you going until we get started."

Bryce looked shocked until the sweet, brandy-flavoured centre reached his taste buds and as usual, personal gratification overcame all other considerations.

Not long after that, the joyful sound of the carol singing filled the air. Several passers-by wandered through the alley and stood enchanted as they watched the scene in the garden. Others, who had witnessed the occasion before, came along especially to join in or just watch. Reverend Tiplady had also spread the word, although he made it sound as though the whole thing was his very own creation. He stood slightly to one side and made like a conductor. No one took a blind bit of notice of him but, in his mind, he was leading the way to choral excellence. Except of course, there was nothing expert in the delivery of the songs. They were just belted out for the pure joy of singing together. And it was this that created an atmosphere that literally made people smile and feel all was right with the world after all.

Only a few were missing. Patrick had already gone abroad and Catriona had spread the word that she was coming down with the flu so would be unlikely to attend. No one gave her excuse much credence except Linda Pugh who had marched round to the Penworthy's that very afternoon, bearing a bag of lemons, a jar of honey and a packet of Paracetomol. Catriona didn't know whether to be annoyed or touched by her neighbour's apparent concern.

"I've heard there's a really nasty bug going round," declared Linda, genuinely sympathetic to Catriona's situation despite their differences. "And I know what it's like when you're a mum. You struggle on, putting everyone else first, so I thought I'd make sure you got a bit of TLC. You won't be able to go to the carol singing of course, so I'm offering to take the kids for you."

It was pretty pointless to put up any sort of protest against the determination of Linda Pugh when she'd set her mind on something and Catriona was only too grateful that her excuse of illness appeared to have been accepted. Nigel was more than happy to go along, although he was wary of being anywhere near Freddie. Linda was puzzled at the boy's obvious anxiety when enquiring if Freddie was likely to be joining them.

"Don't you two get along?" she asked in her direct way.

Nigel didn't know what to say to that. It was a big thing to tell tales on anyone, even someone who made your life hell whenever possible. He gave a nervous smile and shrugged his shoulders before replying.

"I er- I don't think I'm hith cup of tea," he stammered.

Linda had difficulty in keeping a straight face at the boy's old-fashioned way of putting things. It was the sort of thing Catriona would say in an attempt to keep her natural vitriol at bay. But underlying the eccentricity, Linda could tell that Nigel was deeply uncomfortable.

"Don't worry, darlin'," she said. "Freddie won't stop around for long even if he does show his face. He'll most likely just turn up for the food, if I know him. But you stick with me and Baz and you'll be fine."

Sonia refused point blank to accompany the Pughs and said she would stay home and look after her mother. Linda wasn't falling for that but felt it wasn't the time to make a point about it.

Nigel, on the other hand, needed a careful eye and Linda made sure she knew where he was at all times. She shared a song sheet with him during the carols and was not surprised to hear a sweet, melodic voice coming from his direction. Apart from basic social skills, Nigel really was very good at everything. As she'd predicted, Freddie appeared soon after the singing ended. He waded into the buffet, grabbing handfuls of sausage rolls, crisps and other festive fare brought along when various residents joined the gathering.

"Why don't you go and get yourself something to eat, Nigel?" suggested Linda.

He looked at her, doubtfully.

"Go ahead. I'll just be here. Pop on a mince pie for me too."

Nigel trotted off obediently and began to fill a paper plate with some goodies. Linda stood back, melting into a group of people with whom Baz was chatting. She gave her husband a grin and turned her gaze to the tableful of food. She could see Freddie devouring his plateful and that done, he went back for more. It was then he spotted Nigel balancing his plate on one hand while carefully picking his choices with the other. Nigel was about to make his way back to her when Freddie pounced. Like a cat on a defenceless, baby bird, he shot forward and hit the hand, with which Nigel held his plate, from underneath so that everything shot upwards before cascading down onto the ground below. Linda saw her foster-child's mouth open in laughter and she quickly turned away, her stomach contracting with disappointment at his behaviour. She'd been so sure she was getting through to him. Then, she felt Nigel's presence as he moved to her side, vibrations of stress emanating from him and, putting her arm around his shoulders, she walked him up to Baz.

"Don't worry, Nigel," she said softly. "I'll get us something. You stay with your Uncle Baz."

Baz, who was quite used to his wife bringing him children to keep an eye on, took Nigel's hand in his own big paw with barely a pause in his conversation. He acknowledged her, 'I'll be back in a minute', with a brief nod.

Linda made her way over to the food. She picked up a plate noting, out of the corner of her eye, that Freddie was doing the same at the other end, whilst having a chat with Finn. She moved swiftly to join them.

"Alright, Freddie?" she said brightly. "Got enough there, have you?"

"Always room for more, ain't there?" he said, turning to her with a grin.

"Oh yes," agreed his foster-mother. "And if you get too full up, there's always something else you can do."

"What?"

A puzzled look came over the lad's face which quickly turned to shock as Linda brought up her hand and smacked it into the back of his so, like Nigel, he had the experience of seeing all his food shooting upwards before falling onto the ground below.

"What the...?" he gasped.

"Don't you dare say a word," snarled Linda. "Get yourself home and stay there and just you reflect on what that felt like. Tomorrow you'll be clearing up every bit of mess up from this garden. You've let me down, Freddie and you have certainly let yourself down."

Despite the cliché, Linda's words drove home and, as angry as he was with her for showing him up, Freddie knew exactly why she had done what she had and it was the very least he deserved. Aware of the stares now coming their way, he scowled back at her but, knowing she would never back down, he sloped off back to their house. Baz, who'd finally caught on to the unfolding drama, handed Nigel over to Linda and followed Freddie home. He made no bones about it, despite having his evening's entertainment interrupted. Like Linda, Baz always put the children in their care, first, and knew the boy would need support whatever he had done. Linda smiled after him, thanking her lucky stars she had such a man and took Nigel to reload another plate of food. It was he who needed her attention now. Sorting out Freddie would come later.

* * *

People who'd wandered through to listen to the Christmas songs began to disperse but not before spending a few moments offering their appreciation. The Reverend Tiplady, recipient of many compliments, smiled and nodded graciously, his white, skinny hands hanging down from his wrists in the weird doggy way that had almost become his trademark. Commendably, none of the residents of the Harly enlightened the audience that Tiplady was as much an onlooker as the rest of them.

In a dark corner, a man stood, the hood of his anorak pulled up over his head and a thick scarf tied on the outside to hold it firmly in place. He held a roll-up cigarette in one hand and had to pull the scarf away from his mouth every time he needed a puff. His eyes darted continuously over the proceedings until they came to rest on one person, when they grew hard and glittery with spite. Eventually, the man ground out his cigarette beneath one of his trainers with unnecessary viciousness and moved forward a few steps. He then appeared to have a change of heart, turned and disappeared into the blackness of the alley.

* * *

Barbara Harris was another standing in a dark corner. She'd watched with fierce resentment, as the residents of the Harlequin triangle sang joyously into the frosty night air. Like so many unhappy people, Barbara assumed all those who smiled and spoke with a positive attitude had been blessed with good fortune and didn't know the misery of tragedy and heartache as she did. Her mouth tightened into a thin, hard line as she watched Daisy look up at Finn as he dropped a kiss on her smiling lips. It should have been her holding his hand and singing, anticipating going back to his home and enjoying the intimacy of his bed. She felt the unfairness of it well up inside her but she even shocked herself as the words, 'I wish you were dead' hissed, whispered but forceful, from her mouth, But deep in her heart, she knew Daisy's demise wouldn't make Finn love her. And she, too, turned on her heel and made for home.

* * *

During the singing, one other person with a connection to the Harly had crept up the alleyway and looked longingly at the happy group of friends and neighbours. Sally and Megan had been late-night shopping with a friend and her daughter at the market, a few minutes away from the triangular courtyard. Making an excuse of calling on an elderly acquaintance, Sally begged half an hour to go and visit. It had worked and Sally had thanked her obliging friend, kissed Megan and hurried off as fast as her legs would carry her. She hadn't known about the carol singing but had hoped she might bump into Linus. In her pocket was a Christmas card she'd been carrying around for a couple of weeks, waiting for an opportunity to deliver it. She didn't know Linus's surname or his actual address and her worry, however unlikely, was that it would somehow fall into the wrong hands. Such was her fear, she wouldn't risk anything other than delivering it personally.

The beauty of the scene before her, took her breath away. The light from the lanterns created silvery sparkles on the frost and surrounded the carollers in a warm glow. Having abandoned the tired, old decorations, the tree was now adorned with items that also served as food for the creatures and birds frequenting the area; little bunches of millet tied with red ribbons; fat balls instead of the usual glass baubles;

pine cones and various Christmassy shapes covered with seeds and other titbits to which birds were rather partial. The smell of Christmas spices from the food and mulled wine wafted past Sally's nostrils and made her gasp appreciatively. And when the joyful sound of people's voices lifted in song rang out, tears rolled down her cheeks. She wiped them away with a bemittened hand but more came to take their place. She pulled her knitted bobble hat down further, hoping to hide as much of her tear-stained face as possible. It hit her forcibly that this was what she wanted for her daughter and herself; to be surrounded by decent, caring people. Of course they'd have their challenges and flaws but basically, they were people who, despite their differing age, race and beliefs, would offer solace when you were in trouble; people with whom you could laugh or cry and would listen and support you in your hour of need; people who would stand next to you at a Christmas gathering and sing their hearts out. Desperately, she looked around and spotted Finn and Benson but no Linus. She suddenly felt a deep need to see him and to tell him that, above all, she wanted to find a way out of her awful situation and be with him. But she knew in her gut he wasn't there. When the singing finished and people began milling about, wishing each other the blessings of the season, she made a decision. She ran over to Benson and thrust the now dog-eared envelope into his hand.

"Please," she said. "Make sure Linus gets this. Don't give it to anyone else but Linus."

And she was gone; off down the gardens and through the alleyway as though a pack of wolves were after her.

* * *

A few miles away, Linus sat in his car just around the corner from where Sally lived. He looked down at the two parcels on the passenger seat, agonising over whether he should deliver them or not. In the end, he got out of the car, pulled a knitted beanie down over his ears and put up his collar. He stopped just before the entrance to her front garden. What if that man was there and spotted him? How could he knock on the door if it was going to bring her grief. His heart started beating fast and he knew he couldn't bring himself to take the chance. His gifts, however well-meant, were for his own gratification and without a thought for the present circumstances. Wandering back to his car, he glanced up at the silver crescent moon and made a wish that, one day soon, he'd be able to give them their presents, safely and in the comfort of a home they shared.

* * *

Freddie listened to Baz and Linda as they put forward every possible argument against the bullying of a younger and smaller child. The worst of it was, although he knew they were right, at the same time, his former conditioning kept clamouring its insistence that it was just the way of the world and they were making a fuss about nothing. But Freddie was smart enough to keep quiet and nod and smile and agree to behave better in the future. He was finally allowed to escape to his room which, he was assured, he'd be seeing quite a lot over the next few days. There were times when Freddie considered a few cuffs around his ears would have been preferable to the removal of his privileges.

He knew he wouldn't be able to sleep so he waited until all was quiet in the house before carefully sliding up the sash-cord window and climbing out onto the kitchen extension roof below; an act which he'd completed many times before. He made his way over to the gardens, now bathed in silvery moonlight, and looked around, taking it all in; the lights strung from the apple tree to a post on the other side of the triangular plot and the lovingly decorated fir and its edible ornaments. His emotions became a turmoil of longing and resentment. Freddie wasn't a stupid boy and knew he was messed up but the anger inside him always won over the more sensible decisions he could have made and he didn't know how to change that. He felt his fury rise as he remembered the last lot of damage he'd wreaked and the residents' quiet determination to sort things out whatever happened; to keep smiling above all else and to forgive and forget every bad thing done to them. Why didn't they feel like him and want to destroy and hurt back and even things out a bit? What made them so bloody patient and kind all the time? His insides churned sickly as he felt the violence build up and burst out of him. He grabbed hold of the fir tree and began to shake it with all his might, sobs of hate emitting from his throat as he did so.

At first, he barely felt the arm that came across his chest but then realised he was being pulled backwards, away from the tree. He shouted and began to struggle but his captor refused to let go until he was dragged to one of the benches and forced to sit down. And Freddie found himself looking into the deep ebony of Benson's eyes.

"You're one angry boy, ain't you?" Benson gave a wry smile.

Freddie was tempted to spit in his face but something stopped him. Benson was nodding his head as though he knew exactly how Freddie was feeling.

"Someone hurt you very bad, eh son?"

"Whadyou fuckin' care?" snarled Freddie, looking away.

"Well, I don't know that I do," replied Benson, stretching and leaning back onto the bench as though he was there for a cosy, Sunday afternoon get together. "Not a lot of point me caring unless you do."

Freddie sighed and rolled his eyes. More psych chat coming, he thought.

"You wouldn't understand. You've no idea, you lot and your stupid theories."

"Aah, I know what you're thinking," said Benson calmly. "Heard it all before, haven't you? People trying to fix you, all the do-gooders, the know-it-alls. They've read the books but they haven't lived what you and I have, eh? They don't know what it's like to be treated as though your life meant nothing. Or like your feelings, however bad, don't matter to anyone else in this world. Makes you wonder why you were born, doesn't it and makes you wanna hurt everyone else just as bad, so they know and understand what you feel like?"

Freddie became very still. Only his eyes moved as, slowly, they slid in Benson's direction.

"I'm not bull-shitting you, mate," said Benson quietly. "My early years were an absolute fucking nightmare, so don't tell me I don't understand."

"Yeah, well..." Freddie was stumped. He hadn't expected that and he certainly hadn't expected Benson to be using 'inappropriate language', as Linda called it.

"What difference does it make anyway?" he said finally, having waited for Benson to speak again to no avail. "So you know. So what? You can't make it go away."

"Oh, come on, Freddie," said Benson, with a sigh. "You're not stupid. You know no one else can do that but you. But actually, no! You can't even do it for yourself. Well, if you can, you might give me a heads up cos I've never been able to do that."

Freddie looked puzzled. He started to speak but stopped and just shook his head.

"Look mate, the brutal truth is, your life's your life. All that's happened to you is now in your brain, yeah? Sort of in a file marked, 'the shit that happened'. But what you *can* do, is learn not to get that file out. Well, not often anyway."

"Oh and it's as easy as that, is it?"

"No, of course it's not easy. I've had my stuff filed away for a while, until tonight when I recognised yours and it brought it all back. No, it takes time and effort, as do most things in life. But you can do it. I mean, you're not a wimp, are you? You don't strike me that way. Anyway, it's either that or fuck up your life completely and then, the bastards who made you feel worthless have won, haven't they?"

"Maybe I am worthless so why bother?" said Freddie, his voice tightening with emotion.

"Well, we're all worthless, Freddie. None of this life means anything. You know that, don't you? The thing is, it's up to us to give it meaning and worth. Hey!"

Benson swivelled in his seat and grabbed Freddie's arms, making him jump.

"D'you know the one thing you have that's exactly equal to everyone else on this planet?"

Freddie shook his head, his eyes wide with alarm at Benson's sudden enthusiasm.

"Choice! That's what you have -that's what we all have."

Freddie began to shake his head. "No, you got that wrong. Them rich buggers are the ones with the choices. Most of us got no choices."

"Freddie, circumstances may be different, I'll grant you that, but I'm talking about the freedom to choose with whatever you're given.

Think about it. If I was standing here with a gun to your head, you still have a choice."

"Nah, what you talking about?"

"Well, you could scream and shout, beg for mercy, agree to do whatever I wanted. You could have a go at fighting for your life or you could just accept the situation and take whatever comes."

"What, even if you're gonna die?"

"We're all gonna die, Fred, but most of us don't know when, that's all. But d'you see, you could just take a deep breath and accept whatever happens next? It's still a choice."

There was a long silence as Freddie thought about this then he reached into his pocket.

"D'you mind if I smoke?" he said.

Benson shrugged. "Your choice, mate," he said, with a grin.

Thirty minutes later, Benson was giving Freddie a leg-up onto the icy kitchen roof so he could get back into his bedroom. The boy's wiry body felt almost weightless and Benson's heart melted with pity for what he'd endured. Still, he'd got him to talk a little and he'd agreed to come along to the boxing lessons Benson gave each week, even though he wasn't yet convinced it would help with his anger problems. As Benson made his way back to his home, Arlo appeared from the gardens and made him jump out of his skin.

"I heard all that," he said, putting a steadying hand on Benson's shoulder. "I had a feeling we were going to get a repeat performance to our garden so I came back out, just in time to see you grab Freddie. What you said...?" Arlo shook his head sadly, as if in denial at what he'd heard.

"Yeah, it was all true, mate," said Benson, with a wry smile. "I was Freddie a few years ago. What can you expect when a kid's had every bit of self-esteem ripped out of him? Linda and Baz are doing a great job but really, unless you've lived that life, Arlo, you can't possibly know what it does to you. That's why I do what I do for the kids I come across today. I know."

Arlo shook his head, his face full of admiration. He pulled Benson close and hugged him.

"Merry Christmas, mate," he said. "A very, merry Christmas."

Chapter 15

SCARLET

Christmas day dawned and a light dusting of snow obligingly turned the grey streets into a picture of festive perfection. All seemed well with the world. But, of course, it wasn't.

Linus refused all offers of company. He sometimes went home to Lincoln for Christmas but, mercifully, his parents had a full house with his sister and her brood visiting so he had an easy excuse to stay away. When, in the past, he'd chosen to stay and spend the holiday with Finn and Benson, some memorable, raucous times had been enjoyed, although often followed by the searing discomfort of the inevitable hangover. One boxing day, a tinfoil-wrapped turkey had been discovered in the oven, still waiting patiently to be cooked; and yet all three of them had vague memories of sitting down to Christmas dinner the day before. The mystery remained and Linus sat ruminating on these occasions as he waited, hoping for his mobile to ring. The card from Sally lay on the table before him and his eyes repeatedly scanned the words written beneath the traditional printed greeting. They simply said – 'With love and hope, Sally'. Longing and worry drove all possibility of Christmas cheer from Linus's mind but, he reminded himself, at least she and her little daughter were in the world, living not too far away and, most important of all, she loved him. All he had to do was figure out a way to remove the obstacles between them. As Benson had recently pointed out, things constantly changed. It was the one thing you could bank on so, in time, things could change. Linus was a patient sort of person but he knew, without a shadow of doubt, that his patience was likely to run out a lot sooner than normal. For him, change couldn't come quick enough.

* * *

Finn was across the way with Daisy. As they prepared dinner together, still in their night attire, he noticed the way they moved smoothly around each other in the small kitchen. They were so in harmony, it was ridiculous, he thought. He remembered the gaily wrapped box tucked into the branches of the tree that he would take down and give her later and grinned in anticipation.

* * *

Trish had gone to visit a cousin in the country. The idea hadn't filled her with unbridled excitement but she was very aware that Finn and Daisy wanted to spend the holiday together and had no desire to play gooseberry. Part of her was envious her new friend had so quickly found love whilst she, Trish, went from one disastrous relationship to another. Plus, she now knew Daisy was wealthy which was something Trish desired above all else. But, despite Daisy's enviable situation, she couldn't help but love her and was very grateful she'd come into her life; even more now she was offering Trish a way out of her previous chaotic and unfulfilling existence.

* * *

Benson had managed to persuade Florence to stay home in her flat so they could be together. He'd had to promise they would visit her parents later in the afternoon which doubtless meant a trip to church. It really went against the grain with him but, he had to concede, one good turn deserved another and so had capitulated. The differences in their beliefs was the one sticking point between them and they tended to avoid the subject. Although unspoken, both knew it could be what Finn would call a 'deal breaker'. Deep down, Florence felt the good Lord would find a way to enlighten Benson and bring him into the fold. Benson, on the other hand, puzzled over how a few differing opinions could hold such weight over a situation where two people patently loved each other and belonged together. Refusing to let anything spoil their Christmas, Benson pushed all doubt to the back of his mind and focused on making his beloved as happy as he could.

* * *

Trevor and Bryce had invited Arlo round for dinner, late afternoon. Arlo had no qualms about being on his own on Christmas day but hadn't worked out an excuse to refuse their invitation. He couldn't say he was looking forward to it although, from past experience, he knew Trevor was an excellent cook. It was just Bryce he couldn't stomach.

* * *

Giselle, who had been trying to summon the courage to also invite Arlo, found herself being asked to join the Marshmallow for the festive meal. Reluctantly, she accepted.

* * *

Hilary was joining Reg Prodger with the proviso that the person with the best frock was exempt from washing up. Hilary brought along a home-made Christmas pudding and was going to help prepare vegetables whilst Reg was taking on the cooking. Hilary only ate meat on high days and holidays and had insisted on humanely reared, free range. This had cost Reg more than he would normally have spent but he had to admit the taste was vastly superior to his usual cheap, factory-farmed bird. And, as Hilary was quick to point out, if you only ate meat on rare occasions, you could afford to get the best.

* * *

Valerie Figgis was committed to give her sister everything she wanted and more. After the initial struggle with her own bad-temper and negative thinking, she'd started to see some benefits in going along with Frances. There was a rhythm to the way Frances lived her life. The days started with a light breakfast at nine followed by a general clear up, making beds and a dust round and on Mondays, Wednesdays and Fridays vacuuming the carpets. Eleven o'clock was coffee time and a read of the papers before lunch was prepared to be eaten at one. Once a week, on a Thursday, a trip to the shops to get their supplies and on these occasions, they would dine out. Afternoons consisted of a short nap and then, if the weather was clement, a little potter in their small back garden, seeing to the plants, and maybe, a walk around the communal area followed by a sit on one of its colourful benches. A cup of tea was taken at four and some reading or crosswords attempted until supper at six thirty. The evening was spent watching TV, listening to music or more reading. Frances retired to bed at ten, leaving Valerie some time to do her own thing. It was during these times that Valerie reflected on her past and life in general and slowly began to realise that the tranquil simplicity of her sister's days were bringing a peace to her heart she hadn't thought possible. She'd finally relaxed and stopped wanting things to be different. Such was the enormity of her gratitude towards Frances, she'd vowed to give her the best Christmas ever.

* * *

Freddie had once again given Linda and Baz Pugh great concern but this time, it was mainly his change in attitude that bothered them. He was far too quiet for their liking and it was too much to accept that the dressing down he'd received, after the incident with Nigel, had made that much difference. It wasn't until Benson informed Baz there was space for Freddie to join the boxing group that they realised someone else was influencing their difficult foster-child. They were delighted to encourage Freddie with anything that might help him and couldn't wait for him to open a large parcel under their Christmas tree containing a pair of boxing gloves.

* * *

Catriona was dreading Christmas. Sonia was becoming more introverted and spent a great deal of time in her bedroom either on the computer or her phone to her few remaining friends. Nigel was always reasonably cheerful and, as he was so interested in absolutely everything, was rarely bored or troublesome; just too talkative at times. Catriona didn't know how to play the big day. Tom had offered to call round in the morning with presents for them all but part of her wanted nothing to do with him. It would be too painful to sit there and act like everything was normal when she knew he would be itching to get back to the woman with whom he was now living. Catriona had discovered that the other woman was Susan Milcroft who had worked with Tom in the past. It was bad enough, Catriona realised, that the attraction was likely to have started some years before their break-up but, even worse, the woman was dumpy! Catriona was very proud of her slim figure and could not, for the life of her, understand why her husband had gone for a homely looking female with a weight problem. It just added insult to injury and she found it very hard to bear. So Catriona did nothing. She didn't reply to Tom's email suggesting he call round on Christmas morning and she left the answer machine on and ignored his messages. It was partly out of spite as she knew he was trying to plan out his day but mostly, it was because she just didn't know what she wanted anymore and was too weary to think about it.

* * *

Only Harry Footlik was left completely on his own. He knew several places he would have been welcomed but he was still missing Anya and not in the mood for making merry and pretending all was right with the world. He'd descended into a bout of depression, suddenly aware of his mortality and had begun to ponder on the meaning of life, his own in particular. No answers came to him in the quiet of his home and so it was that he found himself wandering by the church on Christmas Eve in the hope that some miracle may befall him and leave him enlightened, joyful and at peace. He hesitated outside when he heard the singing and spotted a notice informing the community of the midnight carol service to which all were most welcome. Harry had managed to avoid the carol singing evening at the Harly and was in no hurry to participate in another. However, after a few moments in the frosty night air, he began to shiver so he crept into St Saviour's and sidled along the back pew, hoping to remain unnoticed. He sat quietly and closed his eyes, letting the voices of his fellow man wash soothingly over him.

"Are you alright, Mr er... F - F.. .er Foot...?"

Harry's eyes sprang open and he sat up with a start. The church was empty and the Reverend Ernest Tiplady's bespectacled face was just a few inches from his own.

"Yes! I er- yes, of course. I must have dropped off, you know! Can't think why."

"Oh, not to worry. It's just so good to see you here."

"Well, look here, don't get the wrong impression. I'm not religious in any way, shape or form."

"I'm not sure I am," said Tiplady rather mournfully.

"I just... well, I just heard the singing and thought I'd... you *what*?"

The reverend gave a wry smile. "There are questions, Mr er... Footle – Foot... even for a man committed to this work such as I. Many, many questions."

"Good Lord! Yes. Yes, indeed there are. I've been asking some myself of late but I never expected you to... Good Lord!"

"Quite. Look, I don't suppose you would care to join me in a little Christmas tipple, Mr er... F-Foo...?" He said it as though he already knew the answer would be negative.

"Just call me Harry, for God's sake," snapped Harry irascibly. "If we're going to drink together, we really should drop the mister, don't you know!"

And he followed Ernest through the church into a back room where tea and coffee making facilities were clearly visible. To Harry's relief, the Reverend Tiplady did not switch on the kettle but reached instead for a bottle of scotch, squirrelled away on the top shelf of a cupboard. And thus began an unexpectedly enjoyable evening.

* * *

Not far from the church, The Beekeeper's Arms finally saw the last drunken reveller ejected from its premises. Barbara Harris dragged her ever more cumbersome body around the bar in an attempt to assist with the process of clearing up. Eventually, sick of her moans and groans, her parents insisted she get herself to bed. Once in her room, Barbara sat on a chair by the window and looked out at the twinkling lights of the street below, registering the laughter of passers-by as they staggered home, anticipating the Christmas celebrations. Barbara hated happy people. She imagined leaning out of her window, a machine gun in her hands, mowing down every joy-filled human being who went by. Why were they all so happy when she struggled to find just a few seconds-worth? She hadn't asked for much; just a decent bloke to brighten up her life and adore her a little. She felt movement in her belly and automatically put her hand there. She never gave the child much thought, apart from considering she'd made a great sacrifice in allowing herself to get pregnant; a sacrifice because it wasn't something she'd ever wanted but had been prepared to do in order to get her man. But it hadn't worked. Maybe if that little bitch hadn't come along, she'd have got him. How she longed to turn her imaginary machine gun on Daisy's neat little figure and pretty face and blow her to kingdom come. The bile rose in her and, yanking her curtains shut, she slipped into bed to try and get some sleep. The baby moved inside her again as though asking its existence to be acknowledged. It never occurred to Barbara to consider her child or that this new addition to her life might bring her some comfort and happiness as yet unknown. No, it was just another misery to be endured - a mistake of monumental proportions she resented with every fibre of her being.

* * *

Christmas day brought with it a variety of emotions for the residents of the Harlequin triangle. The ground still twinkled with frosty crystals as it had for several days and there was that strange silence which only happened on one day of the year; a sort of collective agreement that it was okay to slow down and take a moment, just because it was Christmas day. And whatever the truth of the biblical story of the birth of Christ, the day had a power about it that brought people together and made them reflect, one way or another, on what was important to them. So thought Frances, as she watched her sister clear away the breakfast things.

"I thought perhaps we could open our presents when we have our coffee," Valerie was saying. "That way, it gives me time to get the vegetables done and the turkey in the oven."

It came to Frances just how hard her sister was trying to please and fit in with her wishes.

"Of course, dear," she said, smiling. "But look, it's Christmas day. Let's go with the flow. I don't want you wearing yourself out just to accommodate my silly routines. And I can help with the veg if you bring me a colander full and something to put the peelings in. But first, I'd like you to open a present, the small one with the scarlet bow. Please, it would mean a lot to me."

Valerie, a puzzled frown creasing her forehead, took the little parcel down from the tree and unwrapped it. It contained a blue, hinged box with a clasp. She glanced up at Frances who gave her an encouraging nod and upon opening it, Valerie gave a cry of joy.

"Mother's watch! Frances, why? I mean..."

Frances took the watch, which was attached to a long, gold chain, and clicked it open. It was exquisitely decorated on the face with tiny gold and red flowers and the numbers, also in gold, were formed as roman numerals.

"I've had it for long enough," she said. "I know Mother would have wanted you to share it so it's your turn now. She loved you very much you know, Valerie."

She handed the watch back to her sister who cradled it lovingly in her hand.

"I was the bane of her life, Frances. We both know that. But you - you could do no wrong."

"That didn't mean she loved me more though. We were very different. But so are cheese and chocolate and you can love two things the same but for very different reasons. Father was more down on you, I know, but he could see you were a risk taker and I think he was just scared for you."

"I can see what you mean," Valerie said thoughtfully. "And he was right to be, wasn't he? I mean, he couldn't stand Hugh and he was right. He was an awful man and I wasted so many years with him."

Her eyes were bright with tears and she looked small and vulnerable as she sat on the rug in front of Frances. Frances put out a hand and held her shoulder.

"Don't look at it like that," she said. "Just see it as something you had to experience this lifetime. Try to remember how well you coped in the circumstances. And you've done well, Val, really. I chose the easy way out, too afraid to take the chances you took. And, of course, your life hardened you and you felt bitter and sad but I've watched you fight against those feelings - so you could be there for me. And I want to thank you for that, Valerie, with all my heart. That's why I've given you Mother's watch."

"Thanks, Fran," said Valerie, reaching up to hug her sister. "Thank you so, so much."

They held the hug for a long time, each feeling old scores settling and melting into their newly found affection for each other.

* * *

For Harry Footlik, Christmas started when he knocked back a glass of fine whisky at the vicarage, after leaving the back room of the church on Christmas Eve. The Reverend Tiplady joined him enthusiastically, as they sat in companionable silence in front of the fire in the vicar's sitting room. It was a pleasant enough room in a fusty sort of way but Harry found himself comparing it to Anya's light and airy home.

"I guess you've never married, Tiplady," he stated gruffly.

"I don't know why you should think that," came the reply, instantly making Harry concerned he may have misjudged the situation.

"It's just, us chaps, we decorate differently. You know, the feminine touch, it gives... well, I didn't mean..." he blustered.

"I know exactly what you mean, Harry," laughed the vicar. "I was teasing you. I think anyone could see why I wasn't married. I'm not exactly a catch, am I?"

Harry looked sideways at the other man. He certainly wasn't God's gift to women. He had pale, thinning hair and somewhat bulbous, watery blue eyes. His skin was pale too and dotted with freckles and his body, slightly bent with rounded shoulders. He was a thin man with a pot belly that looked as though it had been stuck on rather than actually belonging to him. His feet were large, as were his strange, dangling hands but Harry, not wanting to offend him, was at a loss to know what to say.

"You just look sort of - well, vicarish," he offered eventually and was taken aback when Ernest burst out laughing. The laughter actually transformed the vicar's features, wreathing his face in smile lines and Harry was treated to a view of what the man might have been.

"Thank you for your diplomacy," chuckled Ernest. "Have another drink."

"Don't mind if I do." Harry held up his glass. "Of course, I never married either but neither did I go without - you know-" And he immediately went into his routine of regaling his audience with the sexual exploits he'd enjoyed during his life.

"I suppose I should envy you," shrugged the vicar. "But you must have realised that sexual gratification is one thing and a loving relationship quite another."

Somewhere in the back of his mind, Ernest was aware that he was imbibing too much alcohol as this was a subject with which he was extremely uncomfortable.

"Of course, it's inbred in men to spread their seed, is it not?" he forged on, turning his reddening face to the fire. "To continue the species, as it were. But as we now begin to realise that too much spreading of that seed is becoming a problem, as in the overpopulation of our planet, we have to try and change that impulse, don't you think?"

Harry, equally surprised at the vicar's words, stared at his new companion over the top of his glass. He hardly expected to have such a conversation with the man at any time, let alone over a friendly Christmas drink.

"You're not suggesting we need a new Nazi party, are you, old boy?" he said, with a weak chuckle.

"Good Lord, no. A master race would be unremittingly dull, I believe. Variety is the spice of life, no doubt in my mind about that. Where was I? I forget but you already have the elite seeking more and more power and wealth. It will lead to revolution. No doubt in my mind about that either."

"Really? But surely, we have learned to become more peaceful in the way we try to change things, Tiplady?"

"But it's getting us nowhere. Do call me Ernest. When those in power take too much, it always leads to revolution in the end. You can't tell me there's any justice in the enormous sums of money taken by the bosses of big conglomerates, the bankers, footballers and the like, while those at the bottom of the pile struggle to pay for food and heating!"

"Well, I'm seeing another side to you er - Ernest. You appear very animated, passionate and full of life. Perhaps you should take a drink more often."

"Oh believe me, it would be very easy. I have to be careful," admitted Ernest ruefully.

"And where does God come into all this?" said Harry, after swigging the last drop in his glass.

"Hmm, not too sure," said the vicar, moving to fill it up again. "I have a constant battle, Harry. A constant battle going on inside of me. A constant battle..."

He sat down and shook his head slowly from side to side, the whisky bottle hanging from one hand and his glass from the other. For a few moments, there was silence when all that could be heard was the old-fashioned clock on the mantelpiece, ticking off the seconds and the logs crackling and fizzing on the fire. Harry shifted uncomfortably in his chair and jumped when Ernest spoke again.

"This must go no further, my friend, but I think the church may have some things horribly wrong."

Harry's eyes widened and his mouth fell open but Ernest didn't give him the opportunity to speak.

"It's not that I don't believe in a higher power," he continued. "I just think the interpretation of what Jesus taught was distorted by those in charge at the time. I read, you see, Harry and *they* don't like it if you explore other philosophies but what I've discovered in those philosophies makes a lot of sense. And God, as they say, works in mysterious ways so who's to say He didn't guide me to other schools of thought. There is, I believe, only one God but a million different ways of reaching him."

Harry nodded and cleared his throat, not quite sure what to say. He was spared the trouble of inventing a reply but again, his companion's response surprised him.

"I know what you're thinking, Harry. I'm an awkward man and I see in people's eyes what they think of me and that makes me more awkward. I try to please people and say the sort of wise things they want to hear and rarely do I manage even that simple task. Also, I am blighted by bad thoughts. Probably the same thoughts that you and most other people have but then, I beat myself up for not being a good person." Here, the Reverend Tiplady stopped and rubbed his face with his large, ungainly hands.

Harry, concerned he may have to deal with the dreaded emotions, cleared his throat and began to search his brain for answers to bring the vicar into line. But, once again, Ernest got in first with his next surprising words.

"My dilemma is I've discovered other ways of thinking that bring me more peace than my own religion," he said with some alacrity. "I've been having conversations with Mr Kshatryia from the shop, whom I persuaded to enlighten me on his own beliefs. He and his wife are a most amazing couple and he is kindness personified, once you get through that rather haughty veneer. He's a clever man, very high caste back in India. Not that I hold with such things. He's helped me look at things rather differently."

Harry, who was becoming really interested, leaned forward in his chair. His recent state of melancholy was in need of answers and it suddenly felt as though this most unlikely of men might be able to give them to him. Ernest topped up their glasses before continuing.

"From what I can gather, both from the Kshatryias and my own reading, it's thinking that causes all our problems."

Harry's forehead folded into lines of confusion.

"How can I put this?" mused Ernest, noticing Harry's expression. "Look, maybe, on the other side of the world somewhere, a plane is crashing but -" He held up his hand to stop Harry from interrupting. "It doesn't affect us until we know about it. Right? And then, it's only our thoughts about the situation that affect us because we are not actually involved. Do you see?"

"You make it sound as though we shouldn't care," said Harry, still puzzled.

"Of course we should care, Harry, but we can't do anything about it, can we? Once upon a time, we lived in tribes and only had a small amount of tragedy to deal with but balanced with good stuff too. Whereas now, we're expected to take on the troubles of the whole planet and so we're all worrying or *thinking* ourselves into an early grave. We have to learn to live in the moment, my friend, and to do what we can within our capabilities."

"I think about Anya all the time and mourn the fact that she's dead. Surely, that's in the moment, isn't it?"

A smile spread across the vicar's face, once again transforming him into a vibrant and more attractive human being.

"Thank you, Harry, for asking that question. This is just what I need to cement my new concepts of life. So..." He rubbed his hands together before taking a hefty gulp of his whisky. "Is Anya in any discomfort? No. Can you bring her back to life? Sadly, no. Is thinking about something of which you can do nothing about making you happy? No, no, no! So you are dwelling on a past event over which you have no control. Hence, it is your thoughts that are making you unhappy."

"Are you saying that mourning the loss of a friend is a waste of time?" roared Harry, suddenly incensed.

"No, of course not," cried Ernest, quickly recovering from Harry's outburst. "When you're sad, you're sad but it's hanging onto the sadness by bringing the cause of it constantly back into your mind that is damaging. It's happened. You've been sad and now, you're here, having a Christmas drink with me. All is well. You're safe. There's nothing to be done but there are other things to focus on, just as Anya would want you to do. Does that make any sense?"

Harry leaned back in his chair. He held his glass up to his mouth but paused before drinking. He stared ahead, his mouth falling open and his brows drawing momentarily together. Then, suddenly, his head shot round to the vicar and he began to smile. The smile became a chuckle and gradually grew into great guffaws of laughter.

"By Christ, vicar!" he wheezed, his cheeks as scarlet as the baubles on the Christmas tree. "It bloody well does!"

And he leaned forward and clinked the vicar's glass with his own and Ernest, giggling helplessly, clinked back.

"Here's to enlightenment and peace," Harry began.

"And freedom and fun and friendship and everything this world can offer!" yelled Ernest and downed the rest of his drink.

Christmas day had dawned, heralding the start of a new and surprising friendship.

* * *

Catriona shuffled through to the kitchen in her slippers and dressing gown to make some coffee and gird her loins to face the day. Normally, she would have been panicking about getting the Christmas bird in the oven but now, they only had a turkey crown between the three of them and that would take no time at all in comparison. She could hear the television in the front room and rubbed at her face, trying to clear her thoughts. Somehow, she had to make the day go smoothly to make up for the dreadful year they'd had. She was in the middle of pouring hot water into the cafetiere when she heard Nigel's cry of excitement and his feet running down the hallway to open the front door. There was no time to call out for him to leave it and anyway, what explanation could she have given for not wanting to let anyone in? She held her breath, praying it would be a neighbour and not him but suddenly, there he was, her Tom, standing in the kitchen just like he used to; only this time he had a worried look on his face instead of his old, slightly apologetic smile.

"I er... I hope this is okay," he began. "Only you didn't let me know."

"Dad, are you coming through to open prethenth?" Nigel's face appeared round the door.

"You go and sort out the parcels for everyone," said Catriona. "Dad will be through in a minute."

Nigel skipped happily away and Catriona turned and poured herself a coffee. She didn't offer Tom one and when she turned back to face him, her expression was stony.

"What do you want from me, Tom? What were you expecting? You made your choice and you have what you want. But I don't. Nothing is the way I want it and yet you expect me to make life easy for you, just so you don't have to suffer any consequences. I don't want to see you and be reminded of what I no longer have. Please go and be with Nigel. I'll get Sonia to come down and then, just go. Get away from me. I'll need time to obliterate you from my mind all over again."

Tom looked shocked but did what she'd suggested. Sonia joined them shortly, her hair all mussed and her face devoid of the layers of make-up she usually applied. She looked very young with her skin all fresh and pink and Tom felt a sadness well up inside of him as he remembered the good times they'd had when the children were little. He turned his head away and grabbed a tissue, pretending to sneeze in order to hide the sobs that threatened to erupt from his throat. Finally, when all the parcels were opened, Tom got to his feet.

"Well kids, thank you so much for my gifts," he said as cheerfully as he could. "I'd better get off and... well, your mum-"

"Mum helped choothe your prethenth," Nigel stated happily. He was the only one who seemed oblivious to the tensions swirling around.

"Oh well, very nice too," said Tom, ruffling his hair. "Look, you guys have a great day, yeah? I'm going to arrange for us to meet up soon and we'll do something really cool, I promise. Okay?"

He hugged and kissed them both and made his way into the hallway. Catriona was walking out of the kitchen.

"Er, thanks," said Tom lamely. "I hope you have a lov..."

He stopped. The look she gave him spoke volumes.

"I wondered if, maybe, I could have them over sometimes?" he ventured, taking his courage in both hands. "We've... I've got tickets for the ice show and we... I thought..."

Catriona met his gaze with such loathing that he actually took a step backwards. She wanted to let him have both barrels; to tell him that never, NEVER, would she allow her children anywhere near his fat, ugly girlfriend and, if she had her way, he would have very little access too. But something in his face stopped her; something that reminded her of how very much she loved him, despite everything, and she knew, in that moment, she would never be able to keep up such a campaign of hate without damaging herself and her children in the process. So, she turned to go back into the kitchen.

"Whatever you want, Tom. Do whatever you want."

He stood in the hallway and felt the cutting of the ties between them; felt it so deeply that he became nauseous. But he had no idea how to sort it all out; none at all. It was beyond him. He pulled the dampness from his eyes with his thumb and forefinger and made for the front door, turning at the last minute to look back at the little house he'd called home for so long. Sonia was standing in the doorway of the sitting room, watching him.

"I'm never getting married," she said darkly. "Never, ever."

And a little voice piped up from somewhere behind her. "Me neither."

* * *

The shiny, new boxing gloves lay discarded beneath the Christmas tree and Freddie stood staring out of the window. Delicious aromas wafted in from the kitchen, where Linda was clattering about and singing carols in her loud, unmelodic voice. Baz was clearing up wrapping paper and ribbons, a fuchsia pink, paper hat balanced precariously on his balding head. He stuffed the detritus into a black bin bag and chuckled from time to time at a re-run of the Morecambe and Wise Show on the television. Freddie, lost in his own thoughts, wished they hadn't presumed he was going to like boxing. He now felt under pressure to take it up, whatever his feelings. He'd only been to two sessions and, whilst he'd enjoyed venting his pent-up frustrations on the punch bag, he was not inclined to get pally with the other members. He'd had run-ins with some of them at school and could already feel a certain amount of animosity emanating from them. He turned away from the window and looked at Baz. He did feel affection towards the couple who'd given him a home, along with a lot of patience and understanding, but that affection was bound up with irritation from the amount of obligation such love generated. Deep down, the troubled youngster was yearning to be his own person and answer to no one but himself. He had a year or so to wait and then, he would be off but, in the meantime, he would have to make the best of things which he knew, in his heart of hearts, could be so much worse. He bent down and picked up the gloves and pushed his hand inside one. Baz looked up from his task and grinned approvingly. Freddie nodded and smiled back.

* * *

It was gone six when Arlo finally managed to extricate himself from the company of Trevor and Bryce. Dinner had been excellent despite the constant bickering of his hosts. For once, he managed to keep silent and not try to smooth things over. Strangely, it had the effect of making them feel awkward and, after a while, even Bryce stuck a smile on his face and began to talk in a more positive vein.

"How about a brandy, Arlo?" he asked. "Or a glass of port maybe?"

Arlo bit his lip and racked his brains for a means of escape.

"Look guys, you've been most generous and the food, as always, perfectly delicious. If you weren't in the antique business, I would suggest opening a restaurant," he blustered, hoping for inspiration.

The couple opposite him beamed with pleasure at his words. Lie after lie presented themselves to Arlo but he was a fan of honesty and, in the end, words burst from his lips, coming close to revealing a truth he, himself, had not yet realised.

"But, I've got to be honest, I was hoping to see something of Giselle this evening."

"Oh, she's having dinner with the Marshmallow," said Bryce quickly. He was enjoying his neighbour's compliments and the alcohol he'd consumed allowed him to indulge in a suspicion that Arlo's somewhat harsh words in the past, were due to a growing attraction for Bryce himself. "Although, why she spends so much time with that woman, God only knows. I mean, what can they possibly have in common? I don't see what Giselle gets from such a connection."

Arlo felt his stomach churn in disgust at Bryce's assessment of things.

"There doesn't always have to be a pay-off, Bryce," he said, trying to keep any sharpness out of his tone. "Maybe, they just get on."

Bryce pulled a face suggesting he doubted any such thing was possible but Trevor, with his usual sensitivity to discordant nuances, jumped in.

"Well, that's hardly the point," he said. "If Arlo has made an arrangement to see Giselle, then he'll be needing to get off. It's been great to have your company, my friend, and thanks for the gift. We'll see you at Hogmanay, no doubt."

Arlo gave a little half smile at Trevor's clever manipulations. He certainly hadn't mentioned any arrangement but Bryce missed the deliberate mistake and finally accepted that their guest was leaving. He took Arlo's outstretched hand but, instead of shaking it, pulled Arlo towards him and hugged him close.

"New Year's Eve it is then," he said huskily.

Arlo pushed himself away, his smile frosty as he gave a curt nod of agreement. Trevor seemed oblivious, putting an arm around Arlo's shoulder to give him a quick squeeze. Arlo wondered, once again, how often Trevor turned a blind eye to his partner's flirtations – or possibly worse – and what it was he saw in Bryce that made it so impossible to end the relationship.

Greatly relieved to be out in the crisp air of the Christmas evening, Arlo wandered over to his beloved bench. It was good to enjoy some peace without the rumble of traffic from the roads beyond. He took a cigar from his pocket - a present from Trevor and Bryce - and lit it, savouring the aroma that twirled around his nostrils and the calming effect of inhaling deeply. Shame Giselle wasn't available. He enjoyed her company more than he could say. Fleetingly, the thought of romance crossed his mind but it didn't linger and carried on out into the ether to maybe visit another day. Arlo wasn't someone who craved another person with whom to share his life, being perfectly happy with his own company. But then, just as if to dispute that fact, she was there in front of him, her eyes shining and her even teeth gleaming in the moonlight. She wore a dress in Christmassy scarlet which looked grand enough for a red carpet event but the illusion was somewhat spoiled by what appeared to be a rather ancient cardigan and a pair of fluffy slippers in the shape of monster feet.

"Arlo," she squeaked excitedly. "I thought you were holed up with Tryce."

"Oh, that's good. I like that. Tryce!"

"I know. The Marshmallow came up with it. Apparently, it's the thing to do with couples these days, meld their names. I told her she watches too much telly. That's where she gets all these ideas from."

"Oh right. Anyway, yes, I had dinner and just managed to escape. I think Bryce is developing feelings for me which, I can assure you, are not reciprocated. God knows why he's picked me."

"Yeah, God knows... I mean, you're not in the least fanciable, are you?"

She plonked herself down on the bench and giggled up at him.

"Aren't you spending the evening with the Marshmallow then?" said Arlo, suddenly unsure of himself. Her boldness made him wonder if she'd had a little too much to drink. There was a whiff of awkwardness as he hadn't responded in the way she'd expected but then, Giselle just shrugged.

"No, I managed to wriggle out of it which wasn't difficult as she had loads of programmes she wanted to watch. What I really want is to spend Christmas evening with my friend so I can relax and have a laugh and say what I want, when I want. You know?"

Arlo got to his feet, cigar in one hand and took Giselle's with his other, pulling her up with him.

"Yes," he said, with a smile. "I know."

* * *

Finn got up from the table and went to the Christmas tree. He reached into its branches and withdrew a beautifully wrapped parcel.

"Here," he said, handing it to Daisy. "I forgot to give you this."

He sat down nonchalantly and ran his finger round his dessert dish in order to collect remnants of Christmas pudding and brandy butter to put in his mouth. Daisy squealed with delight as she stared at the scarlet paper and the silver, gauze ribbon holding it together.

"Ooh, lovely. I thought we'd opened everything. Did you really forget it or do you just know me so well and realise how much I'd love an extra presie halfway through the day?"

"Aah, you'll never know," grinned Finn, watching her undo the bow and take the first layer of paper off. Inside was a box and inside that, another wrapped container. He roared with laughter at her shrieks of frustration until she got to the last layer. Daisy stopped and didn't look up; nor did she utter a sound as she eventually unwrapped the tissue and the content lay in her hand. The silence enveloped them until Finn could stand it no longer.

"Well?" he said, his voice husky with nerves. "Will you?"

Daisy looked up and Finn saw tears sparkling in her eyes, echoing the sparkles from the diamond ring he'd given her.

"Finn, I..."

"You can't say no, Daisy. Surely you can't. I know you love me as much as I love you. We're so good together."

"But Finn, you don't know everything about me. If you did..." Daisy stood up and there was an air of finality about her.

"Daisy, there is nothing, *nothing,* you could say to me, that could make me change my mind about you. Whatever you might have done, I see who you are. You are wonderful, noble, kind-"

"Sick," interrupted Daisy, her face a mask of stone. "I'm a sick person."

"In what way? D'you have some weird fantasy you haven't told me about?" laughed Finn. "I promise you we can work through it. I'm very liberal."

His laughter fizzled out as he watched the girl he loved crumple before his eyes. Her body literally folded as though she had melted and she lay, curled on the floor, a heap of sheer misery, convulsed with sobs. Finn felt a shudder of fear run through him as he dropped down next to her and hauled her into his arms. He held her while she cried; cried as though she would never stop and finally, he took her shoulders and brought her upright to look at him.

"Oh dear, what a face!" he said, hearing the tremble in his own voice. "Perhaps I made mistake after all - asking you to marry me."

He forced himself to smile and was rewarded with a weak one

back. But that courageous effort nearly caused him to lose his own self-control. Somewhere, deep down, Finn realised he was going to have to find the sort of strength he wasn't sure he possessed; but find it he would, or die trying.

"Now then, Miss May, you're going to come clean. No! Don't shake your head. If you don't tell me, life will be impossible because I'll always be trying to work it out. If you do tell me, at least I have a chance of coming to terms with whatever it is. So, a chance - or no chance? Which do you choose?"

"I don't want to cause you pain." Her voice came out in a whisper.

"Pain I can take," said Finn firmly. "Being rejected and not knowing why, I can't - so please..."

Daisy took a deep breath and ran her hand over her face to wipe away the wetness. Her eyes dropped to the ring in her other hand, before going back to Finn's face which she looked over lovingly before she spoke.

"I love you, Finn, so much." She took another deep, shuddering breath. "But, you see, I've got a condition known as mesothelioma. I have, maybe, only months to live. Up until meeting you, I'd learned to accept it. I come from a wealthy family and had all the tests and treatments money could buy until no more could be done. But my family are also pretty dysfunctional and I wanted to spend whatever time I had, in a different way. I wanted just to be ordinary, with normal people, leading a mundane sort of life. I wanted to see how it felt so I had to get away and it felt wonderful. I've learnt so much, especially from Frances. I've been visiting her and she's lent me some of her books. We've discovered we think along the same lines. It's all been amazing and I've met you. You are both the best thing that's ever happened to me and the worst. The best, because I've experienced true love and the worst, because now I have so much more reason to not want to die."

"But that's a good thing," burst out Finn. "We can fight it together."

"There's no cure, Finn. If we stay together, all you have to look forward to is watching me die."

Finn bit the insides of his cheeks as hard as he could. He could not break now; couldn't let her down. The pain took his mind off the welling emotions as he grabbed her and held her tightly to him.

"So be it then. But we do this together. Whatever time we have left, we do it all together. So fix a date, Daisy May and order your dress. We're getting married."

He felt her body shake with emotion and held her even tighter.

"I've got you, Dais," he said. "Don't worry. I've got you."

* * *

The sky over the Harlequin triangle was velvety black as clouds crept in and covered the stars. Christmas was over and another year coming to an end. As ever, problems had been recognised, challenges overcome and new ones to be faced. Friends had come and gone and lessons learned but Anya's picture was the only one to be completed that year. The outlines of other lives around the Harlequin triangle had yet to be coloured in.

To follow, by the same author:-

MORE COLOURING IN

New Year's Eve and residents around the Harlequin triangle share celebrations in their communal garden. The body in the alley, found only months before with neither killer nor cause yet identified, has many of the neighbours unsettled. Further concerns grow when some friends fail to show and, as the bells ring out at midnight, dramatic events play out just across town. An unwanted pregnancy, an unhappy prognosis, an unresolved past and the joys and heartaches of love – the 'Harly' is full of secrets as the old year turns to new and those living there go forward to colour in more of their lives.

OVER THE LINES

Life can be complicated but most try to keep within the boundaries society has put in place. On the whole, the residents living around the Harlequin triangle in London were a decent, law-abiding lot but, for some, the boundary lines had become a little blurred and the only answer was to take the law into their own hands. The perpetrator of a local murder had still to be apprehended and concerns regarding safety was escalating – and yet, love, laughter and romance still abounded. The colourful little corner of London had become even more precious and the residents of the 'Harly' were ready to defend it against any who tried to darken its brightness.

Acknowledgments

My grateful thanks go to my daughter, Elizabeth, for all her help; her honesty in telling me what didn't work; her dedication to the English language in correcting any grammatical or spelling errors and her support throughout the process. Special thanks to Colin Murray for his professional appraisal which gave me the confidence to go ahead and publish. Also, to Duncan, Tony, Patsy, Leonie, George and John at the Writer's Group for their support; to dear friends Annie, Perrin, Karen and Paul for their encouragement and to my friend Janine Calder. "I can't put it down but I don't want it to end", were the sweetest words a writer could wish to hear. And finally, thanks to my writing buddy, Jane Lambert, who, being a step ahead in the game, pulled me along when I was flagging.

Contact: cloudcuckooland9@gmail.com

Blog: penleagarret.wordpress.com

Printed in Poland
by Amazon Fulfillment
Poland Sp. z o.o., Wrocław